I0749948

Rick Gangraw

Deathly Silent

Published by White Feather Press, LLC

ISBN 978-1-61808-085-1

Printed in the United States of America

Cover design created by Ron Bell of AdVision Design Group (www.advisiondesigngroup.com)

Reaffirming Faith in God, Family, and Country!

Acknowledgments

Thanks to my wife and kids for giving me the time to write this story, and for providing feedback along the way.

My bones and I,

Standing on an edge;

Standing against;

In contemplative thought,

Recall past laughter;

Hear past echoes ringing,

Stingingly ringing,

And bringing me nearer to be...

— Paige Cutshaw

Chapter One

"I ALWAYS KNEW YOU'D BURN IN Hell for what you did to me, but I never dreamed I'd be given the opportunity to help you feel the lick of the flames while you were still alive."

Erik stood over the well-dressed man, speaking softly, looking intently at the older man's face almost as though he expected a response, but he knew there would be none. The man laid on his back in a magnificent, open casket, not moving, expressionless, eyes closed. He appeared to be dead, and in fact, was dressed for his own funeral.

State Senator Jerry Grant stayed silent, while Erik spoke to him like an old friend.

"Mr. Grant, I want to make sure you catch every word I say."

His voice was pleasant, although a little biting with sarcasm at times, and he kept his face close to the older man's ear, whispering secrets that only Grant would hear.

"I know you're actually still alive, but you're in such a state that it looks like you're very dead. You're a smart fellow, so you've already figured that out. I've been waiting a long time to talk with you like this, because what you did to me ruined my life and it's taken me fifteen years to finally get my revenge. I think you know exactly what I'm talking about, don't you?"

Erik's thoughts raced as he went over the hours and hours of rehearsal for this moment, and his excitement was difficult to contain. He had planned this discussion for a very long time, and wondered if this was the real thing or just in his mind. Did he truly have this man from the past right here in front of him at the funeral home? Erik stared at the man's face as he touched it to be certain. This was really happening.

The overhead light cast shadows on the wall and floors as Erik stepped around the casket, and for a second he watched his own shadow move across the sparkling tiles. It wasn't easy to recognize that this was a crematorium, but one look at Jerry Grant in his elegant casket near the large furnace gave it away. The room where the furnace resided was in the back of the funeral home, on the other side of the viewing area, but still connected as part of the same building so Erik was able to roll the cart with Grant's casket over to the crematorium with no problem.

The door opened on the opposite side of the room, and his co-worker, Keith Ellis, stepped in. He was a tall man, but very thin, and was dressed in baggy jeans and a flannel shirt. Keith's eyes darted from Erik to Grant and back again.

"I wondered where you took him. Are you teasing the man by showing him where he'll get to go after the funeral?" and Keith laughed.

Erik faked a laugh because that's exactly what he had done to add to Grant's terror, but he didn't have to respond.

Keith continued, "Let's get the show on the road. I just came in to help you get him ready for the funeral and then for the fire. I don't want to be here all day."

Erik nodded, and they set the wheels in motion to get the senator's casket to the viewing room down the hall where the service would soon begin.

&&&

THE FUNERAL WAS RESPECTABLE, HONORing a man that the community believed for many years to be a trustworthy public servant. Even though the family wanted to keep it private, the viewing room was filled to capacity with mostly relatives and close friends. Erik studied the people in the room, noticing that most of the faces were solemn, but no tears fell for this politician.

What kind of a husband was this man, and did his wife even know of the senator's dark side? Did his children really love him, or was he despised by those who knew him best? Was he cold and self-centered?

Glancing across the room, Erik noticed his own bearded, weathered face reflected in the ornate mirror on the opposite wall, and wondered if people who trusted him would ask the same things if they knew what he was doing to the former congressman. As he stared into his own eyes, it almost seemed as though he looked at someone else. He watched his reflection for another second and then he had to look away. Realizing that his breathing had become noticeable, Erik forced himself to relax and become more controlled. Briefly, he sensed a twinge of guilt and suddenly felt like a hypocrite, so he did what he figured anyone else in his shoes would do. He buried the warnings of his conscience deep within and focused on the funeral. He had to be in complete control of his emotions and couldn't let anything interfere with his well-thought out plans.

Some of the words spoken in praise of this man angered Erik as he stood in the back of the room listening. Control the emotions.

"Senator Grant was a model citizen and a selfless public servant."

Erik gritted his teeth. He needed to be in control of his

emotions.

"Jerry Grant made Stockton a better place to live, and we're thankful for his years of service to our community."

Erik tightly closed his eyes and clenched his fists. This wasn't easy, but his feelings must be contained.

"He will be missed by his family and friends."

Erik tried to suppress a cough.

He wanted so much to open their eyes now and let them all know the truth, but he remained patient, relaxing his hands and his jaw, trying to read people's faces when he re-opened his eyes to look around the room. He was glad to see his months of planning finally coming to fruition.

Erik realized how fortunate he was to be the employee who prepared the body for today's viewing. With a decade of experience, he had been an employee here at the funeral home for almost a year, and he knew everything about body preparation. Even how to get one of the funeral home guests to his funeral without an embalming. His manager mentioned last week how impressed he was with the respect Erik provided to those who passed on, so Erik asked if he could work with the former senator's family on the funeral. He was pleased to be granted this honor. Everything fell into place perfectly. Almost too perfectly. He hoped he had thought of everything so there would be no surprises.

Erik paced a little bit, stepping quietly on the soft carpet in the back of the room. He dressed in an average black suit, which looked sharp, although his own outfit was not as splendid as his victim's attire. He noticed his co-worker standing across the room, and figured that Keith's suit was no match for this monster's expensive shroud either. Erik held in a chuckle, since it was always interesting to see Keith dressed up. He hadn't shaved, his hair was unkempt, and he seemed uncomfortable in a suit and tie. Erik considered the suit a necessary part of the act, and played the role like a professional.

He admired the many colorful flowers that had been delivered, and took a few minutes to see how they looked from the back of the room as people continued to stroll by the casket up front. He and Keith had lined them up on each side of the casket, and had discussed earlier how much some of the arrangements must have cost. As he surveyed the room, he listened to the conversations as several guests walked by him toward the exit door.

"It looks as though Senator Grant could be sleeping," one of the man's friends said, and Erik smiled with pride. Apparently he'd done a good job of faking the man's death and convincing many that the former senator's life had indeed already ended.

He desperately wanted to get up now and tell Senator Grant's family and friends what he knew about the man's past, how Grant had accepted payoffs from powerful business men who asked the senator to help cover up certain things. But Erik knew this was not the time or place to expose this man's deeds. He would continue to wait a little longer, until the stage was set and everything was just right. The waiting was painful after coming this far.

When the service ended and the family finally left the funeral home, Erik and Keith removed their formal jackets and carefully lifted Grant from his elaborate funeral casket to the flammable casket, wheeling him back over to the crematorium. They placed the casket onto the conveyer belt next to the furnace and when they were finished, both Keith and Erik exhaled.

"Politicians always seem so much heavier. Must be all of that hot air."

Erik laughed and replied, "Yeah, they're full of something, aren't they?"

Keith nodded and said, "I need to go pick up my wife.

All that's left is to start the flame thrower. Do you mind if I head out now?"

"Not at all. Thanks for your help."

Keith grabbed his jacket and left through the door to the reception area. As the door slowly closed, Erik glanced back over his shoulder at the former senator in his small, unimpressive box. Time seemed to stand still at that moment.

"Not so mighty and powerful anymore, eh?"

No response. An overwhelming silence filled every corner of the room, the same way darkness reaches out to consume every crack and crevice when the light goes out. He smiled as he considered that his old adversary, usually outspoken, was now deathly silent.

Erik and Senator Grant were alone, giving them time for a final conversation. Actually, today had been the only time Erik was offered such a one-on-one opportunity, since the senator never returned his calls or letters, even fifteen years ago. It was a little one-sided this evening as well, with Grant medicated to the point where he could only listen, but that's exactly what Erik intended. He had a captive audience and took full advantage of it.

He eased up to the box and looked at the senator's face from a different angle, leaning on Grant's chest and gazing straight at him. Grant's greying hair and sideburns framed the many wrinkles that etched his face.

"I don't remember these deep lines. I'll bet they were probably caused by tremendous guilt you felt about your illegal schemes over the years. You look older than you really are. I suspect your crimes and fears of getting caught have aged you prematurely. That gives me some satisfaction."

Erik straightened Grant's collar as if he realigned a picture on the wall or fluffed up a flower arrangement. In fact, Grant was more like a piece of decor in the room now than part of the conversation.

"Do you mind if I call you 'Jerry'? Good. I didn't think you'd object. I want you to understand that people will soon find out about your illegal activities while in office, and you'll finally be disgraced, as you should have been years ago. Even more important, I want to remind you, Jerry, that the bribes you took affected many innocent people. The truth has been hidden for a long time, but it's about to be exposed."

Erik stepped back from the casket and slammed his fist down onto the table, gritting his teeth with a rage that seemed to come out of nowhere, but promptly controlled his temper and slowed his breathing. He glanced up at the oil painting on the wall to his left, his eyes reaching into the scene of a cabin on a lake for a few seconds, and then back at Grant, who of course, didn't appear to have noticed the outburst. The soft lighting in the small beige room provided a relaxing atmosphere with the various paintings of nature scenes on each wall. Erik, however, didn't feel relaxed at this moment and dealt with many emotions.

He hated this man and was angry that he got away with his under-the-table payment plan for probably more than twenty years. He felt relief that this evil man would finally be brought to justice, thanks to Erik's involvement in the case now, but he also was afraid of what he had become. He wasn't a murderer, but what was he going to do in a few minutes with Senator Grant? He was about to murder this man, even though the rest of the world thought Grant was already dead. These emotions combined into one tight knot, and it was almost too much for one person to handle. Erik ran his hand along the sleeve of Grant's jacket to relax his fingers out of the clenched fist it was in again.

The senator's fine black pin-striped suit and expensive red silk tie caught his attention, impressing Erik, as he carefully smoothed out any wrinkles along the man's arms and admired the quality of the cloth. His hand shook as he struggled to take his mind away from the anger. He recalled that the tag inside the suit said this was a luxurious Anderson & Sheppard from London's Saville Row, and suspected it probably cost over $5,000. He could feel the difference in the material between Grant's funeral shroud and his own cheap suit.

"What a waste to burn up such a fine piece of material."

Erik considered the abuses of power that this man had committed during his terms in office, and then shook his head; not out of jealousy for what the man could afford, but out of frustration that this slippery politician had gotten away with such manipulations for so long. After he found out that Grant had been involved with a payoff in Erik's case all those years ago, he followed up on the man's activities and was glad that good citizens had tried to expose his actions several times over in the past decade. People should have been able to see a trend, but everything was quietly swept under a rug with each incident, never to surface again. Until now.

"Jerry, I hate to tell you this, but I didn't vote for you."

Erik laughed at his own comment.

"You see, I have a problem supporting someone I can't trust, someone who accepts bribes as part of his job. I just couldn't live with myself if I had given you my vote, knowing you would betray the good people of our state. Unfortunately, you still won," Erik said while patting the former senator on the chest, "and you fooled a lot of people for a long time. I think they'll be surprised when they find out over the next few weeks about some of the cover-ups you were involved in."

Erik strolled across the room to the cupboard and picked out a colorful coffee mug, filling it with water while Grant continued to lay motionless.

"I figure you're probably staring at the back of your own

eyelids, panicking because you can't move, speak, open your eyes, or give any sign of life. I'll bet you're trying to scream and move your hands, wondering why your heart's not pounding out of your chest. The mixture I gave you a couple days ago worked better than I could have ever expected."

Erik opened a cabinet door about eye-level, and selected a bright yellow package. He gently closed the cabinet door, and proceeded to heat the mug of water in the microwave while tearing open the package.

"Would you like some herbal tea, Senator? Oh, you probably don't like tea. You'd prefer expensive wines. Isn't that right?"

Stepping back toward the furnace, Erik made sure Grant was in the proper position, and slowly closed the lid of the flammable casket. He then bent close to the lid of the box.

"You may already be aware, but I wanted to point out that I just closed your tomb. If you could open your eyes, you would still see nothing but darkness, much like what you've been seeing, but this time it's a bit more final. This door has closed for the last time, old man."

He waited to let that sink in and took a few steps toward the wall to press a large, green button, which started a loud hissing noise from inside the furnace.

"Jerry, I just turned on the incinerator, and I'm watching the temperature gauge climb up to over 1,000 degrees Fahrenheit. Are you feeling a little warmer yet? I'll bet you can't even sweat now, but you should be so nervous that beads of sweat would cover your face. I can't imagine the pain you're about to feel. Can you imagine it?"

Erik placed a chair close to the casket, within reach of the controls, and then picked up a newspaper and his cup of tea. Slowly steeping it, he placed the tea bag in the small trash can and then sat down in the chair.

"Goodbye, Senator Grant. Consider this your punishment for crimes committed in secret, and realize that they're about to be made public. Remember, this is only a taste of what you'll be feeling in Hell this evening and for all eternity."

Erik knocked on the casket lid and pushed another button, which opened the door to the furnace and began moving the flammable box along the conveyer belt into the fire. Intense heat poured out through the open door but Erik casually sipped his tea as if he didn't notice. Sweat appeared on Erik's forehead, but he ignored it. Within a couple of seconds, the casket was completely inside and the door closed. A pitiful cry came from within the incinerator as Jerry Grant was finally able to show a sign of life, however briefly, but when the main jet-engine flame ignited, it immediately engulfed the casket along with its contents, silencing this politician forever.

Except for the calming sound of the continuous flames, similar to sitting in front of a fireplace and hearing the fire work its magic on a few logs, it became eerily quiet again while Erik took another sip of the tea and read his newspaper, not even looking up. He was relieved his manager had installed the sound reduction boxes to minimize the noise of the combustion air fans on the furnace, since this used to be a very loud process in the past. These new devices made it much more pleasant for those on the outside of the furnace.

"Hmm. I didn't expect Grant to be able to make any sounds, even when the flames got to him. I may need to slightly modify the dosage next time."

Chapter Two

ERIK'S SHADOW KEPT IN STEP AS he walked along the sidewalk. He was happy to see his shadow today, as though it was an old friend and companion. The sun wasn't high in the sky yet, but it felt good as it warmed him under his jacket. His connected follower was a reminder that the sun was out and he hoped his life would be better today as a result. Days without the sun always seemed to end up badly for him so he craved the sun and everything that came along with it.

Occasionally, he glanced up at one of the old buildings across the street and smiled at some memory he had from this part of town many years ago. He could see him and his wife walking hand–in-hand with their little girl into the bank or coming out of the ice cream shop. This was the old section of the city now, since most of the businesses had built up in other areas over the past decade, leaving this part looking run-down. It was only a shell of its former glory when this street had been one of the busiest streets in Stockton, Illinois. Fifteen years ago, it had been filled with voices, laughter, traffic, and life. Now it seemed like a ghost town everywhere he walked.

He stopped at the steps of a church, and slowly raised his head to his right to take in the massive structure and the grounds around it. The tallest windows reached several stories high, and he couldn't even tell where the steeple ended, since it almost appeared to reach the clouds. From the sidewalk where he stood, the steps led to a peaceful path that wound its way for about twenty feet up to the front of St Mark's Cathedral. This was the largest church in town and it covered the entire block, even maintaining a small cemetery behind it for many years before requiring more space a few blocks over for a larger cemetery. The rectangular stones that made up the cathedral could have each weighed a ton and the building walls seemed to reach up to Heaven.

He had been in this church several years ago, when his life was much happier, and he allowed some of those pleasant memories to escape the dungeons where he had kept them locked for so long. Faces from the past came to him, friends who were once members of this church. Clouds moved out from in front of the sun again, providing a striking light on the large building, making it appear to be filled with God's presence. The rays spread across the front yard, spotlighting trees and landscaped flowers, and for a moment he was filled with awe. He imagined the sun shining light on his memories that had been kept in the dark for some time now.

He wondered if he should continue walking past the church, afraid of what might happen if he stepped inside at this phase in his life. He used to feel comfort in a church, yet with the direction his life had now taken, there was hesitation. He had come this far today, almost allowing his nerves to make him keep going, but decided to wander along the path between several century-old pine trees up to the front door. His legs wouldn't move at first, but determination won out and he took the first steps toward the church.

The cheerful sounds of birds chirping set his mind at ease and he relaxed for the first time in quite a while. Keeping his gaze on the front of the building, he admired the architecture that he had once photographed for a magazine when he was much younger. He had forgotten all about that until just now. He briefly thought about the building the way he did back then, wondering how to take the best pictures here. The long, thin stained glass windows were lit up by the natural light, and the entrance was framed with many small, intricate sculptures. There were still numerous postcard scenes here, waiting to be photographed.

It didn't take long to get to the front door and when he realized he was already there, he wished he had taken it slower. He turned his head to look back over his shoulder toward the sidewalk and retraced his footsteps up to where he was now frozen. He must have been focused on the outside of the building as he walked and time had escaped him. That's what time always seemed to do and then it was already in the past, never to be recovered.

The door was inviting, but he was hesitant to reach out and open it. Maybe it would be closed today and he would have to come back again. Or maybe never. For a second, he stared at one of the designs on the door when it quickly moved away from him. He briefly saw absolution retreating from him, moving out of his reach, when he comprehended that someone inside had opened the large, decorative door and strode through it toward him. The man smiled at Erik as he stepped around him and into the sunlight.

"Good morning."

"Good morning," Erik was somehow able to respond. He studied the younger man who came through the door, but didn't recognize him. He must just be someone who went to this church now. He probably wasn't even born when Erik was here last time.

Now Erik faced a decision. The entrance was open and the church wasn't closed this day. He reluctantly glided through the ancient passageway before the large door could slam in front of him and leave him outside. For a moment, however, he felt as though he had been sealed inside permanently, but he buried the thought as soon as it came up.

The last time he had gone through that door was almost twenty years ago, toting his camera and lights. It was coming back to him now. The church celebrated its 100th birthday and Erik had been asked to photograph inside and out to put together their Centennial Edition of the church directory. He enjoyed those kinds of jobs and liked working with the pastors and other church leaders to point out the historic aspects of their building. Often, there were interesting stories about the buildings that very few people knew about. He tried to remember some of the stories people told him about this church, but he couldn't focus. His mind was elsewhere.

Erik's breathing increased and he wondered what a guy like him was doing in a place like this. He looked around, pondering whether he was being watched by someone who knew what he was truly capable of. If he was going to be caught for his crimes, this would be the place they would catch him because they could see into his heart here. He considered running out the door, but tried his best to relax and stifle his fears. Pushing those thoughts deep inside, he examined every aspect of the large room, concentrating on the second floor, removing the guilt from his mind while he brought back enjoyable memories. He remembered taking pictures of the sanctuary from up there and being fascinated by the massive pipe organ upstairs.

As he stepped forward, the impressive interior captivated his eyes, especially the streams of light shining through all of the stained glass windows. He stopped to let it all sink in as his head slowly turned from the left to the right. If God wasn't in a place like this, where would He be? Certainly not in his own little apartment or unimpressive life. Maybe someone could truly find God in a church like this. Unfortunately, he figured that God had deserted him years ago so it was too late for him.

He stopped when he saw the dark wooden structure on the right side, recognizing the confessional, and unconsciously walked toward it. He wasn't sure why he insisted on coming here, but he didn't fight it, letting his legs take him down the side aisle. He studied the outside of the little room, hesitating, and wondered if someone would be inside now as he opened the door to step in. Erik could tell someone was definitely in the partition next to him and he sat down feeling apprehensive, already wondering if he should walk out of the church and keep going down the street.

Erik savored the silence for a few seconds as he looked around and positioned himself to get comfortable. The dark wood inside the little room had its own beauty but the red carpeting seemed to conflict with the wood rather than complement it. It made him a bit uneasy at first. He wished it had been beige carpeting instead, but acknowledged it while taking a deep breath.

"I've never been to a confession and I'm not Catholic, but I feel the need to come here and confess something I've done. Is that OK?"

"Yes of course. Since you're not Catholic, I won't be able to offer you the full Sacrament of Reconciliation, but ..."

"That's fine."

"What is it that you would like to confess?"

Erik tried to look at the priest in the room next door, already feeling reassured by his kind voice. The man sounded young and willing to listen. Maybe this wouldn't be so bad after all.

"I've held a lot of anger toward someone for many years and I recently had the opportunity to get revenge on him."

"When you take revenge into your own hands, you don't give God the opportunity to work in the other person's life and bring about positive change."

"Well, this person had over fifteen years to change. He kept taking bribes. Breaking laws. And he messed up people's lives like mine!"

Erik could tell his outburst took the priest by surprise and reminded himself that he needed to control his temper. He rubbed his bearded chin and cheek with his right hand, took another deep breath and continued, looking toward the priest, but not clearly seeing his face.

"I'm sorry. It's just that this man had a history of doing bad things and the police didn't do anything about it. I had to step in and take some action in order to bring him to justice."

"What exactly did this person do to you?"

"He accepted money from a rich man to cover up mistakes made by this guy's business, and swept it all under the rug. Meanwhile a small professional like me suffered at the hands of the wealthy men and politicians. All he had to do was hold the powerful business owners accountable for their actions and carelessness, but he helped them cover it up."

"So what did you do?"

"Well, I figured this person would spend eternity in Hell, so I helped him reach this goal a little early."

Silence.

"Did you harm the man in any way?"

Erik heard concern in the priest's voice and wondered if he had mentioned too much. However, he knew the priest had to keep this kind of information private, so he continued.

"I read yesterday that he passed away due to natural causes."

"Hmm. I see."

Erik noticed a bit of relief from the priest's voice, but he wanted to say more.

"I did get a chance to talk to the man before he went into the flames and hopefully made a deep impression on him before he passed on."

"You seem convinced this person went into the flames of Hell."

"Yes, I'm certain he burned in agony for his many crimes." Erik had to stifle a laugh at his comment, since he truly was certain of this.

"It's always best to pray for the person and the situation, then look for an opportunity for reconciliation. Even when you don't see it, God is working and can bring about a change in people's lives."

"Well, I guess God gave me an opportunity to speed things along, because the man is now dead, burning in Hell, and I feel a lot better."

Erik knew these words would be unsettling for the priest and waited with a smile for his response. His eyes explored the surroundings as he considered that his revenge on Senator Grant was only partially complete. He still needed to publicly reveal the man's involvement in illegal activities. That would be soon. Very soon.

"You should only feel better if the man repented from his past deeds and changed for the better, apologizing to you and those that he had hurt. Are you happy that he's in Hell?"

"The man had the chance to admit he had done wrong and confess his crimes, but never made an effort for the past fifteen years or more. He wasn't going to change and would never have made things right again. I think he deserves to burn in Hell."

"God can bring about change in anyone, no matter what they've done in the past. There are so many examples of that in history. You should have given Him an opportunity to bring about this change, while you looked inside yourself to forgive this person. Sometimes the change that's needed is in you and not just the person who has hurt you."

Now Erik was at a loss for words, and thought frantically

of how to respond to this priest. "Listen. I didn't come here for a sermon. The man was bad news, took bribes from rich and powerful business owners, and would not have changed his ways. He's dead now. Too bad, so sad. It's over, and I'm moving on. I don't feel remorse for him, although maybe I should. I'm here to confess that I hated this man for what he did to me and now that he's dead, frying for all eternity, I don't feel guilty at all."

Erik found himself breathing hard, although he didn't understand why, and it finally occurred to him that he must have come here for that confession he just made. He had just taken someone's life and didn't feel guilty about it. Or did he?

"I'll pray for you, and ask that you feel compassion for those who have hurt you in the past. You have a tremendous amount of anger and I hope you're willing to let forgiveness work in your life."

Erik was surprised again at the priest's comments, but didn't know what he had expected the man to say. This guy just wasn't getting it. He had already waited for God, but God never lifted a finger to straighten things out again. Revenge was what he wanted, not compassion. He suddenly became claustrophobic and needed to break free of this place. Stepping out of the door hastily, he glanced to his left and then walked down the aisle toward his escape into the sunshine.

Feeling invisible eyes watching every step he took, he was afraid to remove his focus from the door in front of him, keeping his own eyes from straying to the left or to the right. He didn't pay attention to his surroundings this time as he marched through the church and could think of nothing, but getting out of here before God struck him down with a bolt of lightning or a heart attack or whatever God used these days to take care of people like him. His heart pounded and he breathed hard, but he wasn't sure why. He burst through the door at almost a run and his body absorbed the sunlight as if it was a healing potion, surging through his veins and giving him relief from this experience.

Chapter Three

HE WALKED BRISKLY, LOOKING over his shoulder as if trying to avoid something in pursuit, not thinking about where he headed. Autumn leaves fell, blanketing the sidewalk and surrounding areas with a decorative orange, yellow, and brown pattern. Even though he looked directly at the natural carpet, he hardly even acknowledged it. His mind churned, trying to sort out what to do next. His meeting with the priest didn't go as well as he'd expected and he didn't know what to think about some of the man's responses. It seemed as though he was preaching to him and Erik was in no mood for that now. He put it all in the back of his brain to let it smolder for a while until he could sift through it again.

The cold breeze coming out of the alleys between buildings made his eyes water and reached right through his jacket, chilling his heart, while he nervously turned his attention across the street, concerned about what he might see. He didn't want to fix his gaze on anything for long and constantly darted his eyes back and forth as he walked. The buildings looked like a drab grey when the sun wasn't shining on them, but they seemed to come alive with color when it was. Must just be an optical illusion, since they're still grey either way.

The sounds of children laughing at the nearby playground caught his attention and he realized where he was. A smile spread across his face as he noticed his wife sitting on his favorite park bench, and he walked over to join her, kissing her on the cheek as he sat next to her.

"Where's Brita?" he asked, and she pointed to the swings.

Erik's eyes followed her finger and lit up when he saw his little girl swinging high and laughing. Nothing brought him more happiness than being with his wife and daughter. They were his entire world and everything was better when they were around him. He watched the kids racing down the slide and enjoyed seeing them on the swings. This was a nice park, just down the street from the office where he used to work. It was a great place to meet his wife and daughter for a lunch break.

"I should have known you would be here, Kiersten. This has always been one of the best places to relax and enjoy the breezes and sunshine while Brita plays with her friends."

His wife looked up at him and nodded with a smile.

He stared at her face and admired the curve of her cheeks, her thin yet alluring lips, and the most beautiful deep blue eyes he had ever seen. He could look into her eyes forever. Reaching out to her, he rubbed the back of her hand and stared at her dark red nail polish. She did have the most perfect hands and fingers, and her hair was stunning as sunlight gave her the appearance of an angel. He was truly blessed to have her in his life.

He watched Brita swing for a few minutes more and then his eyes wandered down the street a little ways. He recognized the store that sold wonderful Swedish decorations, ornaments, and household items, and wondered how the owners were doing. Mrs. Petersson used to babysit Brita when Erik and Kiersten went out to dinner or a movie several years ago, and Brita loved to explore the shop. There were so many things in there to interest a young child and the Peterssons were patient to show her anything that fascinated her. It was like another world for her in their shop. He could tell that the Peterssons also adored seeing Brita's eyes light up over something new.

Across the street was an empty lot, covered with grass. It seemed out of place now with the other buildings open for business around that spot. It was surprising the city hadn't complained more about getting something rebuilt on this prime piece of property years ago, but after only a few initial comments about it, city officials stopped pushing to get a new business put up on that lot. It was a little suspicious, since this was the busy downtown area at the time, and he figured there must have been some kind of political payoff so there wouldn't be a big deal about it after what had happened there.

A small white picket fence stretched beside the alley behind the empty lot, running all the way from the street to the next building. It seemed like such a small piece of property now that it had no structure on it, but there used to be an elegant three story building in this place at one time. He had parked his little red Fiat in that alley every day before the fence was put up, and he supposed the new white fence running along the back of the property now looked nice.

Erik recalled many years ago when there was a building on that spot, his photography studio with many rented offices and a restaurant, and he saw scenes almost like something from an old home movie camera without sound. The colors were brighter than normal and people moved a bit faster than in real life, but he savored these scenes from his memories. His wife and daughter sat at the little restaurant, sipping root beer floats and giggling together. He watched himself get up, kiss them both and walk out the front of the restaurant. He wished he could hear their voices, but it was silent as the scene progressed.

On the sidewalk outside of the restaurant's large window, Erik made silly faces to watch his precious Brita burst out with laughter. His daughter blew him a kiss through the window, which he pretended to catch and planted it onto his cheek, causing her to smile with pride at her father. The restaurant's owners waved at Erik as he continued next door to his adjoining studio, and he waved back at all of them before disappearing into his studio's front door. His little home movie was over, but it was quite a treat. Back to reality.

Still sitting on the bench across the street, Erik recalled how much he had enjoyed the little restaurant and was saddened it was no longer there. It used to be on part of that empty lot, sharing the first floor with his photography studio lobby. The other shop owners were such good people, and he missed their company and friendships. He tried to remember the names of the restaurant owners and was surprised at how long it took him to pull their names from deep within the recesses of his mind. Their names were Carl and Violet, and they were so full of life back then. Both were a generation older than Erik and they accepted his little family as if they were Carl and Violet's own son, daughter-in-law, and granddaughter. A person couldn't ask for better neighbors and Brita loved them very much as well.

Erik wondered whatever happened to them, but couldn't remember where the couple had moved on to after their restaurant closed down. It just seemed so long ago and this area had gone through many changes over the years. He gazed up at the cloudless blue sky, smiling as the sun warmed his face, and watched a few pigeons fly around to roost near the top of one of the other buildings. He reminisced about his family and friends sitting on the roof near those birds, relishing the opportunities to watch parades go by.

"Isn't this a beautiful day today?" he asked his wife, but then realized she had got up and left already. Sitting up, he looked over toward the playground and noticed the kids were gone as well. He sat in silence as he glanced around to see where Kiersten and Brita had wandered off to, but didn't see them anywhere up or down the street.

"They must have slipped into the Swedish shop while I was daydreaming," he said to himself. "Strange that the kids all went away at the same time." The swings swayed, moved by the welcome autumn breezes, almost as if they were in use by ghosts from years past. That sent a chill down his spine or maybe it was just a cold breeze that went through his jacket. The weather had been cooling off significantly over the past couple of days.

He stood from the bench and briskly walked one block to the old Swedish shop to see if he could catch up with his wife and daughter. Something in the front window got his attention and he stopped by the large door. Where he expected to see little red wooden horses and blonde dolls with white cloths on their heads, there were mannequins modeling the latest fall fashions. The blue and yellow Swedish flags in the window had been replaced with credit card symbols and a shoplifting sign. The most disturbing item was that the wooden sign with the writing, 'The Swedish Shop' was no longer hanging over the front door, and instead a new sign that said, 'Eighth Street Dress Shop' was in its place.

Erik glanced behind him, stepped backward into the road to look up and make sure he was where he thought he should be. It sure seemed correct. He then had to go inside to look around, determining that this was indeed the right building, and he couldn't believe his eyes. The interior walls were the same and the large, dark mahogany counter where Mr. and Mrs. Petersson always stood was still there, but the store had been transformed into a modern clothes store, many of which he would never want his wife to wear. The dark wood floors and red brick walls were the same, but the Swedish Shop was gone, transformed into something without a soul. Nothing could replace his daughter's favorite store, yet only a few hints of the old place remained.

"Excuse me," Erik asked one of the girls behind the counter. "Do you remember the people who used to work here when this was 'The Swedish Shop'?"

"Yeah, I think my mom told me they both died several years ago. Mr. P had a heart attack a while back and Mrs. P passed away in the past couple of years. I'm not sure what she died of. I always loved coming here as a kid. She taught me how to play the piano."

Erik's heart sank as he grieved the loss of his former neighbors. He turned away from the girl, hiding the obvious surprise that must have been visible in his eyes, but he feared that his increased breathing and staggered steps might cause her to be alarmed. In a daze, he wandered back outside, not even noticing that it was overcast now. This day was turning out to be too much for him as he shuffled through leaves on the sidewalk for a minute, not knowing what to think. His head ached so he hurried over and sat down on the bench again, cradling his head in his hands. He closed his eyes and clenched his teeth, leaning forward in agony.

It wasn't the typical migraine, but was the kind of headache that required a specialist to run tests to determine the cause. Something was seriously wrong and he was no longer able to ignore the discomfort. It wasn't the first time he experienced this kind of pain and he needed to see a doctor again soon. He let out an audible groan, but fortunately there was nobody around to hear it. Unsure about how much time had passed, the pain eventually subsided and he could finally sit up straight again and open his eyes. The past two days had been an emotional roller coaster, and adding the agony of this headache was unbearable. He wondered how much longer he could take this.

Chapter Four

At the Stockton Police Department, Officer Tami Anderson looked over a strange package she had received and tried to make sense of it. Opening the envelope, she saw several newspaper clippings inside and she noticed the date on one of the articles was 1996. It mentioned an old court case in which Illinois Representative Jerry Grant was somehow involved and had taken sides with the gas company. She read the piece, but nothing jumped out at her. She took a few minutes to spread out each of the articles across her desk and skimmed the various stories. People walked by, but she stayed focused on these stories and ignored the rest of the world as she went back in time with every little rectangular clipping. Without looking up, she called to her partner.

"John, didn't Senator Jerry Grant just die recently?"

Officer John Hultgren looked up at her, and paused for a second.

"Yeah, I heard he had a heart attack a few days back. Why do you ask?"

"This envelope came to me today, with an old newspaper clipping about something he worked on about fifteen years ago. There's also several other small articles over the years accusing him of taking bribes, perjury, etc, but they all appear to have been proven false."

"It figures. Now that he's dead, people will try to slander his name when he can't defend himself. Probably just a quack that didn't get something his way."

Tami thought about that while reading one of the clippings.

"Yeah, I suppose so. It's interesting, though, that there are so many different articles over the past few years that accuse him of illegal activities. It's also interesting that he got out of each one. It looks like a pattern that doesn't paint a pretty picture of this guy. Either he had a lot of enemies who kept trying to pin false charges on him or he was a slick politician who didn't let anything stick to him."

"Who sent the package?"

"Doesn't say. Just a bunch of newspaper articles with a typed letter, no signature or return address. If I didn't know better, I'd say he was a shady politician who had a knack of getting away with a lot of bribes and cover-ups, both when he was local Representative Grant and after he became a state senator."

"Interesting theory if someone wanted to pursue it. I just don't see any value in dragging his name through the mud after he's dead."

John turned back and looked through papers on his desk while Tami pondered the clippings a bit more. After several minutes, she put them back in the envelope and filed it in her desk drawer, picking up the current newspaper. She leaned back in her chair and a name on the front page caught her attention.

"Long-time judge, Frank Lewis, passed away last evening," she read out loud.

Tami sat up, opening her drawer to pull out the envelope she just filed away. She reviewed the different newspaper articles again and stopped when she found the one she was searching for.

"Local Representative Jerry Grant praised the Honorable Judge Frank Lewis in the recent decision exonerating the Stockton Gas Company of any wrong-doing in the explosion on Eighth Street last August," she again read out loud to nobody but herself.

She looked at the current newspaper headline that mentioned the judge's death, then back to the fifteen year old clipping that mentioned this same judge with the former senator who was accused in today's anonymous package. It seemed too coincidental to see this man's name twice in one day, in articles that were more than a decade apart.

There could actually be something with these accusations, but she let it go at that. She ripped out the current headline announcing the judge's recent death, putting it into the file folder with the rest of the package, and shut her desk drawer a second time. She would come back to this when she got a few minutes this week.

She glanced over at her partner, noticing that he appeared to be too large for the chair at his desk, and stared at his buzzed haircut. At six-foot-five and over 250 pounds of muscle, he was a daunting character and she wondered if she should discuss this more with him. He had a way of pushing his weight around and intimidating her in conversations, and he seemed to like the effect he had on people. She noticed that he brushed aside any possibility of this package being a potential lead on a new case, but she couldn't help but wonder if this was something worth pursuing. She was young, but had already started climbing the ladder in this office, gaining the respect of many of Stockton's finest. She didn't get here by ignoring her instincts.

&&&

Father Bill Ljunglof sat at his oak desk at St. Mark's Cathedral, not really reading any of the papers he held in his hands. His eyes glanced around his meticulously clean office, but he didn't focus on anything his eyes touched upon. Ignoring his bookcase, disregarding the colorful wallpaper, paying no attention to the impressive wooden door to his office. He was deep in thought about the man who came to visit him for confession and disappointed that this fellow had left so abruptly. The rays of sunlight peered through the high, colorful windows, giving warmth to the cold room, but the priest didn't seem to feel it. He had been bothered by the man's words ever since he left the confessional in a hurry and wished he could have said more.

He realized a man in an old oil painting stared down on him and he thought someone else watched him through his office window. Turning his head, he found that there was nobody outside. Of course not. Who would be staring at him through the window? He hated feeling as though he had done something wrong. Should he be worried someone would discover his past and bring him in front of the church leaders? He was a respectable man, but something constantly made him feel as though he was just not good enough to be in this job. Maybe the confessing man would be the true test that would help him redeem himself and prove that he should indeed be in a position of leadership in the church. Or maybe this man would help to reveal Father Bill's past to the world and show that he wasn't worthy of being a priest.

He briefly and inconspicuously glanced up at the older man in the oil painting, locking in on his eyes for only a moment. This man's hair was gone on top, with a little silver on each side, and his smile was gentle and trustworthy. He was a priest from years ago, long since passed away, but was one

Father Bill had remembered when he was younger. Could the eyes in this painting reach into Bill's other life and see what was buried there, hidden away for no one to see? Nonsense. That past was gone and he was a new man. Bill pleaded with the eyes from the painting to look into his heart now and see the change in him over the past few years. No, he needed to concentrate on the man from the confession. That was the priority right now.

Father Bill couldn't get the angry man out of his mind and was deeply concerned that this guy had indeed done something terrible. The man was protected from being turned in to the police by the rules of privacy with confession. However, he also knew that if this man was a threat to the community, the priest hearing the confession had an obligation to at least report a potential danger posed by this man, even though he could legally keep the details of the confession from the police.

"What would I say to the police? That some man, I don't know his name and I don't really know what he looked like, came to me and said he had taken revenge on someone, and that this victim was now dead? Oh, and by the way, I don't know the victim's name either."

Since they were both sitting in the confessional, he couldn't really tell how tall the man was but guessed he was close to six feet based on where his face was while sitting. Bill was about five-ten and this man sat a couple of inches higher than him. It looked like he had a dark beard, no glasses, but that's about all he had to go on. He did seem to lose his temper a couple of times, so apparently he had some anger problems. Not much information to even give to the police.

He wondered if someone had been killed in Stockton in the past couple of days and thought that if there was an unsolved murder, then he could believe this angry man was truly a threat. He knew one of the police officers in town and considered calling her to see if she believed this was something to be concerned about, but decided against it. The man in confession mentioned that the person he had taken revenge on had died of natural causes.

Father Bill closed his eyes, put down the papers, and prayed for his confessor and for himself. After a minute or so, he opened his eyes and looked around his office, even up at the ceiling as if he expected to see someone watching him. Unfortunately, Father Bill Ljunglof felt very alone lately and he wondered if anyone was listening up there.

Chapter Five

JUDGE FRANK LEWIS WOKE UP only to find his surroundings were dark and quiet. Feeling cold all over, he wondered if he needed to get up and set the thermostat. He figured that he must have had too much to drink the previous night since he didn't remember going to bed. He thought for a few seconds and realized that he couldn't see any light at all coming into the room. This was odd because there was usually a little light in here, even when the moon wasn't out.

He wanted to look over at the window but found that he couldn't turn his head or lift his arms. He desperately tried to sit up and figure out what was happening but he was unable to move his legs. Laying there on his back, he soon discovered that he couldn't move any part of his body. He wasn't even sure if his eyes were open. He attempted to call out to his wife but nothing happened. His mouth wouldn't open and he couldn't make any noises.

He recognized it was cold, so his senses still worked. As his mind went through all kinds of scenarios, he smelled a strange aroma that wasn't pleasant. It was like a combination of hospital and burnt toast, but even worse. Where was he? This obviously wasn't his home, which always smelled like apple pies, cinnamon, or pine, thanks to his wife's creative use of candles. He noticed a slight pain in his head, as well as discomfort in his stomach, so he hoped he could move as soon as he woke up from this state. It's almost as though he was starting to come out of anesthesia after surgery, except that he hadn't gone in for surgery. At least not that he was aware of.

At this point, Frank had serious concerns and needed to know what was going on with him. He didn't even know if he was breathing, and seriously wondered if he had died, still stuck in his body for some reason. Now he feared that if there was life after death, he was not on his way to Heaven and would soon be taken to the other extreme. That couldn't be what the burnt smell was, could it?

Wait. He heard someone whistling and walking around. If only he could get this person's attention. Just then, the door opened and someone stepped into the room. Frank listened as somebody's hard-soled shoes tread lightly on the tile floor and thought he might have been a doctor coming to check up on him. Maybe he was indeed in a hospital, which was infinitely better than waiting to be transported to you-know-where for all eternity. Hopefully this man could revive him.

"Help me please!" was what he tried to say, but it was only in his mind, since his lips didn't move and no voice was heard.

The man walked over to a cabinet and then came up very close, standing still, probably right next to Frank.

"Hi, Judge Lewis. I'm very glad to see you today. You've been asleep for a couple of days already. I was afraid you might not wake up at all since I gave you a little bit more than I gave Senator Grant, but I'm thinking that you may be able to hear me now. Is that right?"

The man paused, then added, "Nod your head once for yes, twice for no. Ha ha ha, just kidding."

"Who is this man?" Frank wondered, as his mind raced

to distinguish the man's voice.

"Your funeral should turn out well today. Maybe you'll recognize the voices of some of the people who show up. I want to tell them all what a lying, untrustworthy cheat you were all those years but I'm going to hold my tongue until the timing is just right. I won't be quite as silent as you are now, though," and the man laughed.

As Frank took in those words, he tried to remember what happened after he went out to eat. He went to 'Bella's Italian Ristorante' in the downtown area, and had ordered manicotti. Everyone knew this was his favorite place and he liked the owners. He and his wife had a nice, quiet table and talked about their plans for the next few months.

"Well, I want to remind you now that I didn't appreciate what you did to me a few years back. I'll be helping you understand that I'm going to get my revenge in a way you won't like very much."

Frank was really nervous now as he listened closely to his mysterious visitor. He remembered eating out and thought that he did recognize the man's voice. The waiter at the restaurant had said the same thing to him, "Hi Judge Lewis. I'm very glad to see you." This must be the same man from Bella's. He had a dark brown beard and mustache and was friendly. Very personable. Yes, this had to be the same person, but what did he do to me? Did the waiter poison me? His mind raced to figure out why this man would want revenge on him. He had to get out of this stupor before this guy did anything crazy, but nothing moved. He couldn't even give some kind of sign that he was still alive.

"You may not remember me, Frank, but you took a bribe a few years ago and judged against me, even though I was plainly innocent of any wrong-doing and should have been compensated for all damages."

That took Frank by surprise and he strained to remember which case this could have been. He had taken so many bribes over the years it was impossible to know which one this guy was talking about. Frank finally regretted his unethical actions as a judge but it was too late. He wanted to cry but couldn't even create a tear.

"I trusted that you would have ruled in my favor, but I guess the gas company was so powerful and so generous that you couldn't resist an incentive from them. Isn't that right?"

Okay, so it was one of the gas company cases. He should have done something about them a long time ago. They always tried to cover up some negligence on their part and he let them use his position as a judge to do it. Now he was going to suffer for his involvement with them. None of their money was worth what he was going through now.

The man adjusted Frank's glasses and they pressed against his face before the man gently slapped his cheek. This person appeared to have a sense of humor and seemed as though he enjoyed this but Judge Lewis certainly did not. Something in his voice had an edge to it that was extremely frightening, and the judge hoped to get out of this right away. Now the man poked his finger into the judge's chest.

"I'll tell you what I did to Senator Grant and then maybe you'll understand why I brought you here, Frank. You see, your good buddy, the senator, came here to visit me recently, and I put him through the crematorium while he was still alive. Oh, you thought he died after the theater last week? Well, think again. He only appeared to be dead, very much like you are now. He was alive for his own funeral, just like you'll be today, and he came back here to let me share some of my grievances with his work as an elected official. We had a nice discussion and then he got all heated up, so to speak. Yet, there was nothing he could do about it, if you know what I mean. Yes, I think you know exactly what I mean. You should have heard him scream when the fire really got hot."

If the judge could have cried, tears would have poured out now, but all he could do was lay there, motionless with a solemn look on his face. He now knew that he was indeed alive but everyone thought he was dead. Plus, he was at the mercy of an angry man who was probably the innocent victim of a cover-up, one in which he himself was most likely involved.

"You see Frank, my little business was the victim of the gas company's carelessness and you should have clearly seen that. I'm sure you did, but you turned a blind eye to justice. When you covered for them and ruled against me, I lost everything!"

Frank sensed that the man banged his fist on the table next to him and let fear take over his mind completely. He expected this guy to punch him and wondered if he was really going to incinerate him alive in the crematorium. He always had such a fear of burning in a fire that he was scared to death at this point. Maybe he would have a heart attack now and be spared the torture of burning alive. That would be merciful, but he didn't deserve mercy for what he had done. Why wasn't he able to move? He wanted to plead with the man, get up and run away, anything but lay there motionless. His body gave no sign of life.

He listened carefully for what his captor was going to do next, waiting with more apprehension than he'd ever experienced in his whole life. The man calmed down, controlled his temper, and straightened out Frank's jacket. He now knew that he had no chance of escape and would suffer immeasurably before being killed by this guy. What could be worse than being burned alive in a crematorium fire?

"I was a little surprised when I found that you didn't want to be cremated, but it gave me some other ideas. I almost considered embalming you while you were still alive but I wasn't sure you would really feel pain with that. It's only right that you suffer immensely for your crimes. You know what I decided on, Frankie ol' boy? I decided to bury you alive in your new, expensive casket and see how you like that. We'll be moving you to the cemetery right after your funeral. Just wait until you see what I rigged up to keep you alive for a day or so while you're six feet under."

Chapter Six

AFTER THE GRAVESIDE FUNERAL, which was stereotypically overcast and threatened by rain, the group of dark-clothed visitors paid their last respects and stopped to read names from the cards on the group of flower arrangements standing around the casket. The colorful flowers contrasted with the dreary weather and black attire, but they were so beautiful that people appeared to be drawn to them. With the sun concealed behind a black veil of clouds, there was a distinct chill to the air as many of the people shivered and cursed at the cold wind.

Erik couldn't clearly see the expressions of these people as each one walked by the grave site, but he did wonder if anyone honestly cared about this man. He was a judge who accepted bribes and allowed innocent people to take the blame while the true guilty parties were exonerated. This kind of person couldn't be a good family man, could he? Someone this deceitful in a court of law had to be just as corrupt and untrustworthy at home in his personal life. At least that's what Erik kept telling himself.

He watched from a distance as the family and friends of Judge Lewis slowly left the gravesite, and he smiled as they all eventually drove the winding path out of the cemetery. He always enjoyed the summer sunshine, but he also had an affinity for the autumn winds, the multi-colored leaves on the ground, and the feeling that things once full of life were now giving in to death. It was fitting that they were at the cemetery on a day like this, where people lay like the fallen leaves and the cold ground claimed them all.

Erik enjoyed the change of the seasons from summer to autumn, but wished the sun would stay out more than it had been. Lately, the sunshine seemed to comfort him more than ever and dreary days threw a damper on any outdoor plans he made. He struggled to convince himself that it was not that bad out today, but he wasn't very successful. Trying to take his mind off of the overcast skies and lack of sunlight, he looked out across the property. He admired the green grass speckled with small white headstones and was glad to see great oaks and maples placed strategically throughout. A cemetery could be a peaceful and relaxing place if a person was in the right state of mind, but Erik undoubtedly wasn't in that state right now. Any peace he might have had today seemed to have left with the sunshine, regardless of how hard he tried to relax outside and take advantage of some cooler, fall weather.

He looked over at Keith and asked, "Are you ready to start lowering him into the grave?"

Keith glanced up at the fast-moving dark clouds and shook his head with a bit of frustration.

"Yeah, let's get it over with. I'd like to take my son fishing before it rains tonight, and if we hurry, I can get at least an hour or two in before then."

Erik admired Keith and the dedication he had for his family, and felt some kind of connection to him as a result. They were alike in many ways, since Erik also loved his wife and daughter more than anything in the world. However, Keith would probably never bury someone alive out of revenge, would he? Maybe if he had gone through what Erik experienced at the hands of these monsters. People just don't realize what they're capable of until they're put into some kind of irreparable situation like he was. Does that make it justifiable to become a monster then, just like those who did it to him? Again, he forced those thoughts out of his cluttered mind.

They both walked toward the judge's grave, neither paying attention as thousands of red and yellow leaves blew from the trees along the edge of the cemetery, providing a spectacular fireworks display of color for nobody in particular, except maybe for the hundreds of long-term residents of Stockton Cemetery. The strong fragrances of local flowers, probably Jasmine and Gardenia, were carried throughout the cemetery as Erik breathed it in. He wanted to convince himself that the day was not as bad as he thought it was.

"This truly is a great time of year, isn't it Keith?"

"It's getting a little too cold for my tastes. Give me some more of the sixty and seventy degree weather that we had last month and I'd be happy. I don't like the time change either, since it gets dark too early now."

Erik nodded in agreement, as the conversation stopped and they focused on the job at hand. Working quickly and quietly, they lowered Judge Lewis into the ground with no problems, and the casket settled firmly in its final resting place.

"If you want to take off now, I'll finish up here."

"That would be perfect, Erik. I appreciate it. You should come with us next time."

He nodded with a grin, and then watched his co-worker leave the cemetery. Emptying his mind of pleasant thoughts of family and friends, Erik slowly turned his head back to the grave and his smile gave way to wrath. He wondered what went through Judge Lewis' mind now, as the man surely realized he had just been placed into his own grave. The two were quite possibly the only living people on the entire grounds now that Keith was gone.

Erik carefully climbed down on top of the light grey casket, pulled some kind of connector from his jacket pocket, and worked on attaching the device to an unseen part at the end of the casket. He then coupled it to a hose that was covered up in the ground. His expectations were that this hose, which he set up earlier, would provide air for the judge and keep him alive for a while after the grave was filled in with dirt. Pleased with himself that it seemed to attach with ease, he sat up with a smirk as he thought about the Judge lying trapped in a lifeless body at the bottom of this hole. The judge would be coming back to life in the next eight hours or so and would be able to move, scream, and panic like never before. It'll be the middle of the night, so he'll be singing to an audience of one – himself.

"Judge Lewis. Can you hear me? I'm sitting on your tomb, and people will be covering you up with hundreds of pounds of dirt soon. You'll be able to hear the workers, but the problem will be that you won't be able to get out of this coffin. Nobody will be around to help you. Besides, they all think you're dead anyway. It's quite a predicament."

Erik knocked on the lid of the casket, and then stood up. He looked at the walls of dirt all around him and it gave him chills thinking about these walls closing in on him. He became claustrophobic as he finished getting someone ready to be buried alive. Ironic. Feeling the need to get out of the grave as soon as he could, he made sure the air hose was buried at the head of the casket and was out of sight in the dirt wall all the way up to the surface before he climbed out of the grave. He had to confirm that when the grave was filled in with dirt, the cemetery workers didn't damage his life-sustaining contraption. Yet he thought he should keep it all hidden so nobody suspected anything unusual was going on.

Once he had climbed out of the grave, Erik knelt down, felt around in the nearby grass, and found the top of the air hose that he had covered up so it couldn't be seen or tripped over. He blew into it to make sure there was a clear, unobstructed flow of air, and was glad to find no resistance. It occurred to him that he might have just blown dirt all over the judge's face, but there was nothing he could do about that now. That was the least of the judge's worries. He left the top of the hose open, but had concerns that when the grave was filled in later in the afternoon, some dirt could accidentally clog it up. This could ruin the plan to keep the judge breathing for a while down there, which was unacceptable.

He stood and looked around the gravesite, trying to think of the best way to protect the judge's air flow. One of the floral arrangements caught his eye as he briefly admired the pink and yellow colors in the shape of a cross. It wasn't very far from the opening of the tube at the surface, so he walked over to it and carefully moved the arrangement about eighteen inches. He scooted over two more arrangements slightly, which made them all still look positioned just right for a funeral. Best of all, they also concealed the air hose in a way Erik believed would protect it from getting covered up or damaged by the gravediggers.

Kneeling down once again, he leaned over by the flowers that had just been moved.

"Hello down there," Erik jokingly called into the hose as though he was talking to someone down in a mine shaft. "I have to leave for a little while, and the cemetery workers are going to disturb your slumber soon. I'll be back in a few hours to check on you and chat some more about how you messed up my life. You may be awake enough to actually respond to me at that time, but I doubt it. Don't go anywhere, OK? Talk to you later, buddy."

He gathered his tools and other belongings then walked

down to his car. Giving the new gravesite one more glance, he looked up at the cloudy sky and got in his car, driving slowly along the curved road that weaved around the judge's new neighbors.

&&&

A FEW HOURS LATER, ERIK CAME BACK THE same way he left and parked his white Volkswagen camper in the usual spot. It was nearly dark now. He wanted to check on the air hose and get out before they closed the cemetery gates. The winds were considerably colder, so he tightened up his jacket and quickened his steps. Looking around as he walked to the gravesite, he noticed there was still nobody around. They were alone again, but this time Judge Lewis was buried completely. The cemetery workers had done a good job of filling in the grave, and they didn't appear to have caused any problems with the air hose. Perfect.

"Hello Judge Lewis. It's me again. You'd be thrilled with how your grave looks now, and the flowers are very nice. I think you'll like it here. Hopefully, the snakes, moles, and bugs won't give you a hard time. There are some pesky underground critters here, you know. Come to think of it, you're a dirty rat so you might be the one ruining the neighborhood."

Erik shifted and sat down on the grass to get more comfortable.

"I'm not sure if you remember my case or not, but it should have been an easy one where I was reimbursed for all damages caused by the Stockton Gas Company's negligence. Instead, I was made out to be the villain and lost everything. My business, my friends, my whole life! I have you to thank for that, since you could have judged fairly, but you chose to judge in favor of whoever gave you the most. Not the best strategy for someone whose whole job description is to do the right thing and provide justice. People relied on you to be honest and fair but you chose to do the wrong thing, time after time, didn't you? I've recently discovered that my case was only one out of many, so I'm going to make sure the details of your involvement with Jerry Grant and some of the other players will be made public very soon. Lucky for you, you won't be around to face the music, but it will happen. Mark my words."

Erik saw someone at the front gate and knew he had to leave.

"Anyway, I need to get going but I'll stop by tomorrow and see how you're doing. We still have quite a lot to catch up on. Have a nice evening, and don't let the bedbugs bite."

Erik got up and hurried down to his car, driving his noisy camper to the gate in time to leave before it closed. He waved at the guard as he passed through and turned on the radio. All in all, it had been a very productive and satisfying day, despite the gloomy weather and constant lack of sunshine.

"Revenge is sweet," he tried hard to convince himself, though something still bothered him about what he had done to this man. He looked into his own tired eyes in his rear-view mirror and tried to recognize the man he once was.

Chapter Seven

THE RAIN OUTSIDE LASHED against the windows, waking Erik from a restless sleep. He lay in bed for a while with his eyes open but it was too dark to see anything. Listening to the sounds, feeling as though he was within the belly of the beast outside these walls, he wondered if this was going to be a miserable day, cold with no sunshine. That didn't make him very happy but not much did anymore. He thought back into the dream he was just awoken from and wondered if it was really a dream or some kind of memory. The two were often difficult to distinguish these days.

&&&

HE HAD DRIVEN THROUGH WISCONSIN and into Upper Michigan years ago, trying to get away from it all when things had gone bad for him. Although he couldn't remember what 'bad' actually meant in his case, he knew he had lost everything and had to start his life over again. He had several childhood memories but nothing from his adult life. It was as though he went straight from being a kid to the man he now was. This time of year was very cold, almost Christmas, and he expected to see quite a bit more snow than was on the ground. He had contacted a travel agent while he was still in Stockton, who found a small cabin for him to stay at for a while, maybe indefinitely, and was glad when he finally arrived. Some of the roads could have used a little repair, but they were better than when his parents brought him up here as a kid. Wisconsin was indeed a beautiful state, especially when painted white all over the countryside with snow, but he just wanted to get through it to his destination.

His parents and grandparents always seemed to come to Upper Michigan for vacations back then and it was like a second home to him. This visit was near the top part of Lake Michigan and he just needed to begin anew. There was no joy, no feelings at all, and he settled here for a long winter getaway.

Erik did a good job of blending in with the small town and stayed to himself most of the time, making just a few acquaintances while he fished and hunted the area throughout the year. The only job he could find initially was at the local funeral home, and at first he didn't think he could work with dead bodies. To his surprise, it wasn't very difficult and he found that it was peaceful work that gave him a lot of time alone. There was never a shortage of business, so it was good job security if he chose to keep working there. He didn't have much money, but he found that he truly didn't need it. After a few years, he saved up enough and purchased himself a small cabin, actually planning to live out the rest of his life there with what little memories he had of his past. If only he had kept to his plans.

&&&

As he stared up into the darkness in the apartment, listening to the howling winds, Erik thought about those days in the UP, or Upper Peninsula of Michigan. He wondered why he eventually came back to Stockton after fifteen years of almost pure solitude. He had a good life up there and should have stayed where he was. He rubbed his eyes, realizing that he wasn't getting back to sleep any time in the near future. This didn't seem like a dream, so he figured it must have been another memory that was slowly coming back to him. Occasionally, his memories were unpleasant experiences that brought pain and resentment but this one seemed serene. He wanted to dwell on it more so he concentrated, blocking out the action of the wind and rain.

&&&

THE WINTERS WERE HARSH IN UPPER Michigan, but life was simple for him, without all the complications of business, relationships, and traffic. He had physical aches and pains, especially when the cold came on fiercely, but he learned to accept them as part of his new life. He had been through an accident in his recent past and couldn't remember much of that part of his life. He sometimes uncovered memories of his childhood, visiting the UP, but very little beyond that.

After being in Upper Michigan for at least a dozen years, Erik remembered meeting a man who said he was a Chippewa Indian. The man was very knowledgeable about herbs and healing, both physical and spiritual. They often talked at Erik's cabin in the evenings and the man, who called himself Kajika, taught him much about life and death. This man understood English and spoke it slowly. His long dark hair and simple clothes reminded him of pictures he'd seen of Crazy Horse, one of the Sioux who had helped bring down General Custer at the Battle of Little Big Horn. Erik wondered how this man could fit in today while looking like he had stepped out of the past, but welcomed his company. There were many aspects of Kajika that were mysterious, but he was also fascinating.

&&&

THE SLAMMING OF A SHUDDER AGAINST one of his neighbor's windows reminded Erik that it was the middle of the night, and he still lay in bed awake in Stockton. He needed to get back to sleep but was captivated with the new memories that were drawn out now about his time in Upper Michigan. Keep them coming, as long as there was no pain. So far, they weren't so bad. He dove in headfirst in order to remember more about this man he met in the UP.

&&&

HIS FRIEND MADE ERIK BREATHE IN SMOKE from a mixture he made, and talked to him quite a bit about his past. Erik was intrigued that some of his memory could be restored with this technique but wasn't happy with several of the scenes he remembered. In one instance, he was in a courtroom but everyone seemed to be against him. Public officials had shifted the blame on him, and he was left with nothing. That was one of the events that led to Erik moving to the UP in the first place. He lost his business somehow and needed a fresh start. More of these memories gave Erik feelings of intense anger and he developed a hatred for those people who wronged him back in Stockton.

Kajika told stories about herbs that could be used to make someone appear to be dead and showed Erik how this could be done on a rabbit with a few simple steps and the right mixture. The rabbit did indeed look and feel as though it was dead, but within a day it was back to normal. Erik had never seen anything like this before and the idea fascinated him. It was interesting, but he couldn't believe it would be good enough to truly convince a doctor that a person who was actually alive, was dead. He wanted to experiment more and find out just how realistically someone's death could be faked. Schemes spun in his mind as he combined these herbs with the anger he felt toward those men who caused him to leave Stockton. He knew that he should just release those men from his thoughts and focus on his new life in the UP, but something just couldn't let go.

During one of their discussions, Erik had an episode where he developed a painful headache and this medicine man created a miracle tea for him to drink. The smell of the tea was unbelievably horrid and the taste was even worse, but the pain in his head was so bad that Erik was ready to try anything for relief. To his surprise, the headache eased within minutes and he was back to normal. He learned to never doubt Kajika's mixtures.

&&&

BACK IN STOCKTON WITH THE WINDS KEEPing him company, Erik wondered about Kajika and whether or not this man was real. During the last year he lived in the UP, Erik believed he talked to this Chippewa medicine man many times and experienced genuine healing from him. Their discussions were usually held in his dimly lit living room, shrouded in a hazy smoke that danced like evil spirits in candle light. This man or spirit or demon, whatever he was, pulled out from his locked up memories rare feelings of joy that Erik had forgotten about and he wanted desperately to experience that again. However, his friend also gave him more anger and vengeful thoughts than he ever considered possible, and he hated him for that. These feelings of wrath exploded out of him regularly, and he blamed his healer for bringing it to life. If it wasn't for Kajika, Erik would still be in the UP enjoying life away from the city and free from the emotions that consumed him and gave him the desire to go back to his past.

&&&

One of the last meetings with Kajika exposed a final set of memories, but they included his wife and daughter this time, both whom he didn't even know he had. Once he learned about them, however, he felt love and happiness for the first time in many years. He remembered their names, Kiersten and Brita, and they gave him an intense desire to go back to Stockton and find them both, making them part of his life again. Just like the anger welling up in him, love burst forth like a fountain, yet this love washed him from the hatred and made him feel like a new man. He preferred being filled with love, yet he couldn't control the dark thoughts that crept up on him.

To his surprise, he was unable to find the medicine man after that night and nobody he asked in town had ever heard of the man. It seemed like a big conspiracy to hide this fellow, but Erik had no desire to stick around to investigate further. He had a wife and daughter in Stockton and craved the opportunity to see them again. He might even find those men who ruined his life, and somehow make them pay for what they did to him. Kajika did teach him how to use specific herbs, so he considered the value of trying some of those if the opportunity became available.

&&&

The cold front must have pushed on through the city because winds finally subsided, giving Erik the chance to fall back to sleep. He was ready for it. This memory was not as happy as he had hoped it would be and actually brought out more hostile feelings, which he didn't want to experience right now. He had let this healer draw out facts about the men who conspired against him, but he wished those had remained buried in the recesses of his mind.

The medicine man had also given him a tea that gave him relief from his severe headaches, but he couldn't remember the ingredients that were used. He remembered other mixtures but not this one key potion that would provide relief when he needed it. He was thankful, however, to recall life with his wife and daughter, and Erik knew that was the best thing Kajika did for him.

He rolled over in bed to face away from the window, getting pulled in to the blackness of his bedroom. The silence was now overwhelming as he emptied his mind in an effort to forget everything for a few hours.

Chapter Eight

ERIK STOOD OUTSIDE THE OLD church, staring at the building from across the street. The skies had been overcast all morning and he was chilled by the autumn winds. How he wished the sun would come out. He had been waiting, almost hiding, around the corner of the downtown bank, occasionally peeking out to get a brief glimpse of the stained glass windows or the ornate sculptures. He remembered every interesting aspect of the church, interior and exterior, but was almost afraid of being seen by the holy structure, as though it had eyes and searched the streets for him. Not certain why he had an uneasy feeling about being here, he stayed out of sight for over twenty minutes except for the intermittent glance from his unique vantage point.

Finally, Erik moved out of the shadow of the old bank and stumbled forward toward the street. He hurriedly sat on the bench at the corner, facing the wall, and looked back over his shoulder. The church hadn't moved or changed its position, but the way he acted made it appear as though he expected it to lunge at him and rip him apart. The streets had been vacant of any pedestrians or traffic the entire time he was there, and he remembered how different things had been in the good old days. This was part of the busiest section of Stockton, hustling and bustling with cars and people walking here and there.

An unexpected movement did get his attention from the corner of his eye, as he noticed sunlight creeping near his bench. He watched as the light slowly glided across the street like an animal moving smoothly yet decisively. The clouds were finally clearing away, and the welcome warmth of the sun came out of nowhere.

"It's almost as though you're luring me into the church," Erik muttered to himself.

He raised his head to the sky, squinting as the sun's rays painted his face. A smile came out of the portrait and he looked back across the street. The shadows were chased away as the sunlight took over the street and gained the higher ground at the church property. It was as though the evil had been overcome by good and everything was going to be alright now. Or was it a trap, and once he went inside the church, would he again be tormented by the priest, never to escape this time?

His courage soon came back to him and he stood to his feet at the street corner, facing his destiny but not knowing what the outcome would be.

"It's just a building, right? That's just the sunlight breaking through the clouds, right?"

He wasn't sure why he felt so alone and nervous this morning, but he finally came to his senses, taking the first steps toward the church. He looked both ways, even though the traffic was non-existent this morning, and headed into the street. His eyes followed the sunlight as it moved up the wall of the church and lit up the building as though it was in a spotlight. While the entire roof glowed with the new rays, Erik stopped in the road to take it all in. Transfixed on the scene, unable to free his eyes from the moving light, he thought it appeared as though a curtain was being raised, presenting the church as the star of the show. He had to keep going toward the light.

Realizing he now stood in the road, he looked around quickly and then kept walking toward the front of the church. By this time, the sun was completely set free from the clouds and appeared to be advertising that this was indeed a beautiful day, telling people to come outside and enjoy what had been covered up all morning. This was such a relief after last night's wind and rain show that led him to believe it would be miserable weather all day.

Erik's footsteps slowed as he came to the sidewalk at the edge of the church property, and he cautiously scanned the walls, remembering every design, sculpture, and change in the roof. There was indeed a lot of history in this church, and he was impressed that it had been through so much over the years and still thrived. Then he remembered that he himself had been through a lot over the years, as well.

He passed the first set of stained glass windows and was mesmerized by them, as though it was the first time he had ever seen them. Looking all the way to the top, then slowly moving his eyes down to the bottom, he absorbed it all. Like a tourist, he saw everything he could in case he never came back this way again. Ignoring the sounds of his own footsteps on the sidewalk, he had to grab it all as he made his way past several more windows with similar designs and colors. It was like cramming for a test, trying to retain as much as he could before he faced his next tribulation.

He stopped when he found himself standing at the front door, and instantly remembered the many carvings on the large wooden obstacle. At first, he was glad the double doors were closed, but knew he had no choice but to overcome the impediment. Staring through the door, knowing what was on the other side, he stood in front of it for another few seconds before reaching out and pushing one of the doors open. Coming into his vision was exactly what he saw while the door was still closed, and it gave him an odd feeling of déjà vu. He had just been here, plus he had visited this church several times when he was younger, but it was still an unusual sense of foreboding.

Crossing the entryway didn't give Erik the feeling of dread that he had expected it to, so he felt relief while walking toward the confessional. Even the soft carpet gave him a welcoming sensation with every muffled step, and he wondered if that was odd. How could he be so calm and relaxed now, when he was in a panic outside for over thirty minutes? Was he being setup?

Trying not to look at the statues on the walls guarding each side of the benches, since they must be watching his every move, he walked purposefully toward the familiar wooden structure where he had just sat in the past week. Barely escaping the last time, he had trouble understanding why he would even try to come back and risk it again. His eyes accidentally caught the eyes of one of the saints portrayed in a stained glass window, so he hastily focused straight ahead again. He almost believed that they were gloating, knowing he was walking right into a trap. Everyone here could see it, so why was he still going ahead with this?

Erik quickened his pace and strained to see if the confessional was empty. It was, so he opened the door and stepped inside, out of sight from the inanimate audience he believed was watching his every move. He found that his breathing was as though he had been running a mile, yet he had only walked briskly down the side aisle of the church.

"Calm down," his mind told his body, and he tried to relax in this confined little room. He had gone from terrified to composed, and now his nerves were on edge again. He took a few deep breaths and slowed his breathing down significantly.

"Good morning. I'm not a member here, and I really

have only been to confession one other time."

"That's quite alright. Are you Catholic?"

Erik's heart jumped when he recognized the priest's voice and he considered leaving right then. No, he convinced himself that he would go through with this.

"I'm not, but I just want to confess something. There's a man who caused me a lot of emotional and physical pain many years ago, and I really wanted to hurt this man for a long time."

"I believe you told me a little about this person in the past week. Have you tried to overcome your feelings of revenge for him, with plans to forgive him?"

"No, actually this is a different person."

The priest was silent for a few seconds, while Erik still worked on regaining his composure.

"This person worked with the other man I told you about last time. They worked together to ruin my life, and I had a positive discussion with this guy recently."

"That's very good to hear. Do you think you'll be able to reconcile your differences with this other man?"

Erik tried to suppress a laugh.

"Yes, I finally feel good about our relationship now. He's had a chance to hear what he did to me, how it made me feel, and I believe he has taken some time to truly think about it."

"I'm so glad to hear this. Have you put the past behind you and can you fully forgive this person, as well as the other man who hurt you?"

"Well that's a different story. I feel good about putting the past behind me, but I still have a problem forgiving what these two did to me."

"But you just said you had a good talk with this man, and it sounded as though you had resolved your differences. You don't still want to cause this man harm, do you?"

"Well, the man's dead now, so I won't cause him any

harm."

Erik noticed a pause, and wondered if he had again said too much.

"How did this man die?"

"Oh, I heard it was a heart attack just the other day. Natural causes, of course. I was fortunate to talk with him before he passed away."

Again the priest paused, and Erik felt concerned again.

"This is the second man you've mentioned in one week who had wronged you in the past and is now dead. I get the feeling that you're not telling me something. Is there more you want to confess regarding these two men?"

Now Erik hesitated, feeling cornered. His eyes darted around the room and his thoughts raced as he put together a response.

"No, my confession is that I'm glad these two men are dead, and I believe they both got what they deserved. My anger toward them has subsided now since I was able to have a heart-to-heart with each of them about what they did to me. I feel better about the whole situation. It's as simple as that."

"No, actually there's more to it. I was hoping you would soften your heart, forgive these men, and release them from whatever guilt you seem to have placed on them. If they didn't change their hearts, then they will be judged..."

"Oh, I'm sure they've both been judged already."

"...yes, I agree, if they're dead, then God has judged them, but there's still work to be done in your own heart. You need to forgive them, and stop the anger from eating you up inside. You're still being held captive by this revenge, and you need to let it go."

Erik had heard enough, and quietly slipped out of the imprisonment of the small room while the priest still talked. He walked to the left, toward the front door, suspecting the priest may come out of the confessional and try to discuss this with him further.

&&&

WHEN THE PRIEST DID STEP OUT, HE WAS surprised to find that his confessor was nowhere to be seen. He didn't see the angry man walk in front of his door, but looked to the right anyway, confused that he could have disappeared so soon. Just to be certain, the priest walked all the way down the aisle to the front door, peering left and right with almost every step, only to wonder if the person who had confessions of revenge didn't even exist. The concept bothered him and he didn't even want to think about that. It wasn't realistic; however this man simply was not in the church anymore, and he couldn't have possibly made it all the way to the front door without being seen.

Standing outside the door, looking across the sidewalk and down the street in front of the church, Father Bill Ljunglof questioned his own sanity, wondering if there were things deep in his past that could bring on a delusion of a man who had vengeful tendencies. Was there something that could be making him reach inside and dig up dark secrets that had been repressed for so many years?

Chapter Nine

AFTER SLIPPING OUT OF THE church without being seen, Erik followed the sidewalk to the north, feeling good about himself and his visit to the priest. The sound of his dress shoes on the old sidewalk kept the time like the ticking of a clock, while he watched the blur of red bricks from each building pass him by with every step. The cool breeze reached in between the buildings to touch everything in its path, but the constant sunshine radiated throughout his body with a warmth that he appreciated immeasurably. The sunshine was his friend this morning and he wanted to take full advantage of it.

The last time he sat in that church, he felt as though his only friend had deserted him, and he was in a state of despair that deeply bothered him. Seeing his wife and daughter at the playground that day instantly lifted him out of the gloom. Today Erik was on top of the world for some reason, and he needed to see his wife again. The park with swans on the lake was probably where she would be by now, so he headed that direction. It was only a few blocks away and since this was such a great day to be outside, he decided to not take his car.

Only a couple of times did he get the feeling someone was watching him from the rooftop of a building across the street or from one of the dark alleys he passed, but he dismissed the thoughts and walked a bit faster each time it happened. He did everything to avoid the darkness and stayed out where the sun covered the sidewalks, cars, office buildings, and shops. Finally reaching the intersection across from the park, he paused and strained his eyes to see the lake through the red, yellow, and orange leaves.

Smiling, he put his hands in his coat pockets, checked traffic, and crossed the street, thinking about the way those orange leaves made it look as though the trees were on fire.

"What a spectacular display," he said as he admired those trees.

Autumn certainly was a beautiful season in so many ways, and he never tired of the fireworks show that the trees gave him every year. He wondered how the people way down south could live without the changing of the leaves each season, where the temperature was not cold enough to turn the leaves different colors and they went from green directly to brown. How fortunate he and his family were to live in such a place as Stockton, where they could celebrate all four seasons annually.

He glanced both ways once more to make sure he wasn't about to walk in front of a car, and kept going toward the sidewalk across the street. The wall by the sidewalk was brick, and looked so elegant under the large trees. He and his wife had walked beside it many times, hand in hand, when they went for a stroll through the park.

Erik considered that it was best to be away from those old buildings now, as he made it to the entrance of the park and saw the acres of grass separated by paths. These trails were where he and Kiersten had so many romantic walks, where Brita would roll down the green hills with her contagious laughter. He loved these memories and tried to open his mind to let more fill the emptiness that had overwhelmed him for years.

Brita ran toward him, and he was under the impression it was one of his memories when he noticed Kiersten waving at him with her gorgeous smile. He waved back and was reminded how incredible her hair looked blowing in the wind. She was the most attractive model he had ever seen, and he constantly reminisced about his days photographing her at the catalog company where she modeled so many years ago. All of his friends considered her to be the greatest catch in town, and he was elated when she finally agreed to start dating him. They hit it off so well and were always together. He got the best end of the bargain when they were married, and he never forgot how fortunate he was to have her as his wife and partner in life.

"The perfect pair," people would comment about her and Erik.

He bent down to scoop up Brita as she ran to give him the most wonderful hug that only a daughter could give. He squeezed her as he lifted her up, spinning around and covering her cheek with 'Daddy kisses' that she loved. They walked over to where Kiersten stood, and he continued to hold Brita while he wrapped his other arm around his better half.

"I'm so glad to be here with my two favorite people of all time," he told the two ladies in his arms. "I don't ever want to let you go."

Setting Brita down and holding her hand, Erik held his wife's hand and they walked along the path for a little ways, enjoying another sunny day together. He leaned over to kiss her neck, breathing in her faint perfume while her long hair smothered his face. He savored the moment until she laughed and pushed him away with her free hand.

"Your beard tickles my neck!"

He stole a glance at her profile and thought about her features. She was pure Swedish, with beautiful light skin, deep blue eyes, and the blondest hair of anyone he had ever seen. Erik was Swedish too, but he had brown hair and his skin was darker. Brita was a miniature mirror image of her mother, and he was so glad she took after Kiersten in every way.

"You're my Svenska Flicka, Brita," he said to his daughter, and she laughed.

"What does that mean, Daddy?"

"It means you're my little Swedish girl," and he leaned over to kiss the top of her head.

They walked under a large shade tree and sat in the grass, while Erik stretched out to lie on his back. His wife stayed sitting up next to him with her arms wrapped around her knees, just looking out over the park, and he softly rubbed her back. He looked up at the yellow leaves that covered this tree above him, and wondered which kind of tree they were from. These looked like leaves from an elm tree.

"Mommy, can I roll down the hill?"

"Of course, Brita. As long as you give us a kiss every time you come back up here to roll down again."

Bursting with happiness, Erik wanted so much for this to never end. He gazed over at the rest of the park to his left, while Brita giggled and rolled in the grass. His mind wandered again as more of his home movie memories came into view. He watched himself moving in fast motion in the grass near where his family rested, with the background showing up in bad greens and blues like an old color movie that was not quite right. In the memory, he rolled down the hill, causing his wife and daughter to laugh, and he focused in on their faces. This was the happiest a family could ever ask for, and he treasured it in his heart.

He then saw himself carrying Brita on his shoulders while his wife walked beside him in the soft grass, holding his arm and carrying her shoes with her other hand. He couldn't place where they were at this time, but there was joy in each of their faces again. They walked by the lake, where Brita threw pieces of bread to swans, and Erik immediately knew where they were. That was the lake here at the park, and was always one of Brita's favorite places to walk.

Next, he was downtown again, walking in front of the little restaurant next door to his studio. He saw himself waving to his wife and daughter as they sat inside the restaurant. He went through the front doors of his studio and saw the reception desk, the large photos of Brita and Kiersten hanging on the walls, and he quickly went into his office. It was his and Kiersten's anniversary and he picked up something from his desk drawer that looked as though it was wrapped like a gift. He remembered they were going out to dinner that evening to celebrate.

Erik watched as he came back through the front door, then walked down the sidewalk to the back of the building for some reason. That's right. The gas company was working in the basement today and he decided to check on the progress. Strolling by his Fiat parked in the alley, he unlocked the back door of his building, went inside, and saw every step leading down to the basement. Things seemed to slow down and his vision became blurred. He heard muffled sounds now as his black dress shoes clacked against the stone steps, and he noticed that voices were distorted slightly as well.

"How's it coming along down here?" he asked the man.

"I don't understand this. Something's not right," he heard the man say.

"What do you mean?"

Then it was deathly silent as the man didn't respond right away. The hush seemed to go on forever until he heard the worker shout and ran toward him.

"Get out of here! It's gonna blow up any minute ..."

&&&

ERIK SAT UP, ONLY TO FIND THAT HE WAS alone on the grass under the tree. He looked around to see where Brita and Kiersten had gone, but they were nowhere to be found. Was he so enthralled by his mind's eye home movie that he didn't even feel Kiersten get up? Thinking back to what he had remembered, he beamed at the times he had with his wife and daughter. Yet his concerns were raised about the basement memory and what the worker had yelled.

"I need to find Kiersten and Brita. Maybe if I walk around the park I'll see them. Brita probably needed to visit the little girl's room and they had to hurry."

That brought another smile to his face, as he got to his feet and determined the best direction to start looking. Remembering where the restrooms were, he headed toward them at a relaxing pace, keeping his eyes moving across the park in case he spotted them somewhere else.

Families walked together in the sunshine, and Erik was mesmerized by the splendor of the fall leaves everywhere he looked. This must have been the peak viewing time for the fall colors, and was a beautiful day to be outside to enjoy it. To his disappointment, he wasn't able to find his wife and daughter inside the park at all, and couldn't see her car in the parking lot. They had vanished again.

Chapter Ten

FATHER BILL LJUNGLOF LOOKED around at the entrance inside the police station, feeling out of place with his very noticeable white collar. He wondered what these blue collar workers thought about white collar workers like him before realizing his joke wasn't that funny. Right away, he masked his attempt at a smile.

He watched several officers walk around the small workplace area and listened to the buzz of the conversations without really hearing what was being said. These men were tough enough to bring down hardened criminals, but he felt safe even in the middle of this group of people. These were the good guys, right? A phone rang as he noticed a man in uniform carrying a handful of papers to another officer's desk and watched them start discussing them. This place had the appearance of a typical office work area, except for the occasional blue uniforms. A lot of paper shuffling, ringing phones, hustle and bustle. Stockton's finest keeping the city safe from people who choose the wrong side of the law.

In all of his years in this town, he had only been here once before, and for some reason he experienced an awkwardness at this situation. He didn't really know if he had something that would require the attention of the Stockton Police Department, but the guilt that practically smothered him by not contacting someone, just in case, ate away at his insides.

"Hi, can I help you Father?" asked the first man that walked by.

Taken by surprise at the man's sudden appearance, he stared at the officer and gave him a weak smile, looking at his name badge. Officer Hoffman.

"Um, good morning. Yes, I was hoping to talk with Officer Tami Anderson. I figured that she'd be in today."

"Can I ask who's here to see her?"

"Father Bill Ljunglof."

"Sure, let me go and see if she's available now. Wait here. I'll be right back."

Father Bill nodded, and the other man headed across the room. This guy seemed young, but gave the impression of being very strong, with a lot of muscles visible through his blue shirt. Not someone he would want to face in a confrontation, but chances are good that he would never have to.

He hadn't talked with Tami in a few months, but was confident he could mention his concerns to her without being treated like an alarmist. They actually went to school together years ago, and were still good friends even after high school. Tami wasn't a member of his church, so they didn't get to talk each week, but based on some of their past conversations, he believed they still had a good relationship from several of their get-togethers over the years. He would soon find out how accurate that belief really was. He watched as a thin officer came around a corner and her eyes lit up when she recognized him.

"Father Bill. It's good to see you again, although unusual for you to be here where I work rather than where you work."

Her elegant smile set him at ease, and he reached out to return her handshake. He forgot how tall she was and realized that her eyes were at his eye-level.

"Good morning, Tami. It's great to see you again. You

look different in uniform."

"So do you."

They both laughed and the priest got straight to the point.

"A few things have happened recently that I have to share with you, and I figured it would be best away from my usual crowd on a Sunday morning. Do you have a few minutes to talk?"

"Of course, let's go back to one of the offices so we can have some quiet."

Father Bill followed Tami as she maneuvered around a few desks and he glanced around to see some of the faces react to a priest walking around in the police station. He gave each of them a friendly smile, of which most of them returned, but he noticed a few who just looked back at their computer screens with no reaction at all. He tried to recognize any of these people, and assumed they didn't go to his church since none of their faces seemed familiar.

His eyes continued to explore the walls and he compared the differences here to the walls at the church. There were no paintings of saints on the walls, no stained glass windows depicting Bible scenes, or familiar hymns playing in the background at the police station. It was so much more comfortable at the church than here, but he reminded himself that this should only take a few minutes. Tami led him into a glass office where she shut the door as soon as he walked inside. The clamor from the busy open room was silenced, like the closing of a catacomb.

"I hope you won't get harassed about being behind closed doors with a priest."

She laughed and said, "Don't worry. I can take anything these guys dish out. Anyway, what brings you over here? It must be pretty serious, so I'm all ears."

Father Bill gazed at her and thought about how different

she looked with her dark hair up. She used to keep her hair down and wore short dresses, but today she was attired as a police officer and seemed much more official in a uniform. He liked the way he remembered her from school better, but she still looked very attractive with her hair this way. He was glad she had long pants on because he remembered how much he used to enjoy staring at her legs in school. That was before he even considered the priesthood, and he promptly pushed that image of himself from his mind. That was in the past.

"I'll get straight to the point. I've had a man come to confession, and I'm concerned he may be a possible threat to some people in the community."

This immediately got Tami's attention, and she sat on the corner of the desk, staring intently into Father Bill's eyes.

"I've never heard of a priest bringing up something from confession."

"Well, I can't give you details because I'm bound to privacy, but I just feel so convinced that this man has either done something terrible already or he soon will do something very bad. He's not a member of the church, and I don't recognize his voice at all. I couldn't tell you who he is even if I knew."

"What has he said that gives you concern?"

"He has a tremendous amount of anger, and it appears to be directed at a couple of people who hurt him years ago. I've tried to talk to him about forgiving these men, but that's out of the question for him right now."

"A lot of people are angry, Father Bill. What makes you think he might truly act on it? Most people don't follow through, even when they have anger issues."

His eyes bore into hers and he moved slightly near the corner of the desk, raising his opened hand.

"I understand that, and I appreciate you pointing that out. This guy said both men are now dead, but added that he's glad these men are burning in Hell."

Father Bill detected the surprised look in her eyes, and before she could say anything, he added, "He also mentioned that he'd talked to them both before they died. At first, I thought he spoke with them and worked out his differences before they died, but I don't think that's the case here."

"Do you believe he killed these men?"

"That was my first impression. I asked how the men died, but he told me they both died of natural causes. I initially thought I could ask you if anyone had been murdered here in town over the past week, but if they died of natural causes, it makes things a bit more challenging to piece together."

Father Bill saw Tami's expression change, looking away momentarily, and could tell the wheels were spinning in her mind. She didn't have a very good poker face, and he had to find out what her thoughts were about this scenario. This story seemed to have hit a nerve.

"What is it Tami? Do you see a possible connection?"

She hesitated, but then found the words she decided to share with him.

"Nothing definite, but I did get an unusual package in the mail about someone who had just passed away, and I saw that another man died a couple of days ago. Both of natural causes and both were popular men in town. I'm not sure if there's anything there, but it's worth looking into. Let me see what I can dig up on them."

"Sounds good, Tami. I appreciate it. Hopefully, it's nothing, and this guy just likes to vocalize his anger. I really don't expect him to go to confession again, but if he does show up, what should I do?"

"Try to focus on the things these men did to hurt him, any clues that we could connect him to someone who is recently deceased. Keep working on helping him to forgive each of them. That's probably what you've been doing, so don't change anything there. I know you'll say the right things. Whatever you ask, don't sound like you're a police officer probing for information. Any details you can pull out of him in the course of your conversation, however, could be helpful."

She reached in her pocket and pulled out a card, handing it to him.

"If he comes by again, or if you think of anything else that might be useful, please call my cell phone, anytime."

He smiled and reached out, taking the card and reading it as she walked past him to open the door.

"Wow. If only it was this easy to get your phone number back in high school. I might not have gone into the priest hood." They both laughed, and he added, "I'm just kidding. Thanks Tami. I appreciate you listening and not thinking I'm crazy."

She offered a genuine smile that made her face look more beautiful than he ever remembered, and then led him back across the room. He followed her past the stares from the wolves waiting to devour them, between the gauntlet of desks, toward the front of the station.

"I'll let you know if I make any connections, and please let me know if he stops by again. Especially if you have any more concerns."

"Will do. Have a great day."

"You too."

&&&

TAMI WATCHED THE PRIEST WALK OUT THE front door, and stood there thinking about the envelope she had received a couple of days ago. It's not that unusual for two public officials to die within a week of each other, even for a medium-sized town like Stockton. However, the fact that she received a package of newspaper clippings on

Senator Grant after his death did make things more interesting.

She ignored several staring eyes on the way back to her desk, and sat down, removing the envelope from her desk drawer. Pulling out one little square at a time and reading the clippings over again, she wondered if Senator Grant had actually done something years ago, maybe even unethical, to hurt the man who visited Father Bill. Even if he had, what would it matter, since Grant died of a heart attack? There was no foul play. It was probably just a coincidence that Judge Lewis had passed away in his sleep soon after that, and there was most likely no connection between the two deaths. In both cases, it was a heart attack anyway.

It was curious, however, to see the trail of suspicious activities for Senator Grant over the years, yet odd that the clippings were newly made copies on crisp paper, not the yellowed original newspapers from back then. May not be significant. She wondered what kind of person kept up with things like that from the newspapers over a ten to fifteen year period.

"Someone who had been wronged by Grant may hold a grudge and gloat over anything that might be potentially troublesome for the Senator," she said out loud.

"What'd you say, Tami?" asked her partner with his booming voice as he walked up to her desk.

Startled, she responded, "Oh sorry. I was thinking out loud. I didn't see you here."

"I just walked in the door. It's a shame you didn't notice my entrance. So Hoffman said you've got something going with a priest, eh? I didn't think they could date."

"No, he's a priest who wanted to get my advice on something that was going on at the church."

Tami didn't want to go into details yet, even with her partner, so she left it at that.

"Must be that handsome collar. You got something for men in white collars?"

She laughed, "No, of course not. Don't be an idiot, although I know that won't be easy for you."

"Touché. Here, you got something in the mail," and he handed Tami a sealed orange 8 ½ x 11 envelope before walking to his desk and sitting down.

Tami absent-mindedly examined it, and started to set it down on her desk before she recognized that it looked similar to the envelope she received just a few days ago. She froze and stared at it briefly, especially at the lack of a return address, and then hastily opened it. Her heart pounded as though she was about to make some kind of great discovery, but received a painful paper cut instead.

"Ow!" she exclaimed, and immediately put her left pointer finger in her mouth. After a few seconds, she examined the finger and noticed the blood trickling from the cut matched her dark red nail polish as she put a tissue on the cut and held it with her thumb to stop the bleeding. Her partner either didn't hear her or just ignored her mild outburst, and she clumsily poured out the contents of the envelope.

Copies of several small, carefully cut out newspaper clippings spilled onto the desk, and she detected that the dates were from quite a few years past. Turning them so she could read each one, she realized the name being discussed in each clipping was Judge Frank Lewis.

Chapter Eleven

THE RESTAURANT WAS BUSY FOR the middle of the week, but Erik didn't mind. Most of the people were friendly, and the day went by faster when he was on the go. He'd only been working here at Bella's Italian Ristorante for a few months, and was pleased with himself for what he had already accomplished here. There were several places at which to eat in Stockton, but this was one of the nicer restaurants, with excellent food, an attentive staff, and a constant need for reservations in advance.

The ambiance included a large open kitchen where guests could watch the food being cooked in brick ovens, as well as listen to romantic Italian music playing in the background. Dim lighting provided privacy inside to diners in tall booths and at the many round tables in the center of the room, and large groups could be accommodated in a couple of dining areas with long rectangular tables. The paintings on the walls showed scenes from various Italian cities and Italy's countryside, and the hanging ivy arrangements received many compliments. There was an open deck out back for outdoor seating when the weather permitted, and the evenings were always busy at this elegant restaurant.

Bella's attracted some of the most important people in Stockton, especially when they entertained out-of-town guests, and Erik hoped to see someone specific this afternoon. Since he had been working there, he already had the pleasure of serving two of the town's most prominent elected officials, former Senator Jerry Grant and Judge Frank Lewis, but he was on the lookout for someone else now. Studying this man's personal habits for over a month, he thought his prey would be out to lunch today. Erik was betting it would be Bella's, but so far there were no signs of him yet.

Filling water glasses and carrying trays of food around to different tables were handled with efficiency as he kept his eyes on the entrance to the restaurant. Even when he wrote down someone's dinner order, he glanced up to make sure he didn't miss his target. It was an interesting atmosphere that gave him a challenge, since there was constant background noise, talking, laughter, sounds of silverware and glasses clinking, while he hunted for someone without letting anyone know he was on the prowl. He found it thrilling, and thrived on the risk of being caught doing something so dangerous in public. He preferred a quiet atmosphere, but recognized this was a necessary part of his plan months ago when the pieces all came together.

Periodically, Erik stopped by the reservation desk to see if the man's name had been added, but was disappointed each time. He hoped not to draw attention to himself, and once even made sure the hostess knew he was looking to see what tables in his area were available on her chart. Careful not to appear to be hitting on her each time he checked, since he was probably old enough to be her father, Erik was popular with the staff and worked well with everyone on the team. He didn't want people to think he was a creepy old man, hovering around teenagers and college girls, even though he wasn't even fifty yet. When he caught his reflection in the mirror at the front of the restaurant, he turned away quickly so he didn't focus on it too deeply. He looked so different with a beard, and at first didn't realize the reflection was his. He saw the fancy uniform of a waiter, but often required a double-take to make the connection that he was the bearded man. He would never get used to seeing himself with hair on his face.

While he worked, Erik compared this job at the restaurant with working at the funeral home, and it was quite a comparison. The funeral home provided a lot of quiet time to reflect, not offering much interaction with live people, but the restaurant had friendly conversations, smiles, children, and a lot of activity. He remembered that he enjoyed being around other people and used to be an outgoing person. Keeping to himself for so long, he had forgotten how nice it was to be in a crowd. "Would you like a refill of iced tea, sir?" he asked.

"Yes, please. Unsweet."

On the other hand, downtime could be helpful as well, and much of the time at the funeral home was peaceful, giving him plenty of opportunities to think. Yet, when he had so much time to think, that was when he was most miserable. It was better to be busy and living his life than to have too much time on his hands, just thinking about living. Pondering his past was a mixed blessing. So much of it was filled with joy, but there was also...

"Could we get some more bread?"

"Of course," Erik replied. "I'll be right back with some."

To his disappointment, the unwelcome and recurring ache in his head started to return, and he tried to cover up his discomfort as much as possible. He checked his watch, and glanced to the front again, not seeing who he was looking for.

His shift was almost over. Not every hunting expedition comes back with a prize, so he would have to try again later this week. If only he had that concoction that took away his headache in less than fifteen minutes. He could already tell this was going to be a bad one.

Making sure all guests at each of his tables were content, and that nobody lacked anything, he made arrangements to transition his responsibilities over to the next shift. It wasn't soon enough, since the headache came on strong now as he slipped out of the restaurant. He had made an appointment to see a doctor after work, so if there was a good time for the head pains to come back, this was it. He wanted the doctor to see him while the headache was in progress, and it looked as though it might work out that way today.

As expected, driving was no pleasant experience, but the doctor's office was close by and it didn't take long to get there. He felt terrible as he walked through the front door, and the receptionist must have noticed right away that something wasn't right with him. She stood up, apparently recognizing Erik, and walked toward him with an appearance of genuine concern.

"Mr. Johnson, why don't you come back and lay down for a few minutes while I tell the doctor you're here? I'll sign you in."

Erik didn't argue, and she led him to a quiet room with the lights dimmed where he could lie down on an exam table. A nurse came in and took his vital signs, which Erik didn't even acknowledge, then she finished up and brought the lights down even lower.

"The doctor should be here in just a few minutes," and she gave him one last sympathetic look before closing the door.

Glad that he didn't have to wait long or talk to anyone, he was relieved but the pain was still overwhelming. With his eyes closed, he imagined himself lying beside a tranquil stream under clear, blue skies, with a cool breeze and the soft sounds of the running water. It was challenging with the feeling of someone taking a sword slowly through his head, pushing in, pulling out, pushing in, and pulling out. His imagery just wasn't working, and he hoped for some kind of relief.

The door opened and the doctor walked in, faced with Erik's expression of torment.

"Hi Erik. I can tell the pills aren't doing you any good. I'd like to get a CT scan today and see if there's anything visible that we can deal with. Is that OK?"

"Yes," was all Erik could mutter.

"I'll go order the scan now, so just lie still for a few more minutes.

No response from Erik as he did what the doctor ordered. Time seemed to pass in days, even weeks, even though he knew it was probably less than fifteen minutes.

The nurse eventually came in and helped Erik get into a wheelchair, and he didn't argue. Full compliance was all he could do as she wheeled him to the radiology department. He trusted that these people would get to the bottom of these massive headaches, and then come up with a fix for them. However, deep in his gut he suspected that something was terribly wrong and he wouldn't be alive much longer.

The nurse handed him over to the technician, who positioned him for the scan of his head, and Erik was oblivious to his adjusting. He only hoped it would end.

"Can you just cut off my head? It feels like I'm being stabbed repeatedly."

"Let's try the scan first and see what that shows. Then maybe we'll try you're idea," responded the technician with no expression.

It didn't take long, and Erik was back in the dark examination room again waiting for the results. The pain lasted longer than any other episode he experienced, but finally subsided as waves of relief poured over him. The nurse came back in and gave him a cool, damp cloth to wipe his face with.

"It's finally going away now, isn't it?"

"Yes, I'm getting back to normal. Did the CT scan find anything that could be causing these headaches?"

"The doctor will be in momentarily. He has some questions for you, so just relax for a few more minutes. He's getting the images ready to bring up on the computer here and show you."

"I'm afraid you'll see that there's merely a brain the size of a walnut in there, but I can't imagine what else has filled in the space."

Touching his shoulder, she replied, "You were smart enough to finally go to the doctor, so there's surely some brains up there."

Erik looked up at her and was reassured by her compassionate smile. She left him a few more minutes by himself. A knock came, and then the doctor entered the room.

"Can you give some details about what happened to you in the past, specifically with regards to your head? If I was guessing, I'd say you were in the military and saw active duty in Iraq during Desert Storm. You look too young to have been in Vietnam."

Giving the doctor a confused look, Erik asked, "Why would you say that?"

Calling up the scan on the computer, he pointed to several dark spots that were visible on the first image.

"Either you're not leveling with me, or someone's been playing cruel games with you while you were sleeping."

"What do you mean? What are those dark marks?"

"Erik, there appears to be metal, stone, and maybe even glass fragments imbedded in your brain, and looks as though you've been through a war zone."

Chapter Twelve

THE DOCTOR STARED INTO ERIK'S eyes, and said, "There's a long metal spike about a half an inch, like part of a small nail, sitting in a bad spot in your brain, and I don't think it can be operated on. In addition, there are almost a dozen other particles embedded in various parts of the skull and brain, but they don't appear to be life threatening. The nail is probably the cause of your headaches, especially if it's moving. I also believe you have frontal lobe damage as the result of some kind of serious injury."

The silence was powerful while the doctor waited for a response. Erik looked at him in amazement, and he could see the doctor was serious. Thoughts flashed through his mind as he struggled to make sense of these statements. Averting his eyes when he noticed his reflection in the doctor's gold framed glasses; he tried to read something from the nurse's expression, but just noticed how pretty her eyes were. She showed concern briefly but gave him a smile when she saw him look up at her, and that brought out the true beauty in her face. He stared at a drawing on the wall and glanced at a medical picture, not knowing how to respond.

"Did you serve in the military?"

"No, I never joined up. I got married, then my wife and I had a baby."

"Were you in some kind of traumatic accident that could have left these small items inside of you? Maybe a car crash, an explosion, or something like that? There's not a lot of ways this could happen to a person."

Erik kept digging through his past, not sure what he was actually seeing, but shook his head in bewilderment as he stared at the spots on the scan images.

"Well, something obviously happened, so you must be suppressing the memories of this event. Let me discuss these results with one of my colleagues and I'll let you know what we come up with. On first glance, our options appear to be limited, but I'll know more tomorrow. Sandy will give you a call to schedule an appointment so we can discuss it further once I've studied this a little more."

Erik nodded and followed them to the reception area. He paid for the visit without thinking, and wandered out to his car in a daze, not sure what to make of today's discovery. He drove around aimlessly for a while, not really paying attention to where he was, with no destination in mind. The skies had become overcast again, almost matching his mood, and he didn't feel good about anything at this point in time. Anger popped up once in a while, sometimes fear, sometimes hopelessness, but he fought to overcome each of them individually as they attacked. Where was the joy that he needed so badly?

Realizing he was near the cemetery, he remembered that he needed to pay the judge one last visit and turned the steering wheel to go toward the entrance.

"Such a dreary day. Seems like the best time to go to the graveyard," he commented as he drove past rows of headstones.

The parking lot was empty, and the grounds showed no signs of life, as usual. Erik was alone with acres of dead bodies again, with the exception of Judge Lewis. Making his way up to the grave site, it was peacefully quiet with no bird songs playing in the background, until he walked up close to the judge's grave. He heard something, so he stood still to listen closely.

Sure enough, the judge had awoken from his simulated death sleep, and was screaming, the sounds of his voice barely audible through his air tube. Erik stood in place a minute, assuming that the judge could tell someone walked up, either through vibrations of his footsteps or the sounds of his car driving up. He stared at the grave trying to picture what the judge looked like inside his dark box under the ground.

"I wonder if I should have left you a flashlight so you could see better. It must be awfully dark down there. Anyway, I don't feel like talking to you anymore, so I'll say goodbye. You've been a dark chapter in my life and I'm putting it behind me now."

Without another thought, Erik walked over to the flowers, reached in his pocket, and kneeled down to the grass. He had no expression as he inserted a plug into the air tube and made sure it was a tight fit. He covered it up completely with dirt and grass to make it look like there was nothing out of place under the flower arrangements, and then stood up. Listening for any kind of sounds, he seemed pleased with the silence and turned to walk back to his car without another glance at the grave site. He was done here and would never return to this spot.

&&&

AT THE POLICE STATION, TAMI TRIED TO piece together the connections between the senator, the judge, and the priest's confessor, looking at the new clippings she had recently received in the mail. These were the same kinds of accusations that were made against Senator Grant, and in each case, Judge Lewis was cleared of any illegal activities. Tami thought it was suspicious that both of these men had so many potentially damaging claims against them, and both were able to get their names cleared. Also interesting is the fact that both had died within a week of each other.

She wasn't sure if there was any relation between the deaths of these two public servants and the angry man that unnerved Father Bill with confessions of being glad two men had died and were both burning in Hell. She made a quick call and figured she could get some basic answers right away.

"Hi, James. This is Officer Tami Anderson."

"Hey, Tami. What's up?"

"I've got some questions on a couple of recent deaths and I wonder if you could give me some information."

"Anything for you. Whose deaths are you looking into?"

"I need the causes of death for Senator Jerry Grant and Judge Frank Lewis, and where the bodies are now."

"That's easy. These guys just died in the past week. Give me a minute."

She waited as her friend looked up the death records, glancing at her watch.

"OK, Grant died of a heart attack and was cremated, and Lewis died of a heart attack and was buried at the Stockton Cemetery two days ago."

"Do you know if an autopsy was performed on either of these men?"

"These were older men and the deaths were natural causes, so no autopsy was done for either. Tami, are you thinking that there's something suspicious about these two deaths?"

"Right now it's just a hunch, James. Nothing concrete to go on, but I'd like to see if we can have Judge Lewis exhumed and an autopsy performed, just in case. Do you think that would be a problem?"

"Well, if this request came from your belligerent partner,

then I'd make sure it's a problem, but since it's you, we can make it happen. I don't think we'll be able to start digging him up right away, since we'll also need the family's permission, then we have to contact the Attorney General, the cemetery director, and the funeral home. Usually this process takes a few weeks."

"We need it ASAP, since other people's lives are in danger if I'm right about this. We can't even wait a week."

"I'll see what we can do. Would that be OK?"

"That's fine. I appreciate your help with this."

"No problem Tami. I'll call you once we have the go-ahead."

Tami sat back and sighed as she considered what she was planning to do. She would be cross-examined about exhuming a dead judge, and needed to have some solid answers ready when the questions started flying later in the afternoon. She put together some details on both men, their deaths, the mysterious envelopes she received in the mail, and the man in confession so she'd be prepared for the gauntlet.

Trouble came sooner than she anticipated when her partner stormed up to her desk with a stern look on his face. She felt like a small quarterback about to be tackled by an enormous linebacker, and braced herself for the onslaught. Surprised at the anger emanating from his body movements, she grew curious about why he would fume so much. This was more than she expected from him.

"Tami, I just heard that you requested to have Judge Frank Lewis' body dug up. What's going on?"

"Hi, John. There's something fishy about the deaths of Lewis and Senator Grant, and I think they both could have been foul play."

"Based on the mail you received a few days ago from that disgruntled quack who wants to bad mouth the senator? Well, I knew Senator Grant personally, and I don't believe a word of it."

"That mail you just gave me today was from the same person, but it was filled with all kinds of articles that showed Judge Lewis being investigated for dishonest activities and potential involvement with known mafia-like criminals. These people are untouchable, but when our public officials, not one but two, start getting linked up with these kinds of people, that's something worth investigating."

"Yeah, but you don't know who's making these accusations, and there's no way for these two men to defend themselves now. It seems like you're climbing up the wrong tree here, and should be focusing your attention elsewhere, maybe even the jerk that's sending you those tips."

"Look John, I've been contacted by someone who believes two men have died in the past week at the hands of a killer out for revenge based on a confession this person gave him. Both Grant and Lewis have died in the past week of 'natural causes'. Plus I've been sent incriminating evidence on these two men implying that both had been involved in illegal activities over the past ten, fifteen years or more. I have justification to follow up on Lewis' death to see if he truly died of natural causes. If he has, then I don't have anything to go on, but if I can prove that he was murdered, then I think we have something here."

John just stared at her, seething, and responded, "OK, let me know what you come up with."

As he walked away, she sat down and opened her desk drawer, pulling out the two envelopes. It was satisfying to stand her ground against this opponent, but she wondered why he pushed to have no investigation. She sat down and skimmed through the contents, pausing occasionally to read entire articles. Tami was hesitant to give her partner any details about Father Bill. She would just leave him as an anonymous source for now and save him from potential interrogations. Her biggest concern was that John seemed to be protecting Grant and/or Lewis.

Chapter Thirteen

ERIK KEPT BUSY THIS EVENING AT Bella's Italian Ristorante with what seemed like continuous refills, bringing out yet another check, and taking a new table's order for the evening meal. The activities took his mind off his quest momentarily, but when he did glance over to the front of the restaurant, there was Ed Stewart. Erik's mind raced, as did his heart, while he made his way to the hostess table. This was who he'd been hoping for, like a lion waiting for a gazelle to stop at the watering hole.

"Hi, Jessica. I've got a table in section A that these folks can sit at," Erik nonchalantly suggested to the hostess. She looked up at him, skimmed the seating charts, and nodded.

"OK, thanks. I'll seat them over there."

Erik moved back toward his area, smiling inside at his success, and planned out his actions over the next few minutes. A memory came up of seeing Ed Stewart up close once, at his trial about fifteen years ago, but the man looked a lot older now. For some reason, however, he had the aura of a celebrity, perhaps due to his money and power in this town, and he was certainly dressed up tonight. Erik's hatred of this man had to be kept secret, so he made sure he put on the charm and assumed the wealthy payoff man would never recognize him.

Erik had been stressed, hoping to start relaxing soon, yet with Mr. Stewart's presence at the restaurant now, this was not the time to wind down yet. There was work to be done. Noticing that the restaurant manager gave Stewart special treatment and welcomed him like royalty, he tried to continue business-as-usual. He gave his other customers the attention they needed, and smiled with them about whatever they discussed, keeping an eye on his gazelle, who was getting closer to the watering hole.

"Good evening, sir," Erik welcomed Mr. Stewart and his two companions.

"Hi. I'll just have ice water with no lemon, please," Stewart replied.

"Coming right up. Anything for you two gentlemen?"

"Just a scotch for me," said the younger man with the mustache.

"I'll take a beer. Whatever you have on tap," added the dark haired man.

"I'll be right back with these."

Erik headed toward the kitchen with the drink order, and looked back at his new customers. He had recognized Ed Stewart, but his dark hair was completely gone, with grey hair definitely taking over. Crow's feet spread from each of his eyes.

Still very classy, and hanging around with other rich people, no doubt. He wondered who these two men were, and just assumed they were involved with the gas company somehow. Ed Stewart had been the CEO for the Stockton Gas Company for many years, and had only recently stepped down to let someone else take over that position. He was still in an advisory role, from what Erik had read in the past few weeks.

He wondered what kinds of advice he'd be giving the new guy. Maybe ways to weasel out of trouble and how to cover it up? Perhaps how to make sure someone else gets blamed and takes the fall?

Anger welled up in Erik's eyes, as he looked forward to serving Mr. Stewart this evening. As it turned out, Stewart ordered a spicy meal, which was perfect; since Erik knew the concoction he planned to give to the former CEO had an unusual, bitter taste and needed something to help disguise the flavor. While he prepared to bring the plates out to the three men, he quickly added his magic potion to Mr. Stewart's meal while nobody looked, and carried the tray out almost as though he was a professional waiter. Erik smiled smugly as he presented the meals to his guests, and blended back into the evening at the restaurant. Now it was a waiting game and Erik was about to win.

It would be another few hours before the mixture took effect, so he went on throughout the evening as though he enjoyed the company of these men. He laughed with them, talked politely with them, and bid them all good night when they left, even though he wanted to strangle Ed Stewart during the whole charade. Erik would have to wait patiently and see this man at his other place of employment in the next day or two in order to continue with his plans.

&&&

FORTUNATELY NO AUTOPSY WAS REQUIRED, and Ed Stewart was pronounced dead, presumably from a heart attack in his sleep.

"Not a bad way to go, really," Erik said as he got the man ready for his funeral. "Unless you're actually not dead, and nobody else was aware of it."

If an autopsy had been requested, traces of certain unusual items would most likely be found in the body, and his game of revenge would be up. However, since these men were older and they appeared to die peacefully in their sleep, the families must have just accepted the initial cause of death and didn't want to go through the extra trauma of putting their 'loved ones' through an autopsy.

"I actually find the idea of you going through an autopsy today while you were still alive a satisfying revenge, but I'll accept this just as well."

He made sure the suit looked just right, and the shine on his forehead was not too glaring under the lights. Staring into his closed eyes, looking past the eyelids and seeing deep within the man's soul, Erik knew that this was an evil man. He had covered up maybe two or three gas explosions over the past twenty years, somehow getting the blame shifted off of his company and employees. Knowing he was at fault each time, Ed Stewart used his money, power, and influences to sweep it under the rug, avoiding investigations that should have come with every incident.

Whispering into the man's ear, Erik tried to send chills down the man's spine.

"Mr. Ed Stewart. Powerful ruler in this town. Let me give you a glimpse of your future. You will soon have your family all around you, but you won't be able to call out to them, reach out to them, or let them know in any way that you're still alive. They all believe you passed away and are a part of history now."

Erik moved around the casket and leaned over him again.

"I have dozens of newspaper articles that I've put together nicely over the past few months to show a pattern of cover-ups, payoffs, involvements with big money people from Chicago, and even some records from your office that you wouldn't want seen in the newspapers. But guess what, Ed? That's exactly what's going to happen. All of your lies, the way you framed people and left them to take the blame, it's all coming out in the next week or two."

To add to the terror, Erik rolled Stewart's casket into the

room with the furnace, and opened the lid again so he could see the man's face. He sat down next to Ed Stewart's head, explaining, "You see, Ed, this place is the crematorium, and what happens is that I put you on this roller that slowly moves you into the fire. I then push a pretty green button to blast out an incredible set of flames, and you get to experience it all up close and personal. It's actually quite impressive and very fitting that it's the last thing you're going to feel today."

Erik looked away for a minute, fuming, wishing he could put this man through the crematorium now, but retained his calm demeanor. This man could have easily reimbursed him for his lost building and equipment and not noticed it in his bank account at all, but instead he spent probably twice that amount to make sure the blame went somewhere else.

"Your good buddies, Senator Grant and Judge Lewis, have already come to visit me, just like you're doing now, and I had a pleasant talk with each of them. Just so you know, it didn't turn out well for either Grant or Lewis, and it's not going to turn out well for you."

Pointing toward the crematorium, Erik added, "We have to wait for your funeral to end first, but I promise you that I'm going to put you through this massive flame thrower and you're going to feel the flames of Hell while you're still alive. Isn't that a neat trick?"

Looking up at the clock, Erik stood up, closed the lid, and rolled the casket toward the door and back into the preparation room.

"I'll be back to help get you there on time. We wouldn't want you to be late for your own funeral, would we?"

He smiled, and then stepped through the door to the other room to make sure everything was ready.

&&&

THE FUNERAL SOON FINISHED, AND FAMily and friends unknowingly deserted the former business tycoon in his time of need. Keith hurriedly helped Erik get Ed Stewart's body ready for cremation in the special flammable casket, and was anxious to finish up his work day to get on to something better.

"Alright man. It's all yours. Mind if I slip out and try to catch the Cubs' game over at Wrigley? They're playing the Cardinals, and I've got some friends who are driving over there in a little while."

"No, go and have a good time. I'll finish up here and close the place when I'm done. See you later."

"Thanks Erik. I owe you one," Keith replied as he grabbed his jacket and went through the front door.

As the door closed, there was a brief echo which quieted down to a complete silence. Erik liked the sound of this silence. He was glad the funeral was over so he could now focus on the next step. He knew Ed Stewart had done everything he could to move or let people find out he wasn't dead, but it was to no avail. This dosage of the special ingredient from his last meal at Bella's Italian Ristorante had proven again to be so effective that nobody could tell its' recipient was still alive.

"I was touched by the kind words of your friends and family, Ed. Weren't you?"

Erik laughed. "No, I'm just kidding. I could tell they were all just being polite because it was your funeral, but I know they all thought you were a self-centered, greedy, jerk and were glad you're about to be fried."

He gave one last look at Ed in his flammable box, and added, "I think it's ironic that you'll be burned alive just like some of the victims of your regime over the past fifteen or twenty years. You deserve this more than you realize, and I'm going to enjoy pushing the buttons for you."

He shut the lid of the casket and started the initial flames, watching the temperature gauge climb to the optimum level. Heat surrounded the casket as it poured out the open door, but Ed Stewart could do nothing but wait. Erik knocked on the lid and pressed the next button which set the casket in motion. Within seconds the box was completely inside the furnace and Erik watched, waiting patiently for the final touch. Knowing Ed Stewart was now burning alive, he searched to see if there were any feelings of guilt at all over his vengeful actions. The jet-engine flame took over, and Erik wondered if he had completely buried his own conscience. He did everything he could to convince himself that he didn't feel guilty, but he still wasn't sure he truly believed it.

Having successfully taken revenge on three of the main conspirators that ruined his life, he still had one to go. There was a lot of work to be done, but Erik knew that he was running out of time.

Chapter Fourteen

OFFICER TAMI ANDERSON WAITed at the Stockton Cemetery while Judge Lewis' body was exhumed, with plans of having tests run to see if the cause of death could have been anything other than a heart attack. Surprisingly, it was no problem getting the family's approval. Tami had expected them to ask that he be left alone in his grave, but her argument was convincing enough that they agreed without any complaints. She got the feeling they suspected someone might have had reasons to kill the retired judge, which strengthened Tami's resolve that she was doing the right thing. Even though she was not glad to see him, she felt some relief when her partner drove up and joined her near the grave. She watched his demeanor as he walked up to her, head covered, jacket enveloping his huge frame, with a scowl on his face.

"I'm glad you could make it. I didn't want to be the only person here from the department."

"Yeah, you owe me one. I still think this is a waste of time."

Tami wasn't surprised that the sun had disappeared, since it always tended to leave an overcast, dreary day for these kinds of activities at a cemetery. The wind seemed to be just a bit on the bitter and uncomfortable side to make it even worse, and she figured that all this day lacked was a cold rain.

"Tami, if this guy was embalmed, wouldn't that corrupt any findings they might make during the autopsy?"

Tami looked up at her partner and replied, "It's possible. I'm still not sure of what it is we're expecting to find, but I believe something is suspicious about this whole thing. Whatever might have been done to kill the judge, if indeed that's what happened, I'm betting it could still be detected with an autopsy and may help prove that it was murder, not natural causes."

She watched John shake his head in disbelief as he added, "I can't understand why the family didn't fight this and let the man rest in peace. I wouldn't want my family members dug up after having a heart attack, funeral, and closure."

"What if there was any kind of doubt that it was foul play? Wouldn't you want to know that for closure?"

"I still don't believe there was anything suspicious about it, and I already have the closure I need on this case. This goes way overboard, in my humble opinion."

Tami turned to watch the workers run the machines that pulled the casket to the surface, and didn't say anything more about his lack of true humility. The thought of a potential murder bothered her, but it also bothered her that John could be right. What if it's determined that this guy did indeed die from a heart attack, and she ordered this whole huge process for nothing? She would have put the family through unnecessary concern and pain, while wasting taxpayer's money with this exhumation. For some reason, John was very much against any kind of investigation into the judge's death, and she couldn't figure that out at all. The evidence she had pieced together appeared to be good enough reason to at least dig into the two recent deaths a little further, no pun intended.

The vehicle was ready nearby to transport the body, as

the casket was placed on solid ground and steadied. Several people put on surgical masks, since the man had been buried for three days, and they knew what to expect when the casket lid was opened. Tami put her mask on as well and waited, nerves on edge, as she now had doubts about her own theories. She glanced over at John, who didn't even put on a mask, and saw that he had stepped farther back away from the grave.

At least the news media hadn't caught wind of this and made it into a big fiasco. She could just see the headlines now that made her out to be some kind of gruesome grave digger, dragging a long-time public official's name through the mud, as her partner had once suggested someone was trying to do to Senator Grant. If nothing came out of the autopsy, she could at least close the case, admit John was right, and hope this incident blew over quickly and quietly.

&&&

FATHER BILL LJUNGLOF SAT IN HIS OFFICE, getting ready to go out into the church to take his turn hearing confession, when his phone rang. It occurred to him that he should let it ring, since he didn't want to be late getting out there, but for some reason he decided to answer it.

"Hi, this is Father Bill. How can I help you?"

"I feel awkward calling you 'Father', since you're younger than I am. Can I just call you 'Bill'?"

The priest instantly recognized the voice at the other end, and stood frozen in place.

"Of course. Wouldn't you rather come in and talk in person? I was just heading out to the confessional when you called."

"No, not today. I've had a really bad headache and don't feel like going outside now. Plus it's overcast and I prefer to be out in the sunshine instead. Do you have a few minutes to talk to me over the phone?"

"I'll be glad to do anything I can if it helps."

"Thanks. I can tell you have a good heart and I truly appreciate it. I do apologize for having to leave so abruptly the last time I visited you."

Father Bill prayed for wisdom and what to say next.

"Listen, let me be honest with you. I'm concerned that you have some terrible guilt and feelings of anger that are consuming you. I want to help you. Can we meet somewhere private where we could talk face to face?"

"That's thoughtful of you. I'm not sure I want to do that yet. I've just met with another past acquaintance of mine and had a good discussion with him. I wanted to tell you about it, like a confession over the phone."

"OK. Is this man also dead now?"

Erik paused and then responded, "Uh, yes he is now. Poor guy's heart just gave out. Maybe it was broken over all of the evil things he'd done to people over the years."

Father Bill's concern about the caller being a potential murderer was on high alert now, and was reminded that he had to be extremely careful about the words he used.

"Whatever this man did to you, it's in the past and can't be undone. What can be done now is for you to forgive him and move on. It'll be a huge burden taken off you once you do that. Have you even considered forgetting about the past and letting it go?"

"Yes, I've tried that, but he ruined my life forever, causing pain to so many people around me. He also did this to several others and got away with it every time. He made some key pay-offs and left innocent people to take the blame." Erik hesitated for a few seconds, and then added, "I can't let it go."

"Yes you can. It's a choice you have to make to free you from needing revenge. This person will be judged on what he's done in his life and you'll be judged for your actions. If you trust God to handle the revenge factor, you'll be free to live your life without guilt or anger eating away at you."

"Bill, I don't feel guilty for being glad these men are dead."

"I don't believe you. Deep down, I think it's tearing you apart and you need to release your anger. Let it go and you'll feel relieved."

Silence.

Father Bill thought he heard sobs at the other end of the line, as his eyes darted around the room, not focusing on his books, the paintings, or anything else.

"It's not too late for you to release your anger and forgive this person. You can ..."

"It is too late! I've already ... This man's already dead and I can't change anything about that. He was an evil man. I tried to talk reasonably with him years ago, and he brushed me aside. I wish things had gone differently, but it's too late for that. The man is dead. What can I do now?"

"If you truly are sorry for what's happened, God will forgive you and it's as simple as that. No matter what you've done, and one day you'll be accepted into Heaven."
Silence again.

The priest wondered if the man was playing a game with him or if he had actually reached something in the man's heart.

"Priest, you don't know what I've done."

"It doesn't matter if I know it or not. God knows what you've done and although it may not make Him happy, if you turn away from the vengeful thoughts and come around in honest forgiveness, whatever actions you've done in the past will be forgotten."

He heard sobs again, and considered what else to say to this man.

"I wish I could believe that."

"You can believe it. I'd be glad to talk in person with you."

Click

Father Bill was surprised the man would have hung up and tried to continue the discussion.

"Hello. Hello. Are you still there?"

Frustrated, he set the phone down a little too hard and slumped at his desk. The sound echoed for a few seconds as his eyes glazed over, staring blindly at the words in the large book on his desk. He couldn't read them if he wanted to at this point.

"What did I say wrong?" he asked himself as he rubbed his eyes and his forehead.

He fought back memories of things he had buried long ago and wondered why they came up now. He had hoped these would be forgotten forever.

&&&

ANOTHER CHILLY BLAST OF AUTUMN WIND hit everyone standing at the gravesite and Tami shivered. She dressed warmly but this air seemed to reach right through her jacket and pants. She hoped to just get this over now and escape back to the office. Two men stepped up to the casket and after a few seconds of trying, the lid was wrested from what was thought to be its final position. As the lid sprang open, time stood still while the faces of those peering into the casket almost looked like they'd seen a ghost. Tami stepped up with her hand over her mask and couldn't believe what she saw. Judge Frank Lewis had been buried alive!

Chapter Fifteen

TAMI WAS HORRIFIED AT THE SCENE her eyes sent to her brain as she looked inside the opened casket in a state of shock. She knew there was some suspicion of foul play with Judge Lewis' death, but this changed everything. She wanted to search inside the casket for anything to help shed light on what had happened here, but her overwhelming fears kept her from it initially. She stared at the flowers around the casket, noticed the ornate designs in the wood, glanced inside briefly, and then turned her eyes away again to look out at the rows of gravestones neatly lined up around them.

Her partner stepped forward with his mask held over his face and cursed when he looked inside at the judge's body.

"How could he have been buried alive? This man was dead and had his funeral in front of dozens of people? What kind of evil, hateful person could do this?"

Tami looked up into John's eyes, but couldn't respond. She had never been involved with something like this and couldn't remember if she had even heard of a real case where a person was presumed dead then buried alive. Her mind raced with so many thoughts that she couldn't grasp on to one of them in order to speak. She stared at the ripped up coffin linings, the position of the body, and the expression on his face. His eyes were filled with terror. He was almost on his knees and elbows, with his head tilted at an unnatural angle as if he was trying to get to something up in the corner. His death, his real death, must have been the worst form of torture she could imagine and it sent chills throughout her body.

"This man's been buried for three days, but it looks like he's only been dead for less than a day," she heard one of the men whisper to the other.

Tami had an intense fear of being buried alive and she trembled as she considered what Judge Lewis went through over the past few days. She was afraid these images in front of her might revisit her thoughts while she tried to sleep over the next week or more and finally had to step away. This poor guy was probably alive for two days in that casket, six feet underground, and that made her hands shake. She promptly put them inside her jacket, hoping nobody else noticed. Tami had to be professional, in control, and couldn't be seen as having any weaknesses now. She observed the men from the funeral home and health department, trying to read something from each of their eyes. They all showed the same fear that she experienced, so that made her feel a little better. However, she had to be decisive and proficient or else her partner would chew her up and spit her out.

"Officer Anderson, I know it sounds morbid, but I'm going to have to photograph Mr. Lewis in this current state before we transport him," one of them said in a hushed voice.

She watched her partner turn his head at the thought and she knew that she had grimaced at the man's comment as well.

"I understand. I hope the family doesn't see these pictures. I don't even know what to tell them at this point. Please don't share with anyone else what you've seen here today, especially the media. Our investigation could be compromised if this gets leaked."

"We have to catch the person who did this!" added John, not really talking to anyone in particular. "I personally want to put a few bullets into this ... this ... psycho."

Tami looked over at John, who stared away from the casket at nothing in particular and she noticed a fury in his eyes that surprised even her. His jaw was set firmly and it seemed like his glare could burn through metal. He wasn't mad at her, which she was thankful for, but he would be challenging to work with now, even more so than usual. His mind set on vigilante revenge for certain, which would make the investigation difficult for her. She wanted justice on the person who did this, but from a judge and jury. She laughed briefly at that thought. An honest judge. Not the kind of justice their suspect apparently received from his judge years ago, but true justice.

"John, when someone dies, doesn't the person have to go through an autopsy to confirm the cause of death?"

"No," he responded without looking at her. In Illinois, and many other states, if the death appears to be natural causes and the person's had similar health issues in the past, like a heart attack, stroke, or something like that, most of the time an autopsy isn't done."

"It just seems as though it should have been required."

"Well, if a seventy year old man dies in his sleep, that's usually not very suspicious, is it? You'll notice that in most cases, an autopsy isn't performed anymore. That itself can put the family through a lot of anxiety."

"Yes, but I think finding that the person was alive in his casket for two days would put the family through more stress."

John looked into her eyes, but didn't speak right away.

"Tami, could you imagine what would have happened to Judge Lewis if they had performed an autopsy on him while he was still alive and couldn't respond? That has to be an even worse form of torture."

She stared at him, letting this ghastly thought sink in, and didn't even try to imagine this scenario. She couldn't respond and just looked away for a few minutes without saying a word.

Tami watched from a distance while the man took the horror-filled pictures and she stepped forward when he turned to her and nodded.

"I'll meet you in a little while to go over the initial results of the autopsy. Make sure you emphasize that the doctor should look for any kind of chemicals that could have made this man appear to be dead for a couple of days."

"You realize it could take weeks to get back the toxicology report."

Tami looked at the man's face and just nodded. She and her partner walked around the casket to make room for the removal of the body and she watched him as he took an interest in something at the head of the casket.

"What is it John?"

"Someone rigged this coffin up with an air hose."

He stepped over to the open hole from where the judge was removed, evidently looking for something, and pointed down into the grave.

"I don't believe this. Look at that clear plastic tube coming into the grave down near the bottom. I'm betting that's how this guy kept the judge alive for so long and that's what the judge was trying to reach."

Tami followed his gaze and saw it too. She looked around to see if she could tell where the air hose came to the surface but couldn't see anything obvious. John walked around the gravesite and scanned the grass for some kind of opening that lined up with the hose inside the grave. He carelessly moved around the head of the grave, kicking up dirt and grass, and she saw what he was searching for. Hidden just under a small clump of grass was the other end to the plastic tube that served as the judge's lifeline, but she realized why the judge eventually ran out of air. That end of the hose had been deliberately plugged up.

&&&

STANDING BY THE POLICE CARS, TAMI watched the transport team drive through the cemetery gate. She looked over at her partner and said, "John, I have to stop and tell Mrs. Lewis what we found. I don't want to scare her but she needs to know that it appears that someone may have actually murdered her husband."

John nodded, and said, "Be sensitive about what you tell her. She's already gone through a lot with her husband dying a couple of days ago, so you may want to leave out the details about him being alive in the grave."

"Yeah, I know. I'm concerned that if this gets leaked to the news, the killer's going to know we're onto him and we'll lose some of our edge. We have a better chance of catching him if he's not aware that we know what he did to Lewis."

"And possibly Senator Grant," John added as she nodded her head. "Do you think he would have actually cremated Grant alive?"

"I don't know. That's a terrible thought. Anyway, thanks for coming up here, John. It's not what I expected to find."

"Yep. Me neither. I'll meet you back at the station later this afternoon."

&&&

OFFICER JOHN HULTGREN MADE A PHONE call to someone he knew at the police station.

"Hey, Gene. This is John. Listen could you do me a favor? I need to find out which funeral home handled the bodies of Jerry Grant and Frank Lewis in the past week. I'm betting it's the same one. Sure, I'll wait."

He drummed his fingers on the steering wheel, gritting his teeth while he waited for the voice to come back on the other end of the line.

"John, you're right. Both funerals were handled by the Stockton Funeral Home."

"That's not far from where I'm at now. You're awesome, man. Thanks. I owe you."

"You seem to stay forever in debt to me. I need to cash these in sometime before I lose my chance."

John laughed and hung up on his friend. He immediately drove over there for some routine questioning. Someone at that funeral home took the time to connect that air tube to keep this guy alive and he was determined to find out who it was.

There was one car in the parking lot, so John was optimistic. He wasn't in a good mood and didn't like the idea that someone could be torturing public officials, even retired ones, and was ready to interrogate a suspect. Opening his car door to a cool autumn breeze, he kept his eyes on the entrance to the funeral home.

"I wonder if there's a back door here. Rats. I should have made sure he couldn't slip out the back first," he said to himself.

Checking his gun, he opened the door and stepped inside. There was nobody in the lobby, so he walked carefully to the next room, glad to find that someone was there.

&&&

TAMI GAVE THE JUDGE'S FAMILY ONLY some details about the exhumation, letting them know she was having an autopsy done and would let them know the results as soon as she received them. She conveniently left out some of the gruesome details that they found when they opened the casket, since she didn't want to unnecessarily upset the family while she still didn't have any answers. She hated this part of her job where she had to talk to the families of someone who died, and never felt like she did a good job of it. On her way back to the station, her cell phone rang.

"Tami, the angry man just called me, saying there's another person who he wanted revenge on, and this person's now dead."

"Father Bill. Did he say who this person was or if he killed this person?"

"No, it was similar to the other two meetings, where he told me about someone who was rich and powerful that ruined his life. I asked if this person was alive and the caller said the man wasn't."

"Rich and powerful. Like a senator or a judge," she whispered to herself. "Did the caller give you anything helpful that might identify who he is, why he wants revenge, or anything else?"

"He said that this person paid off people to let others take the blame. Does that make sense?"

Tami thought about that, looking down at yesterday's newspaper in the passenger seat, and saw something that caught her eye.

"Maybe. Thanks for keeping me up-to-date. I've got some ideas, so I'll follow up on them and let you know what I find out. Thanks again Bill."

She read the headline again out loud, "Former CEO of the Stockton Gas Company, Ed Stewart, passed away in his sleep Tuesday evening."

Chapter Sixteen

OFFICER JOHN HULTGREN stepped quietly into the back room at the funeral home, gun raised and pointing directly at the dark-haired man who had his back to him. The employee appeared to be startled by something behind him but as he turned his head, it was met with a solid object that prevented him from coming around all the way. The policeman had used his handgun to greet the man, who was now on the floor with blood seeping out of the left side of his face.

"OK, buddy. So what do you know about Judge Frank Lewis and Senator Jerry Grant?"

The man tried to look at his assailant from the corner of his eye, which started to swell up already, and Hultgren figured he must be surprised to see an angry policeman aiming a gun at his head.

"I know they both died recently. What's ...?"

Hultgren kicked him hard in the stomach and made sure the gun pointed down at the man's face again, which now showed a teeth-clenching grimace with his eyes closed tight.

"Thanks, wise guy. I know that much. Tell me what dirt you have on these men or I'll make sure you go through what they just went through."

The man on the floor hesitated, and asked, "What do

you mean by 'dirt'? I just know they both died peacefully in their sleep, one was cremated, and one was buried. That's all."

The protector of the law gave him another good kick, causing him to flinch again to try to avoid it. Unsuccessfully, of course.

"Were you ticked off that you didn't get a payout? What did you have against these two?"

"I don't know what you're talking about. I just helped get them ready for their funerals. Nothing more. I never even knew these guys. Look, I don't know what you want from me."

"Judge Lewis was buried alive. That just doesn't happen by accident now, does it?"

Silence. The man stared up at the big police officer.

"He couldn't have been buried alive. The embalming would have killed him first."

"Oh really? Lewis wasn't even embalmed. He was buried alive and had an air tube that kept him breathing while laying six feet under. Explain that."

The man gave him a confused look, and Officer Hultgren saw the genuine expression of surprise on his face.

"No, that couldn't have happened. Erik would have embalmed the man before getting him ready for the funeral."

"Who's Erik? What's his last name?"

"Um, Erik Johnson. He works here with me and handled the preparation for these two men."

Hultgren shifted nervously, realizing he might have made a mistake, and frantically grasped for a way to get out of this gracefully. There was a case for police brutality here, but he also knew how to make sure it never came to that.

"Where is he now?"

"I don't know. Maybe still at home, since he doesn't work until tomorrow."

"If I find out you're lying and covering up something,

I'll be back and you won't get out of this so easily next time. Understand?"

"Yes."

He stepped on the man's hand, crunching it as pain registered in his suspect's face, but Hultgren's expression appeared as though he enjoyed the groans of agony.

The policeman kneeled down near the man's face and spoke threateningly into his ear.

"I'm not taking you in now, but don't leave town and don't try anything stupid. I'm still watching you. If I were you, I wouldn't say anything to anyone about our meeting today."

Without any kind of warning, Hultgren grabbed a clump of the man's hair, and smacked his head on the tile floor for good measure. He really wasn't surprised that the guy didn't move after that.

Officer Hultgren stepped back slowly through the door, never taking his eyes off of the suspect, still lying on the floor with a small puddle of blood by his face but very much unconscious now. He holstered his gun in the hallway, cursing as he left the lobby and got in his car. Looking around to see if anyone watched him come out of the funeral home, he sped out of the parking lot and exhaled some of his anger. This wouldn't go over well if his partner found out about this visit.

&&&

TAMI'S RESEARCH PAID OFF, FINDING OUT from where the call was made to Father Bill, and she planned to pay the caller a visit today. She had also confirmed that both Senator Grant and Judge Lewis had been sent to the same funeral home and was not surprised when she found out that Ed Stewart, the Stockton Gas Company CEO who died a few days ago, had also been sent there before his funeral. She had missed his funeral by one day, discovering that he had already been cremated.

What if the person who buried Judge Lewis alive also put Senator Grant and Ed Stewart through the crematorium flames while they were still alive?

She didn't even want to think about how gruesome that would be. Just like her intense fears of being buried alive, Tami had been afraid of burning since she was a little girl and heard about someone dying in a house fire in her neighborhood. Between burning people alive and burying people alive, this person she dealt with now could very well be her worst nightmare and it sent chills throughout her body. That seemed to happen to her a lot lately and she didn't like it. Tami didn't want anyone to notice but this case was the most frightening thing she had ever considered. She had to get moving and piece things together before someone else suffered the same kind of fate as these three men. How many more enemies could this man have?

She decided to check out the funeral home that was a common link between the three men and drove there first. There was only one car in the parking lot, so she figured someone would be there to talk to. However, Tami wasn't sure if she was prepared to face a person who potentially was involved with the torture and deaths of these three men.

What if the killer is the employee that she was about to meet? She couldn't let her guard down and be taken like them, only to die a horrific death at his hands. That was her greatest concern.

She parked the car, and seriously considered calling for backup now, even though all she had to go on were theories and speculation. She almost called her partner, but was hesitant to involve him at this point. Her gut feeling was that she couldn't confide in him right now but she didn't know why. Maybe she should just go back to the office and let John come out here to question the funeral home employees.

No, the way John had been acting, he might gun down the man to get his own justice and not take him in for questioning. She couldn't risk that, even though it was getting easier for her to agree that they shouldn't take any chances of this killer getting away. He could always come back for her, especially since he knew who she was. What if she doesn't expose the criminal activities of these men like the killer wants her to do? He might want to take out revenge on her. Maybe letting John take care of him would be the best way.

Images of agony, fire, screaming, Judge Lewis trapped in his casket, and more flashed through her mind, causing her hands to tremble. She had to put these thoughts behind her and do her job. Childhood fears of burning alive came to mind, but she promptly brushed them aside, only to find they were replaced by the terror of being buried alive. She just couldn't win.

"No, I'm an officer of the law, and it's my responsibility to investigate these kinds of suspicions. I'm here now. I'll go in and talk to whoever's here."

She stepped out of the car and walked to the front door, her brain still bombarded with thoughts of burning alive and visions of Judge Lewis's face. She prepared her gun and stepped inside while her heart pounded a steady beat that rivaled a very fast hard rock song.

Nobody was at the reception desk and it was eerily quiet, except for her heartbeat. Very neat, professionally decorated to make people feel welcome, but not a soul in sight.

"This is Officer Tami Anderson of the Stockton Police Department. I need to ask you some questions."

Holding her gun level with her eyes, she slowly moved across the room with her back to the wall. The last thing she wanted was someone to step up behind her and surprise her. She realized that she had to focus and be prepared regardless of what she encountered in the next few seconds. She was determined to be ready because there was no way she could let herself be captured by someone who might do those things to her. Her adrenaline was at an all-time high as she worked unsuccessfully to control her nerves.

After one last look around the reception area, she hurriedly opened the door to the back rooms and stepped away. Carefully peeking into the hallway, she rushed in and leaned her back against the wall, quickly sliding toward the first door, which was open. Within a second, she had popped her head inside and pulled it back in, and her eyes almost jumped out of their sockets. There was a man lying on the floor with blood around his head!

Chapter Seventeen

TAMI'S HEART STILL DRUMMED AT an incredible rhythm, as she scanned the room for the person who attacked this man lying on the floor, bleeding from his face. She held the gun so tight that it hurt her fingers, and she bobbed her head through the doorway, pulling it back behind the door in case someone else was in there. With professional skill, she stepped into the room with the gun ready to aim at anything that moved, rapidly turned around to face other areas, and stopped with her back to the wall. The man on the floor was alone with her, so she relaxed a little bit.

Bending down to check the man's neck for a pulse, yet never taking her eyes off of the door she just passed through, Tami kept her gun ready for action.

"Good. He's still alive."

She took out her phone and punched a few numbers.

"I have an injured white male at 2391 Alpine Street who needs medical attention. Please send an ambulance right away."

Still holding the phone to her ear with one hand, she held her gun with the other and carefully walked to the door, lightly kicking it open and looking back into the reception area.

"He's breathing, but appears to be unconscious. There's

a small puddle of blood by his head, but not much. It looks like he was hit in the face by something. Blood's coming out of his nose and his cheek appears to be cut."

Glancing around the room, Tami tried to find any object that could have been used to hit this man, but everything looked all in order. No potential weapon was visible. Nothing disturbed except for this man. She went back into the reception area to make sure the assailant wasn't still in the building somewhere, and systematically went to each room to flush out anyone who could be hiding there.

She stepped into the crematorium and a chill went down her spine. Her eyes opened wide as they explored every aspect of the macabre chamber. She knew what it was used for and immediately got the creeps, slipping back out of the nightmare chamber as swiftly as she had entered.

"OK, thanks. I'll wait here for you," she responded to the voice and hung up the phone.

Satisfied the attacker had left the premises, she holstered her gun as she walked back to check on the man's injuries. Her breathing had slowed back to normal. The pictures she saw in her mind of her being captured by this person who appeared to be burning and burying people alive were still vivid to her, but the fear she faced when she first came up to the funeral home had subsided. She wiped the sweat from her forehead, and knelt down to look closely at the man on the floor.

Relieved he didn't have a weapon in his hands, she still had to make sure he wasn't laying on a gun or knife, ready to pounce on her when she least expected it. As she touched his hand, the man moved slightly and made a groaning noise, momentarily startling Tami.

"I'm Officer Tami Anderson of the Stockton Police Department. An ambulance is on its way and should be here in a few minutes. Can you hear me?"

The man blinked his eyes and opened them to look around, wincing in pain as he moved his hand to touch his face. He felt blood, and looked at Tami squatting next to him.

"Are you able to talk now?"

"Yeah."

He pushed himself up, and Tami handed him some tissues she pulled from the counter nearby.

"Thanks. I'm a mess," he added while he sat on the floor wiping the blood from his nose.

"What's your name?"

"Keith, Keith Ellis."

"Do you know who did this to you?"

He looked at her, apparently examining her uniform and reading her name from her left pocket, shaking his head just a bit. She handed him the box of tissues and he took it, while she watched his painful expressions. Touching the right side of his forehead, she noticed a big bruise visible under his bangs, and she figured he must have hit his head as he fell to the floor. It crossed her mind that he could have a concussion.

"Can you think of anyone who would want to hurt you?"

Looking at the bloody tissues, and setting them on the floor, he pulled out some fresh ones and wiped his nose again.

"Why would someone attack a mortician?" he asked.

"Good question. I was hoping you could answer that. Did you see the person who hit you, what he used, what he was wearing?"

He looked in her eyes, but shook his head. He seemed a little nervous in his responses. Tami wasn't convinced he was being truthful, but went along with it for now. If he was the suspect, who would have attacked him and left him on the floor? This man couldn't have faked these kinds of injuries in an effort to lead people off the scent, right?

"You can't think of anyone who would have done this to you?"

He stood up against her wishes, and replied, "No, I'm just an average guy trying to make a living. Someone came up behind me, and before I could turn and see who it was, I got smacked in the face and woke up with a bloody nose, probably a broken cheekbone, and a bad headache."

"OK. Why don't you go over there and sit down while I ask you some questions. A paramedic will be here to check out your face soon. You may have a concussion and shouldn't be walking around."

He nodded and walked to the nearest chair, sitting down without arguing. She figured he may not be feeling well enough to stand for long, and helped lead him across the room. Her first thought was that the suspect involved with the alleged tortures must have come here and surprised this poor guy. Wrong place at the wrong time. However, she couldn't shake the nagging concern that this man could be the suspect she was looking for – the person she was more afraid of than anyone she had ever feared.

&&&

AT THE POLICE STATION, TAMI READ through her notes as she added some details from today's incident at the funeral home.

"Hi Tami."

Tami jumped when her partner came up to her desk.

"Oh sorry. You surprised me."

"Looks like you got something going. What's up?"

"I found that the three people who died recently, including Judge Lewis, all went through the Stockton Funeral Home."

"Wait a minute. You said 'three'. I thought there was only two."

"I believe Ed Stewart from the Stockton Gas Company is somehow related to this case, and he just had his funeral yesterday."

She watched his expression go from disbelief to fury in a matter of seconds.

"I can't believe this creep! Did Stewart get cremated or buried?"

"Cremated."

"And you think he was cremated while still alive?"

"Yes, I'm almost certain of it."

John rubbed his eyes, and turned to look around the station. Without even looking at Tami, he sat down and picked up one of her paperweights.

"Well, it's obvious this monster is after powerful people. I don't think there's any connection between the three of them, except that they're in positions of influence."

Tami looked at his face and shook her head.

"John, I told you I've been getting some disturbing packages in the mail this past week, and they tie both Senator Grant and Judge Lewis to some interesting illegal activities. I wouldn't be surprised if I get one tomorrow or Monday about Ed Stewart being involved."

He looked at her and set the paperweight down.

"Listen Tami. These men have been pillars of our community for years. I personally knew Ed Stewart, and he was as honest as they come. He truly cared about the people of Stockton and Winnebago County. I don't believe for a minute that they were involved with anything illegal. This guy that's torturing our town's leading citizens is some kind of disgruntled, envious sicko who needs to be stopped. There's no telling who could be next. He's gotten a politician, a judge, and now a company's CEO. He'll probably go after the owner of the TV station or a restaurant owner or our mayor next. I'm going to make sure he's stopped before he gets that far."

Tami sat back and stared into his eyes before he looked around the station again. Her first thought was that he reminded her of a serpent or a shark from the appearance of his eyes, but that had to be just in her mind. She didn't trust anything about him anymore and was certain she had to be careful around him.

"John, you may be right. I'm just looking for more of a connection between these three men."

He focused on her expression and smiled.

"I understand. Say, what exactly is in those packages you've received?"

She hesitated for a moment, but then sat up and opened her desk drawer with the file folders. John watched as she selected a specific file folder, and opened it on her desk.

"Mostly newspaper articles, but what's so compelling is that a clear picture is being drawn of these two men being involved in several shady deals, even though they both somehow got out of all accusations. It's clear they worked together on several cases and knew each other well."

John skimmed some of the articles, and Tami noticed his face frowning in disagreement as he put each one down on the desk.

"I'm still not convinced of any wrong-doing by either of these men. I think this guy is going after the key men in Stockton who are or were once in a position of power. He's probably a weak little man who's jealous of what other people have."

Tami watched as he tossed the last article on the stack, and then stood up without even looking at her.

"Yep. That's probably it. I just hope we can get a lead so we can stop him before he gets another person."

That got his attention, and he turned to look into her eyes, giving away some of his anger.

"Yes, exactly. That's the key, and we need to catch this guy now. I think I could put a few bullets in him just because of how sick the man is and how evil his actions are. I'd sure like to work this guy over and put him through the crematorium while he is still alive."

How ironic that John criticized the suspect for burning and burying people alive, but then commented how he would like to do the same to this man.

John started to walk away, but then turned and added, "Let me know if you find out anything new. Especially if you get another collection in the mail from your mysterious informant."

Tami nodded, causing a friendly smile to spread across her partner's face.

Chapter Eighteen

THE BLACKNESS OF THE EVENING almost suffocated Tami as she awoke from a terrible nightmare. Drenched with sweat and trying to control her breathing, she forced herself to read the time on her digital clock beside the bed. 3:14 AM. Turning on the light by the bedside table, she wondered if she would be able to fall asleep again and get rested up for work in a few hours.

Although she didn't want to remember what was in her dream, she knew exactly what had triggered it tonight. What she saw when those men opened up the judge's casket was enough to give even the bravest man horrific dreams and she wondered if that image would ever vacate her memory. She thought back to what her mind had given her in the dream and it was not a pleasant picture. When the lid of the casket came open, she saw herself inside, the victim of the most unthinkable torture she could imagine. Everything that had happened to the judge in real life was somehow passed on to her in the dream and she experienced the suffering of the man as he lay in the dark box waiting for his slow death to finally arrive.

Despite the coldness of the floor and the air outside of her blankets, she got up out of bed and walked toward the kitchen, apprehensive of her surroundings since she lived alone. Something made her feel as though she was in danger, so she picked up her handgun and made sure it was ready to fire in case this dream had been some kind of warning for her. She didn't even take a few extra seconds to put on a robe or slippers. The place was filled with silence and she hoped to remove any possibility of surprise by flipping on the light switch in every room of her apartment as she stepped into each one. Her eyes quickly adjusted from the darkness to the newly lit rooms and she faced her fears with her eyes wide open and her lips tightly clenched.

She noticed each piece of furniture, looking behind every potential hiding place for the unwelcomed guest from her dream. It was just a dream but the fear was very real. Why did this man scare her so much? He didn't seem the type to come after a police officer, since he was focused on revenge against people from his past who wronged him. Glancing up at the chandelier over her dining room table, she saw nothing and wondered why she would even look up there. She peeked behind the couch and stepped around her recliner, but again nothing out of the ordinary. Uneventful was a good thing tonight. Her eyes peered under the table and around the kitchen counter, glad to see only chairs and a clean kitchen floor.

As she made her way to the last room, the second bedroom which was reserved for guests who never visited, her nerves seemed to take over her senses. She treaded carefully and quietly, gun pointed straight into the black room, while she never took her focus away from the doorway and what awaited her. She imagined this man rushing out of the darkness, ready to put her through the nightmare that wouldn't go away.

Her bare feet felt the cold wood floors with each silent step but the rest of her body was heated with a mixture of adrenaline and fear. She didn't need a robe now, even though the air in the room was chilly. She swallowed and realized that her mouth was dry, and her eyes did everything they could to capture any movement or unusual presence in the second bedroom. Visualizing where everything was situated in that room, Tami tried to remember how the bedroom looked the last time she was in there. Holding in her next breath, she saw something near the right side of the bed, but it could have been a jacket that was placed on the bed post.

Finally with her back up against the wall, she inhaled deeply and reached around the doorframe to flip on the switch, then immediately squatted down. As light instantly engulfed every section of the bedroom, it seemed to move in slow motion. Somehow she saw the light travel across the room while she spun around and ended up in the doorway on one knee with her arms outstretched, gun pointing toward the interior of the bedroom. The remaining darkness soon disappeared and was replaced with a much welcome light.

Nothing. She remained still but on high alert while her eyes darted across the bed, to the closet, beside the dresser, along the walls. Relief flooded her senses and a smile came across her face as she relaxed and stood, clicking on the safety of her gun. Tami recognized that the nightmare had put her on guard and she struggled to forget about the concerns that surfaced as a result of the strange dream. For some reason, it was as though she was in danger from the man who had been torturing those public officials but knew it was an irrational fear. Or was it? Anyway, it was better to be safe than sorry. Tami was most certainly involved, since the alleged killer had sent her incriminating newspaper clippings and other documents about these men. Why send them to her? It was unnerving that this serial killer had singled her out as the recipient of these packages. She preferred being unknown to someone who would burn or bury people while they were still alive.

Checking the closet in the bedroom, just as a precaution, Tami wanted to be certain there was nothing to be afraid of, and she slowly moved the clothes hanging inside to see what was behind them and in the back corner. As suspected, there was nothing but more clothes. She scanned the room one more time before switching off the light and made her way back to the kitchen counter. She sat the gun down and poured herself a glass of milk, glancing around the room with her back to the refrigerator. She heated it up in the microwave for a minute, hoping it would trigger whatever warmed milk did to cause a person to fall asleep sooner. Warm milk always helped people sleep, right? The timer on the microwave startled her for a moment and she took out the mug to stir it before sampling it. The warm liquid tasted good and she closed her eyes, letting down her guard as she drank it. She tried to convince herself that she was already falling back to sleep.

Tami was tempted to go through the case in her mind now, but she wanted to push all of the details as far away as possible. The newspapers, the exhumation of the body, the suspicions about her partner, the horrors of her nightmare. She gazed around the room at her décor and was reminded of her decorating skills, getting her thoughts to a more pleasant state. A smile came to her face as she examined the wood floors, the flowery wallpaper and wooden chair rail, the antique kitchen items placed strategically around the room. She would address each of the case details after a good night's sleep, while she focused her mind on relaxing in bed again. She was in her own apartment and there was nothing for her to be concerned about tonight.

She sipped the rest of the milk and set the cup down on the counter. The room actually felt colder now and she recognized that her mind had let her body get back to normal again. It was probably sixty degrees in the apartment and she was glad to feel goose bumps on her thighs and arms from the cold temperature. Tami decided it was safe to turn off the other lights and picked up her gun as she made her way across the apartment, leaving the familiar blackness behind with every step.

Finally back in her bedroom, she eyed the comfortable bed and blankets. She deliberately didn't want to look at the clock, knowing that she had to get up again in just a few hours. Tami kept telling herself that she could fall right back to sleep, yet her mind knew that remnants of her dream would stay with her as she struggled to doze off again. Sitting down on the bed, she gave one last nervous look around the room before shutting off the lamp and lying down, wrapping the blankets around her. She wondered if she really would be able to fall back to sleep, as she struggled to keep the nightmare from rekindling her fears.

Chapter Nineteen

A FEW HOURS LATER, TAMI WAS AT work, not even acknowledging each thought that came up to get her to concentrate on the dream she had. She would put everything into her investigation and not be intimidated by a childish nightmare. The clues were all there, with the newspapers and the facts she had documented about these men, and she was connecting the dots. Maybe that's why she was picked by this serial killer. Could he have somehow known that Tami had the skills to piece together puzzles like this?

Tami had carefully done her homework this morning, and found that there was another employee at the funeral home who handled the bodies of the three men in question. They called him 'Erik with a k', and said that Erik Johnson, a long-time employee there, was the other person who worked on all three funerals. She planned to meet with him for informal questioning when she got a chance. It was odd that the first employee, Keith Ellis, was beaten up, and she initially thought the other employee, Erik, may have been the one that did this. However, Keith was positive it wasn't Erik, and he had nothing but good things to say about his co-worker. Her new dilemma was to find out who would pound a funeral home employee to the ground, at a place where people were being cremated and buried alive. First things first.

"Tami."

That startled her, and she smiled at her co-worker as she walked toward her desk.

"Oh, hi Gwen. What's up?"

"I traced the calls going in to Father Bill's office at the time the priest said he received it, and I found where the call came from."

Gwen handed her a piece of paper and she read it to herself.

"I'm impressed. Good job. I'll check it out right away."

"Be careful," Gwen added as she headed back to her desk.

This was where the suspected killer called Father Bill from, and Tami was a little bit apprehensive about going there alone in case the person in question was there again. However, she figured the odds were slim, and persuaded herself to check it out. Driving slowly around the neighborhood, she searched for the address of the phone number from where the call was made, but her mind was not entirely focused on locating this phone booth. The fears of being captured and tortured by this person came back in scenes of people being buried alive or cremated alive, and it took several minutes to overcome these deep concerns that haunted her.

"This man is not targeting me. He only selected me because he believes I can figure out what links these men together and expose whatever it is he's convinced these men are guilty of. That's all. He's not after me."

Finally, she stopped at a street corner and saw the street name she was searching for. To her surprise, the call came from a phone booth at the intersection across from Father Bill's church. The suspect had been standing right outside the church when he made the call to Father Bill. She would have liked to capture his fingerprints on the phone, but figured that several people might have used it since then. Cell phones are more common than phone booths, so it was a longshot, but Tami decided it was worth a try. She called a number on her phone.

"Hi James. This is Officer Tami Anderson. I need someone to come out to the intersection of Springwood and Tenth Street to see what prints can be picked up from the phone, phone booth, and the bench by the curb. Yeah, this is the case I was telling you about. I know it may not give us anything, but what if nobody's used this phone since the suspect made the call? Most people use cell phones nowadays, so his prints may still be there. Anyway, it's something to check into. Also, there's a possibility there could be prints inside the church, so ask them to come across the street into St Mark's Cathedral and talk to Father Bill Ljunglof for some potential places to check for prints. Ok, thanks. I appreciate it."

Although nobody was visible in the area, Tami parked the car at the curb and got out to walk around, looking for anything that might have been left by the suspect. She checked the bench for writing that could be a message to the police from him, since he had already left some clues for her, but found nothing useful. She sat on the bench, envisioning what he could have seen from this vantage point, but the only thing that stood out was the church across the street. He must have been staking out St. Mark's Cathedral. Walking around the pay phone, she searched for some kind of hint that could have been left, and let her eyes scan the phone, the phone book, and the small walls on each side of the phone. Nothing.

She casually stepped back, staring at the phone with the church in the background, and noticed an interesting view of the front door with some of the windows along the sidewalk across the street. It was a sunny day now and the designs in each window looked beautiful. This was definitely a large church.

He must have watched the building from here, and decided to call Father Bill this time instead of going in and having confession in person. Maybe he was concerned that Father Bill had called the police last time and thought the church was being scoped out.

She looked up the sidewalk to the left, then across the street to the left, following the sidewalk along the church and beyond, and then crossed the street with her eyes to study the sidewalk to her right. Still nothing out of the ordinary that would point out a vengeful man capable of psychological tortures.

"Where are you and what are you planning next?" she asked out loud.

While she was this close to the church, Tami decided to visit Father Bill. She checked traffic, and then walked across the not-so-busy street to the front of the great structure. She stepped inside, but had no idea where to go to find him. Walking aimlessly, examining the inside of the impressive building, she noticed the confessional and thought about having it dusted for prints, wondering how many people came to confession over the past week. With her head tilted, she looked into the little room as she slowly passed by. It was empty, with the door open, as was the next room.

Hmm. Maybe this isn't the time for confessions.

Just then, someone walked toward her and Tami asked, "Hi, could you tell me where Father Bill Ljunglof would be?"

The man smiled and pointed back and to his left.

"Yes, his office is just through these doors. I think he's about the third room down the hall, and he should be there now."

"Thanks," Tami responded with a smile of her own.

She traced the man's verbal map, and found the first door he alluded to. Beyond that, there was a hallway lined with offices, most of them open, and she inspected the names on each door. Sure enough, a sign fixed on the third room on the left said, "Father Bill Ljunglof."

Peeking inside, she noticed Father Bill writing, not even perceiving her presence. She had never seen him with glasses before.

"Hi Father Bill. Got a minute?"

He looked up and smiled, standing immediately when he recognized her.

"Hi Tami. Come on in. What brings you here?"

"I found that your mysterious stranger called from the pay phone across the street when he made his last confession, and figured while I was in the neighborhood, I'd stop in and see if you had any updates for me."

"Across the street? That's strange. I asked him to come in, but he said he had a headache and didn't want to be out while it was overcast. I figured he must have been inside somewhere and thought the weather might have been giving him a migraine."

"I searched the area, but didn't find any leads. I'll see if any fingerprints or other evidence shows up. Would it be worth dusting the confessional for prints?"

"Well, I don't know what you could find, since dozens of people go through that door each week. My guess is that the prints have been covered up many times over, but you can try if you think it would get something."

"That's what I was afraid of. Has he contacted you since the call?"

"No new visits or calls yet."

"I did want to give you a warning that we do have reason to believe he has killed two people, possibly a third."

Father Bill's eyes narrowed as he took in those words.

"I suspected as much, but I honestly hoped it wasn't true. Can you tell me who these men were?"

Tami hesitated for a second, then said, "Well, Senator Jerry Grant and Judge Frank Lewis are the two I believe were killed by this man. I'm still investigating the third one, so I can't reveal much at this point. Please don't mention these names to anyone else either, OK?"

"I won't. He did say the men who ruined his life were rich and powerful, and although I might be able to see a congressman fitting that description, I always thought judges were not very rich."

"According to what I've seen, there are accusations against the judge that claim he accepted bribes. Maybe they were big bribes, or maybe he was 'influenced' by someone else who was rich and powerful."

The priest nodded slowly as he digested that idea.

"You know Tami, as bad as this person's crimes may appear, I honestly believe he sounded as though he was sorry for what he did, based on the last time I talked to him."

"You know, if he's broken the law and killed someone, I have to take him in and he has to be punished."

"I understand that, but looking back at our conversations, I get the feeling that he's not really a murderer. I think he's a good man who was wronged, and made some bad choices to take the law into his own hands. From our past conversations, it sounds like he went to court to settle this legally, but justice wasn't done."

"I think you're right. I've been sent two packets of newspaper clippings on Grant and Lewis, and it looks like they both had a history of covering up illegal activities. However, they were both somehow able to get cleared of all accusations. I think your confessor is the person who sent these to me."

"Wow. Is there anything in these packages that could identify our man?"

"No, I haven't found anything definite yet. He's been

careful to keep his own name out of the clippings he sent me. I have a friend who's helping me investigate, but so far we haven't come up with any helpful insights. I'm still working on pinpointing something that ties all three of the deaths with a common thread."

"What I'm saying, Tami is that I don't think the man is a threat to the community, even though he may have killed two or three people. I know that sounds strange, but he appears to have targeted those specific individuals who caused his problems, whatever those might be."

"I see what you're saying, but he still can't just go and take someone's life because they ruined his business or took away his profits or whatever they did. He can't take the law into his own hands, and he can't go around killing people. It's as simple as that."

"My gut feeling tells me that he's a good man who's gone astray, and I believe he's close to being brought back to the right path."

"That would be good news, but I've had some of the most terrifying feelings lately relating to this case, and I'm more afraid of this man than anyone I've ever investigated. I'm not to the point where I agree that he's not dangerous. He creeps me out. After seeing what he did to one of the victims, I'm not convinced this man is one of the good guys."

Bill nodded his understanding and added, "Anyway, I'd like to talk to him more since I have a feeling that he's reachable and will be reasonable. Just keep that in mind, OK?"

"I will. Thanks for the reassurance. I'll try to remind myself of that after my next nightmare describing how he's going to torture and kill me the same way he's done the other men."

Bill didn't smile, and Tami wondered if she mentioned too much. She stood and reached out her hand, giving him one of her awesome smiles, while he shook her hand without expression.

"Keep in touch if you think of anything else that could help us identify who this person is or if he contacts you again. I appreciate your help so far."

"I will. Please be careful. I know you're in a difficult spot, not knowing who he is and realizing he's still out there. I just don't think he would take his revenge out on you since you weren't part of that group of people who hurt him years ago."

"Thanks Bill. It does make me feel better. I'm still going to keep my guard up if you don't mind, and I hope you're right about him."

As she walked back down the length of the church, she thought about what Father Bill had mentioned regarding the suspect, and she wondered if he would hide anything to protect the man. She shook her head with that thought, and pushed open the front door as her phone rang.

"This is Tami. What? Are you sure about that? They both ate at Bella's Italian Ristorante the night they died?"

Chapter Twenty

TAMI'S MIND FLOODED WITH NEW ideas as she drove to Bella's Ristorante to meet her partner, putting together the new pieces to this puzzle as she zipped through traffic and went over the details with one of her co-workers on the hands-free speaker phone.

"So far, a priest I know came to me, telling of a man who confessed to him about getting revenge on some wealthy and powerful people."

She sped by the blurred faces of other drivers, not focusing on driving as she played it all out in her head.

"In addition, I've received newspaper clippings on a former state senator and a retired judge, who both supposedly died in the past week of natural causes, and the articles imply that these men were slick public officials who appear to be crooked. It turns out that the judge was buried alive, which leads me to believe the recently-cremated senator may have been cremated alive."

"They did an autopsy on the judge already, right?" asked James.

"Yes, I'm still waiting impatiently for toxicology details from the autopsy, although they told me that the cause of death was asphyxiation."

"The toxicology report could take weeks you know."

"Yeah, but we can't wait that long. I suspect that I'll be receiving another such package of clues on a third man any day now. Also, I believe the person who confessed to the priest might be the same person who sent me the old newspaper clippings, but I haven't made any further connections."

Tami stopped at an intersection and looked around to make sure it was safe to proceed. She glanced at the other drivers as she accelerated past them and wondered if she had stared right at the person who gave Father Bill the confession. She wouldn't even know it if she had.

"We found that the bodies of all three men were handled by the Stockton Funeral Home, which took care of their funerals; two were cremated and one was buried. Someone at that funeral home must have been involved, since the casket of the buried man was rigged to allow air to reach inside, plus that guy was not even embalmed."

"Tami, you know that only someone involved with the funeral home could make sure an embalming didn't happen, allowing the man to be buried alive."

"I know. When I went to the funeral home to investigate, one of the employees was found lying face down, bleeding on the floor after an assault, and although he admitted to helping a co-worker get the bodies in place for their funerals, he claimed to know nothing else. This co-worker's name was Erik Johnson, but he wasn't available for questioning."

"Now it seems as though at least two of the men, maybe even the third, had eaten at the same restaurant the night they 'died of natural causes'. At least that's your theory, right?"

"Yes. Could someone have poisoned these men at the restaurant with a chemical that made them appear to be dead, and then someone at the funeral home made sure these men suffered a horrible death by forcing them to be cremated alive or buried alive? Is there really such a chemical that would be that convincing?"

"I don't know, Tami. I'll dig further and see what I can find out. Maybe some kind of Native American herbs."

"I need that toxicology report now to find out what unusual chemicals or herbs were in the judge's body. We'll probably wrap up the case before the results come back. At least I hope so. I've got to go. Talk to you later."

"Bye Tami. Be careful."

Tami drove into the parking lot of the restaurant, easily finding a spot to park since it was between lunch and dinner, and saw her partner walking across the lot at a fast pace. She ran to catch up, wondering how they must look, walking side by side. She was tall and thin, while he was even taller and much bulkier. They were like an odd couple in a way, but with no feelings for each other. At least no good feelings.

"John, how did you find out that this place served their last meals?"

"I talked to both of the men's wives and interestingly enough they both had dinner here the night they died. Coincidence?"

"Not likely. I'm betting that Ed Stewart also ate here the night he died."

John stopped walking and gave her a look of surprise, while she passed him up. She stopped as well, turning and standing in front of him.

"I forgot about that. You think he might have been killed too, instead of dying of a heart attack in his sleep. Let me check with his family after we finish up here, just to see if he fits in with the other two. Have you received any new love letters from your mystery man, accusing Ed of being in the mafia?"

"I think he may be the third victim, but I haven't seen any new mail yet with the same kinds of articles. I found that Ed's body was also handled by the Stockton Funeral Home and he was cremated. Remember, my guess is that Stewart was cremated alive."

Tami watched as her partner fumed and cursed again before finally regaining his composure.

"OK, let's see how this restaurant ties in with the work of this maniac."

The hostess gave them both a smile as they stepped through the front door, and said, "Hi folks. Just the two of you?"

The thought of a dinner date with her partner immediately repulsed Tami, even though he was a handsome man, and she almost responded with, "You must be kidding!"

John responded with a somber expression and said in his baritone voice, "No, we're here on official police business. Can we speak with the manager?"

"Oh, of course. He's right over there, standing by that table."

Tami smiled her appreciation and the two of them strolled through the restaurant toward the man to whom the hostess pointed.

"Excuse me, sir. I'm Officer John Hultgren and this is my partner, Officer Tami Anderson. We understand you're the manager here. Is that correct?"

"Yes, how can I help you?"

"I'll get straight to the point. It's been brought to our attention that several prominent people who have died recently were reported to have eaten here the night of their death."

Tami noticed the manager's eyes staring through her partner, as his lips tightened and he started to appear defensive. John enjoyed being confrontational, and she could tell he relished in putting this man on the spot.

"What are you implying?"

"Nothing yet, just trying to investigate the commonality of these men being here only hours before they passed away. We have reason to believe someone who works here could have given these men a drug or chemical."

John paused to let that sink in for a second, and then Tami continued the line of questioning.

"We need to see your schedule to find out who was working on each of these three evenings to narrow down our search for the suspect. Also, can you tell us if you have any employees, either in the kitchen or serving the food, who might appear to be suspicious or has had suspicious behavior in the past week?"

The manager looked at her intently but shook his head.

"No, I have a great team of people right now and they're all top-notch employees. I can't even think of one who would be doing something like that. You must be mistaken. This is quite a claim that could really hurt my business here. I think you need to ..."

"Look, has anyone called in sick or not shown up for work in the past day or two?" John interrupted.

The manager looked up at the big man and hesitated.

"Well, Erik, one of my waiters, has called in sick in the past few days, but ..."

"Erik Johnson?" Tami blurted out.

"Uh, yes. That's his name, but he's a great people person and a tremendous team player."

"Tami, how did you know this guy's last name? Is he someone we need to follow up on? It sounds familiar."

John recognized it from his visit to the funeral home, when Keith Ellis mentioned that Erik had helped with the bodies of these two men.

Tami pulled her partner aside and glanced over to the restaurant manager, who was obviously confused and concerned.

"Excuse me sir. My partner and I need to discuss something for a minute."

Turning to John, with her back to the restaurant manager, she looked up into his eyes and then down at the ground as she put her thoughts together.

She whispered, "John, I went to the funeral home that took care of the burial and cremation for all three men, and I talked to an employee there who had been attacked and beaten up while at work." Her eyes moved up to catch his and she noticed some surprise in his expressions. "He told me that he didn't see who hit him but he did mention his co-worker's name was Erik Johnson. Erik with a k. I didn't think anything about it until this manager mentioned the name 'Erik', and bells went off in my head. I didn't think the person here would also be named Erik Johnson but I had to throw it out there and see if I got any bites."

John stepped up to the manager again, assuming his naturally intimidating stance over the smaller man, as the manager did his best to stand up to him.

"This person, Erik Johnson, is a potential suspect in three separate murders, so if you hear from him again, please call us right away."

John handed him a business card while the manager took it and nodded, saying nothing.

Tami asked, "Would you show us the schedules for the three nights in question so we can see if Erik was at least scheduled for one or more of them?"

He nodded again and started walking toward the back of the restaurant. "OK, let's go to the employee break room where the schedules are."

They followed him and Tami noticed the wind seemed to be knocked out of the manager when he learned they were investigating Erik. She felt bad for the man, since he acted like he had just lost his favorite puppy.

The break room was simply a small room between the kitchen and dining room, with a couple of chairs, cabinets, and charts on the wall. Very basic. Could the murderer have stood in this same spot just a few days ago?

"Here are the three nights that we need to check," said Tami, handing the manager a piece of paper with three dates listed.

He took it in silence, as his eyes digested the information. Then paging back a couple of sheets of paper, he looked at the schedule, back to Tami's paper, looked at the schedule, back to Tami's paper. Then he turned the page once more and looked at the third date. He handed the paper back to Tami, shaking his head.

"Yes, Erik worked all three of these nights, but I still can't believe he would be involved in anything that would hurt someone. You must have the wrong guy. He has called in sick a few other times, but that's because of his severe migraines. I think that's why he called in this last time too."

"We appreciate your help sir, and will follow up with Erik. You may be correct and your Erik Johnson may not be the same person we're looking for, but until we're certain, please let us know if you hear from him. Also, we need to know his phone number and address. Would you be able to provide that for us?"

The manager pulled out his phone, searched for a few seconds, and then handed it to Tami.

"I don't have my address book readily available, but this is his number."

She wrote the number down and returned the phone.

"Thanks again. We'll be in touch, and I apologize for the bad news."

The officers walked through the restaurant, and Tami turned to see the manager's sad expression one last time before exiting into the parking lot. Father Bill had mentioned something about the last call he received from his confessor, where he thought the man had a headache and didn't want to come out in bad weather. This Erik Johnson seemed to have migraines bad enough that he couldn't go to work.

Tami was surprised at her partner's excitement and his smile as he exclaimed, "We've got him now!"

Chapter Twenty-One

STANDING BESIDE HIS CAR, JOHN told Tami, "I'm going to check with Ed Stewart's wife to see if he ate at Bella's the night he died. I'll meet you at the station in a little while."

Tami nodded, got into her car and headed back to work. She immediately got on her phone and pressed a sequence of numbers.

"This is Officer Tami Anderson. I need everything you can find on an Erik Johnson. He works at the Stockton Funeral Home and at Bella's Italian Ristorante, and he's the prime suspect for at least three murders. Find out where he lives, who his friends and family are, what kind of car he drives. You know the details I want. Also, once you get his address, I need a search warrant right away. I know. Just get it as soon as possible and let me know once we have it. Great. I appreciate it."

She clicked her phone and put it on the seat while she tried to focus on driving for a few minutes, deep in thought about what she needed to do next. Was there anything else she was missing in this case? Could he have been working with that other funeral home worker to carry out these murders and she just released that other guy by mistake? Is there something else she had missed from the packages sent to her, presumably by Erik? Why had he chosen to send them to her? What did he want her to do with the information on each person? Was he simply playing a game with her and enjoyed the thrill of leading her on? She was overwhelmed and needed to concentrate.

When she marched through the door at the police station and walked over to check her mail, she stopped and stared. This was an old police station, and the mail slots were wooden with dark walnut stain. She didn't pay much attention to it at this point in time, however. Her focus now was with the contents of her mail slot.

There was another orange envelope and she was convinced it had to be something about Ed Stewart. Without further hesitation, she grabbed it and opened the letter, scanning the contents for a highlighted name or something circled. Sure enough, the first article she read mentioned Ed Stewart, as did the second and the third. Walking absent-mindedly to her desk, ignoring the people she moved past, she searched the newspaper clippings for anything useful in this case. Unfortunately, just like the other two packages, there was nothing obvious that revealed who the sender might be. He was smart enough to cover his tracks so far by pointing out activities on each of these men, but leaving out any mention of his own name.

She sat down, taking the other envelopes from her desk and read the rest of the new articles. Wow, this Ed Stewart really was like a mafia king who may have pulled all the strings in this town. He's the one who had the money and did the bribing. How did he keep getting out of these accusations? Somebody else had to be protecting him. Or was his money enough to pay off lawyers, judges, police officers, and more? The other two men, the congressman and the judge, kept getting out of the claims that were made against each of them, just like Ed Stewart. Ed certainly was wealthy enough to hush up anyone who got too close, so this man could be the key player in this game of deceit that she had been dragged into.

Tami grabbed the three envelopes and studied the contents for a while, writing down key names, dates, and court cases in a notebook. She filed the envelopes back in the drawer and got up abruptly from her desk, heading to the front door of the station. She needed to get to the library and link these men together to find some kind of common ground, hopefully leading to someone like Erik Johnson as a person with a grudge and a motive for revenge.

Once in her car, she drove to the older part of town, periodically glancing down at the notebook placed on the passenger seat. The person who sent this information apparently wanted it revealed to the public and hoped to expose their illegal connections. Why would he have selected her as the recipient of this material? Why not send it to the newspaper? Maybe this man knew that someone at the newspaper was also involved and would continue to cover it up. Maybe that person would be the next victim. She couldn't waste any more time.

She turned into the library parking lot and found a spot for the car, getting out quickly, almost running to the entrance. She rushed up and tried to get the attention of the person standing in the room about ten feet behind the desk.

"Excuse me. I need to research several incidents that happened in town over the past twenty years. Can you help me get started?"

An attractive, young brunette with long straight hair came out with a welcoming smile, and walked up close to the desk.

"Hi, I'm Sally. I can help you now if you just follow me."

"Hi, I'm Officer Tami Anderson. I appreciate anything you can help me with," replied Tami as she trailed behind the librarian.

They went into a small room with a lot of file cabinets and large machines, and Sally flipped on the light switch. Darkness scattered into every corner of the room and then disappeared as the light took over.

"It looks like you have the room to yourself for now. These drawers here cover the past twenty years, and the reels should be in chronological order. Do you know how to use the microfilm machines?"

"Yes, I've used them before. I think I'm all set. Thanks for your help."

"No problem. There's a computer there also, since some of the town's history, including newspapers, has been scanned and put online. Our local history seems to be a popular topic lately. A man from Upper Michigan spent a lot of time researching here a few weeks ago. Anyway, if you have any questions, feel free to ask."

The young librarian walked out of the room and vanished, while Tami set up at one of the desks to organize her plan of attack. She had a notebook of facts already written out in some kind of format from the first two packages she received, and started reviewing the items related to Ed Stewart. She hoped to confirm any hint of conspiracy between the three victims, and link them to her suspect somehow. Occasionally circling an item about the court cases, she flipped through her notes from the old newspaper articles that were back at the station. Once she had everything she might need, she took her list to the file cabinets and opened a large drawer.

"Whew!" she exclaimed while exhaling, staring at the dozens of small boxes that were offered for her selection. She read the dates on the boxes, and looked at the dates on her list. After pointing at several boxes in search of the right date, she pulled one out, took her prize to one of the machines, and sat down.

Once she got into a rhythm, it wasn't that bad to look up these dates and incidents, so she was able to get information on everything she searched for. After about two hours, she rubbed her eyes and sat back in the chair to stretch. Spotting the computer in the corner, she decided to search some of the dates there for a while and took her notes with her to sit down across the room.

Tami was surprised with each new discovery she made, but was disappointed that the key missing link was so elusive. There was enough evidence here to show that each of these men were indeed crooked and should have gone to jail for their involvement, even though they somehow escaped justice in every case, and she wondered how these men were connected to her informant. It appeared that when these issues were brought up in the past, they were swept under the rug and the person who had tried to raise a red flag eventually crept away with his tail between his legs. These men were powerful indeed.

It occurred to her that this mystery man may have picked her at random, and maybe it was a coincidence that Father Bill happened to be in confession when her suspect came to the church. Yet, she wondered if this person chose each of them for a reason, still unknown at this point in time.

"Can I get you a coffee or a bottle of pop, Officer Anderson?"

Tami was startled by the interruption, but laughed as she noticed the librarian standing in the doorway.

"Sorry to disturb you. I just thought you could use a break after all this time."

"Yes, thank you. I could use a root beer if you have one."

"Sure do. Come on around the corner and get one. We have a drink machine just outside here."

Tami got up and followed her out the door, and walked up to a machine with a good selection of cold drinks.

"It's on the house, so take your pick."

"Thanks. I'll just take a regular root beer."

Sally offered the required sacrifice to the machine, receiving a cold bottle in return.

Tami gratefully took it from the beast, and opened it while she stood beside it.

"Are you finding what you're looking for?"

Tami took a sip, enjoying the taste immensely, and nodded while she swallowed.

"Yes, actually the records are easy to locate and I've found quite a bit already. I'm still looking for a key element to the case I'm working on, but haven't found the item that ties it all together."

"Well, good luck. I can help with using all of the resources and tools to do the researching, but if you're already proficient, I'm not sure if I can do anymore for you."

"No problem. You've already been a big help. Thanks for the drink too."

Sally walked back to the desk, while Tami made her way back to the research room. She gazed across the empty library, not really looking for anything in particular, and got her mind focused on the search again while she entered the small room and sat down.

Giving her notes a good review, pointing out a few connections between Judge Lewis and Senator Grant, then connections between Ed Stewart and Judge Lewis, she then decided to start with some of the dates that appear to link Ed Stewart with Senator Grant. She made a few notes beside two of the incidents she had identified, and then got back to work on the computer. She spent quite a while searching and found a case that appeared to involve all three men in one way or another. For a long time, she read with great interest, staring in disbelief as she soaked up this newfound knowledge. Her eyes widened and her heart rate increased with the excitement of discovery. This had to be what she was searching for, and Tami knew that she was on to something big. She read voraciously and felt that she couldn't read it all fast enough. This was it. This was really the connection. Finally.

The case went on for days, and was covered thoroughly in the local papers, even making the Chicago Tribune several times. Her adrenaline was going strong and she couldn't take her eyes from the screen while the words entered her brain as though her life depended on them. This story was important, and she finally knew why their suspect had collected these kinds of articles, detailing different events over all these years. There was a conspiracy all right, and these three men were as guilty as sin. How did they get away with this all these years?

All at once, she gasped, eyes wide open, and her hands covered her mouth.

Chapter Twenty-Two

ERIK SAT ON THE GRASS BORDERing Alpine Lake, staring into the water. He warmed himself in the sunshine, welcoming the continuous breeze that gently touched the surface of the lake. It was relaxing to come here and forget about things, and take in the beauty of the park. There was something peaceful about the lake and watching the rippled movement of the dark water as the wind painted patterns on the surface. The trees along the road and throughout the acres of rolling hills were like old acquaintances to him, since they had been there since he was a small boy. They lined up evenly around the lake with a symmetry that he appreciated. Most of the flowers from spring were gone, but some covered large areas of the park, gracing the grounds with different colors. He wondered what the view would be like from the sky today.

Erik just remembered that he used to do a lot of aerial photography and enjoyed seeing the different parks from the air. A memory came to him about taking Brita with him once, and he treasured her excitement of going up into a small plane. She giggled at the feeling in her belly when they ascended, and her eyes were wide open as she looked at the town from a birds-eye view. She actually called it a 'God's-eye view' and Erik was impressed at her perception.

Somewhere, he had a photograph of her sitting in the driver's seat of the aircraft, and he wished he could look at that photograph now. He stared into his mind in an effort to see it once more and was pleased that he could picture her on the plane with her beautiful smile, full of enthusiasm.

He could tell she was so proud of herself after that first plane ride with Erik, since he had told her that some people get sick with the movement of a small plane. Not Brita. She said that she enjoyed the tickle in her belly and seeing everything from that point of view, way up in the sky. Erik was delighted with his little girl and could hardly take his eyes off of her during the flight. He was supposed to be taking photographs of an old farmhouse and surrounding barn, root cellar, and other buildings. Yet he adored his daughter in her exhilaration and had to force himself to focus on his job. He ended up getting his photographs and his payment, but the memories of his daughter's first flight were far more precious.

&&&

TAMI'S HEAD SPUN WITH THE NEW INFORmation she had learned and she thanked the librarian on her way out for her help. Hopefully the librarian didn't notice that she had been wiping tears from her eyes, but it really didn't matter. She had written down the name of a doctor mentioned in one of the newspaper articles and found out that he was retired now but still in the area. She tracked down his current address and stopped by his house after leaving the library.

"Hi Doctor Crain, I'm Officer Tami Anderson from the Stockton Police Department and I'm investigating a case that appears to be related to something that happened over fifteen years ago. Could I ask you a few questions?"

"Of course. I always welcome a pretty lady who knocks at my front door. Please come on inside."

The doctor's accent sounded more Southern than Midwest, and she suspected he was from North Carolina or Virginia. Undoubtedly not from northern Illinois or Wisconsin.

"Thank you. You have a beautiful home. It looks like a woman's touch though, so is it safe to assume your wife did a lot of the decorating?"

"Yes, she is amazing when it comes to those kinds of things. I did the landscaping and the flower garden but she did the wallpaper, picked out the furniture, and arranged all of the pictures on the walls."

Mrs. Crain stepped elegantly into the room, and asked, "Would you two like something to drink?"

"I could use a glass of water, if you don't mind dear."

"Well if you're bringing something for your husband, I could use a glass as well."

She smiled and disappeared into the kitchen. Tami knew the woman had to be over sixty, but she the way she presented herself gave an aura of beauty that most seniors don't have. Mrs. Crain was probably the perfect hostess. Tami looked around the room for a few minutes, enjoying the calm before the storm of ancient history questions that she was about to bring up. She stared into some of the old photographs of the doctor and his wife, feeling an honesty in the eyes of the older gentleman.

"She certainly is good at what she does. I feel very welcome here, and I don't even know either of you."

The doctor smiled as his wife entered the room with a tray of drinks.

"I hope you like ice water with a hint of orange. I sliced an orange into the pitcher of water, so you just get a bit of the fruit flavor."

"Officer Anderson, this is my wife, Julia. I meant to introduce her earlier but I forgot my manners."

"I'm pleased to meet you. I do apologize for intruding this afternoon, but I've recently found some leads on a case that you had some involvement in many years ago."

"Let's sit over here," he said as he led them to a circular couch. "You have my curiosity going. What is it that I can help you with?"

"Dr. Crain, do you remember the explosion on Eighth Street?"

"Who doesn't? Yes, that was a terrible day. What about it?"

Tami paused as she considered what she found at the library. Erik Johnson was a photographer she remembered when she was younger, but it was a difficult concept to accept. She wondered what to say, then just blurted it out.

"There was a man who was hurt that day and I found a newspaper article that said you treated him."

"Yes, I remember him. He was thrown from the building by the force of the explosion and had so many injuries. It was a miracle he survived."

"This man is now a suspect in several recent murders, and I'm trying to understand how such a good person could become a serial killer."

"Very interesting. So that's why you're here. Well, I don't remember all of the details, but I know he did have a serious head injury. I believe he was blasted through a door or a window and the front of his brain suffered a tremendous amount of trauma. You've probably heard it called frontal lobe damage, but not a lot was known about it back then."

"Could that explain how a friendly person could become a murderer?"

Tami noticed that the doctor looked at his wife, who waited for his next words.

"Yes, frontal damage could bring about a dramatic change in this man's social behavior. His personality could change dramatically after an injury to the frontal lobes, especially if both lobes were damaged. Damage to the left frontal lobe could lead to depression and damage to the right frontal lobe could lead to psychopathic behavior. In this man's case, I believe he had damage to both."

Tami looked at the doctor, then to his wife, and nodded quietly.

"It's been a long time since I saw this man, so I can't say anything for certain about his diagnosis, especially since I haven't looked through his charts in over a decade."

"I understand, and I appreciate your confirmation. I wondered if the injuries could have really caused the suspect's recent behavior, but I remember this man from years ago and he was the kindest person I knew. It's just a shock to try to connect the man I remember with this murderer."

"From what I remember, the damage was significant. I'm surprised he's been able to function in society all these years later, especially if he's been undergoing the depression I suspect he's experienced over the years. If he's now psychotic and lashing out at people, that's most likely the results of the right lobe damage, and you may have difficulty trying to find the person you once remembered."

Tami responded with a blank expression, and eventually gave a slight nod as she thought about seeing Erik Johnson at the studio many years ago.

"Thank you both for your time today. It's not what I wanted to hear, but it finally sheds some light on how someone like this man could turn out the way he has."

Tami stood, as did the other two, and she led the doctor to the door. She faked a smile and shook their hands, then walked to her car, still remembering the photographer in a positive light. Did his laughter and pleasant smile really die in that explosion, only to be replaced with anger and vengeance?

&&&

JUST THEN, ERIK SAW TWO PEOPLE ACROSS the lake, and thought they looked like his wife and daughter. He stood up and walked toward them on the path around the water, feeling a big smile spread across his face. This park meant so much to his family and he had memories of being there with them in every season. In winter, they would sled down the snow-covered hills with laughter, and in spring they all marveled at the colors of flowers that adorned the park in the thousands like a spectacular rainbow. The summer brought kites out so they watched the skies to see the wonderful fliers, and even tried their hand at flying kites themselves. Brita loved seeing her kite carry upward, tugging on the string as it soared with a life of its own. In autumn, they kicked up fallen leaves, and Kiersten knew what kind of tree every yellow, orange, and red leaf was from. To his surprise, even his daughter knew more than he did when it came to leaves. How priceless it was to recall these moments with his family.

As he drew near to his wife and daughter, he realized that they were not who he thought they were and could now tell the little one was a boy. The people Erik had seen as Kiersten and Brita were not his loved ones and the disappointment registered immediately. The lady and her son walked toward him while he stared at them as though he had been dejected. Making his way to the closest park bench, he filled the empty seat.

While he sat alone beside the lake, memories came flooding back to him like long lost friends, and he soaked it all in. It was becoming more and more difficult for him to distinguish between reality, memories, and visions and he was almost to the point of not even trying to tell them apart anymore. He watched his daughter laughing in the little restaurant and saw himself go into the front of his studio next door. As usual, the action moved along almost in fast motion and it reminded him of an old silent movie, although it was washed in colors that were not quite right. He beamed at the comedic quality and tried to remember what the occasion was. Erik supposed that his suit looked good, and he could tell he was dressed up to go out somewhere with his wife. Sure enough, he picked up what looked like a small wrapped gift. It must have been for their anniversary. He walked through the lobby, out the front door, and around the corner toward the back of the building, entering the basement door from the alley as he headed down the stairs.

His shoes were silent as they made each step, but he remembered distinctly the clack of his dress shoes whenever he walked down these stairs. The man from the gas company was down there, but he looked concerned, as if something didn't make sense. The gas man made a comment and then was eerily quiet as he looked up in terror. His mouth moved as he waved his arms frantically and Erik instantly ran back up the stairs.

When he reached the top step and reached for the door knob, Erik was pushed with tremendous force from behind, thrown through the glass window in the basement door. He was amazed at how high he was forced through the air, as he sailed over his little red Fiat parked in the alley behind the building. A burning pain radiated throughout his entire back and the backs of his legs, and the back of his head hurt for some reason as though he had been hit with a shotgun blast. He noticed the top of his head hurt too, but he figured that was from crashing through the door head first. His weightlessness was an unusual feeling and he couldn't make sense of it all. There was a terrible roar now that hurt his ears and as he turned in mid-air, his eyes caught glimpses of fire and black smoke behind him. His silent movie now seemed to have sound, but it still had a dreamlike quality to it.

The strangest thing was that all of this happened at once, yet it almost seemed like minutes had gone by as he took time to think about the noise, the burning of his skin, the knock to his head, the smoke, the intense heat, and the sensation of being thrown through the air. Something big had just occurred and he saw it as an observer, even though he was actually a participant in the action.

Time moved slowly as Erik appeared to float for several seconds, but now he felt in his stomach that he was hurtling toward the ground. He turned his head to see where he was going to land and he witnessed a large brick building collapsing in the midst of the smoke and flames. Where was the man from the gas company? He didn't get out of the building. That couldn't be his building, could it? His little red Fiat disappeared as a wall laid down over it like a blanket and the memory ended suddenly.

Erik felt physical pain as he pondered these memories, and he wanted to figure out what he had just seen. Some of it didn't ring a bell at all, yet he distinctly remembered other parts of the memory as if it had just happened. He staggered up from the bench and again it was as though a knife sliced in and out of his head, poking and sawing. The pain was unbearable and he had to get back home as soon as possible so people wouldn't stare at him while he was in this state. A cloud momentarily obscured the rays of sunlight and that bothered Erik. The sunshine always seemed to make things better. If only it would stay out all the time. Thinking he was good at hiding the pain, he noticed the look in people's eyes as he rushed by them. He just knew they could tell something was wrong. He needed help. He needed to hold Kiersten right now. Where were his wife and daughter?

Chapter Twenty-Three

FINALLY BACK IN HIS APARTMENT, the room seemed to spin out of control, while heart-pounding drums, guitars, and vocals screamed in the background. It wasn't really, but that's the way it appeared to Erik as he knelt on the floor by the bed, cradling his head with both hands, suffering for what seemed like an eternity. When these headaches came, they were merciless and attacked with a vengeance greater than his own feelings for the men who hurt him so much all those years ago. They lasted longer and longer and the intensity of each one was much greater now than when they had first started. He wondered how people dealt with these kinds of agonies in their daily lives, since his migraines were so debilitating that he could hardly work, drive, relax, or anything while they were happening.

All he could do was hang on for the ride while it was underway and try to wait it out. If he took the pills given to him by his doctor, they would practically knock him out, which was one way to deal with the pain, but there were things he needed to do. He couldn't just sleep it off.

What was it the specialist told him yesterday?

"The damage to your frontal lobe is so extensive that we're surprised you're even able to function at all. This kind of injury often affects a patient's moods and in a very negative way."

Not very encouraging.

"To make it even worse, the debris embedded in your brain is inoperable due to the difficult locations, and there's nothing we can do to help, except medicate you whenever an episode begins to happen."

Great! What could be done then?

The doctor added, "I'm afraid you may have only a few months to live, since the pain is getting worse and happening more often. I recommend that you get your things in order while you're still able to think clearly."

Erik had let this sink in while the doctor stared at him, waiting for a response, and was at a loss for words. He had figured this out already and suspected something was very wrong with him even before he went to the doctor. His usually easy-going demeanor sometimes gave way to a rage that he had never known before, and once he recognized the anger getting too strong, it was too late. It wasn't like him at all and he hated being so angry all the time. He didn't like the person he had become, but there appeared to be nothing he could do except treat the symptoms with knockout pills. Unfortunately for him, these were not really migraines, although there were some similarities.

He needed to see his family again but since his wife left him years ago, he couldn't see her every day. At least she was kind enough to meet him regularly and let him see their daughter, Brita. When he was with them, everything was back to normal and his life was good again, even if only for a short time. He looked forward to their visits more than anything, but he needed them every day. He couldn't remember any details of their breakup, but he wasn't sure he wanted to know more.

It must have been his severe mood swings that caused her to leave, since she probably couldn't stand to be around during his episodes and he understood that. In a way, he was glad that his wife and daughter weren't around while he had these fits but he also wondered if his rage would be lessened if they were around more often. Probably not if there was indeed a physical problem with his brain that caused the unpleasant incidents, yet still he constantly longed for more time with his two favorite people in the world.

When Erik opened his eyes and waited for the blur to clear up, he noticed the sunshine coming through the windows. It finally started to look like it would be another beautiful day outside and he just had to get out there to feel its healing powers. Unlike a migraine, the light didn't bother his eyes or his head, so he yearned for the warmth of the rays and the splendor of the light shining on everything it touched. The pain slowly subsided and his agony was replaced with joy. He needed to get away from this pain and live what little he had left in his life, so he stood up and put on his jacket to escape into the light. He glanced at his reflection and realized that he looked terrible. Trying to comb his hair didn't help much, since his eyes were red and puffy. He went into the bathroom to see what else he could do to become more presentable.

While splashing water on his face and looking in the mirror, he remembered that he had an appointment with a lawyer today and checked his watch. Rats. He would be a few minutes late but he could still make it. Hopefully the lawyer wouldn't spoil his plans.

&&&

TAMI NEEDED TO GET BACK TO THE STATION and make sure some things happened quickly in order to try and prevent another murder. Now that she understood what happened in the past to Erik Johnson and his business, and she figured out who was involved, she believed she saw the big picture and could tell what his next move would be. She hoped she would be in time.

As she drove to the police station, she put herself in Erik's position and finally felt his pain. She believed that Erik went by 'Victor Johnson' back then, and figured that Erik was probably his middle name. Apparently, his building on Eighth Street was blown up fifteen years ago and Victor Johnson claimed that it was due to a gas leak in the basement of his building. Ed Stewart and the Stockton Gas Company countered that they shouldn't be held accountable and local Representative Jerry Grant, before he became a state senator, initiated an investigation. It was eventually ruled by Judge Frank Lewis that the gas company would not be held responsible and Victor Johnson was left with all of the losses and no compensation. To make things worse, he had no insurance to cover the expenses. She suspected there was more to the story and was determined to get back to the library to follow up, now that she knew the key players and what she was looking for.

While she waited at the intersection, she saw the park and momentarily thought about coming here as a child with her parents and siblings. Tami tried to remain calm as she figured the traffic light taunted her by not changing, and she watched the other cars drive by. Those were good days at the park and she let a smile sneak out in an effort to not get too anxious by this delay. Finally, the light changed and she flew through the intersection, knowing she would just hurry up to wait at the next stop.

Tami actually agreed that the three men who were taken by Erik and tortured deserved to be punished if they did indeed cover up the cause of the explosion. However, she couldn't tell people those thoughts, especially her partner. Officer Hultgren was adamant that Erik needed to be brought to justice, and rightfully so, but she was concerned that he would make their suspect pay for his crimes before being brought to a judge. Hultgren seemed to be overly vengeful himself and she wondered about his own involvement with some of these men. Her partner was not exactly a model police officer and had been reprimanded more than once for overzealous actions. She had also heard rumors of him being a 'bad cop', but didn't know what all that involved. She never did figure out why she had been teamed up with him, since they were complete opposites. He was very experienced as a police officer with a lot of contacts, and she was fairly new, still trying to prove herself. However, she already had an impressive track record in her first few years with the Stockton Police Department and was considered to be the lead member of their team, much to her partner's frustration. Lately, she felt as though she had to watch her back.

The traffic light near the station always took too long before turning green and she reckoned it would be slower than normal today. Tami drummed her fingers on the steering wheel and waited impatiently to make her turn onto State Street. Her friends always reminded her that these kinds of delays come up in her life to help teach her patience and she believed this could actually be true. This always happened when she was in a big hurry. When the light finally changed, she turned and headed to the parking lot at the police station. She found a spot and parked, got out of her car and ran to the door, not saying anything to the people she sped by. She hoped her co-workers wouldn't take offense at being ignored by her rushed coming and going lately.

She looked around the station, noticing that Officer Hultgren was nowhere to be seen, but understood that she would have to meet with him soon to go over these new developments. He said he would meet her at the station this afternoon, so maybe he would show up any minute. Tami wondered if he had already been here and left, and she had concerns that he may be checking out where Erik Johnson lived. Knowing her partner's anger toward this suspect, she feared for the suspect's safety. She figured she should call John or better yet, maybe she would pay Erik's residence a visit next.

She went straight to her desk and sat down, pulling open her left drawer. She reached for the three anonymous packages that she believed to be from Erik Johnson, who she assumed to also be Victor Johnson, the local photographer from years ago. She stopped when her hand touched nothing in the file folder and immediately looked down to see that it was empty. She froze as it occurred to her that someone had taken her anonymous packages tying together the pieces to this case.

Chapter Twenty-Four

TAMI HAD A DIFFICULT TIME CONTROLLING her feelings at this point, knowing that someone had deliberately opened her desk drawer and taken evidence without her permission. The room seemed to be angry and prying now for some reason, as she felt paranoid. These were the same people she worked with every day, but one of them had violated her space and stolen something that belonged to her.

Her eyes scanned the room, looking for anyone with a suspicious expression, but realized the most likely person to have taken these clippings was her partner, who wasn't here right now. He would sure get an earful when she saw him again. She figured he must be trying to cover up evidence that could incriminate him or his unethical friends and was angry at herself for not being more careful with these details.

She sat back and realized that the sender of those packages had done a good job of linking the three men's activities and showing trends that implicate each of them with illegal undertakings. She knew more of the background of this one case with Erik/Victor Johnson and saw the connections better. And now she'd lost these packages with all of this evidence. She could kick herself for being so naive and trusting. At least she had taken notes from the newspapers and had all of the important dates and court details with her in the notebook she took to the library.

Alright, so next she needed to get to Erik Johnson's residence before her partner if she wanted to see this suspect alive, so she made a call right away.

"Hi, this is Tami. Did you find any information on Erik Johnson? Erik with a 'k'."

"Hi Tami. Of course Johnson is one of the most popular names in the city, settled by a large Swedish population over a hundred years ago. There are more than nine pages of Johnsons in the Stockton phone book."

"I know. That's just the way it is. What do you have?"

"Well, I think you should realize just how difficult this request of yours truly is."

"Understood. And?"

"I found four Erik Johnsons, but only one spelled with a 'k'. The others had a 'c'."

Whew. Maybe that 'k' would be the item that helped her find this man. Now that she knew the man's first name was probably Victor, Tami considered asking him to look deeper to see if there were also any Victor Johnsons, but hoped she didn't need to go farther. She guessed that if the Erik she was investigating and the Victor from the explosion was indeed the same person, he was going by Erik Johnson today, but she may still need to check out the Victors too. She kept that in the back of her mind in case the Erik Johnson she would soon meet today turned out to be the wrong one.

"Tami, I already met with Judge Milam and got you a search warrant. Stop by to pick it up on your way out there."

"Thanks again, James. You're awesome. I'll let you know what I find out."

She almost forgot the next piece to the puzzle was with the attorney in the case fifteen years ago in which Victor Johnson's building had exploded. Tami was convinced that the prosecuting attorney had been involved in the conspiracy, since the judge, the gas company executive, and a local representative each had played a part, so she needed to make sure he was protected. She looked through her notes to find out who led the case against Victor Johnson back then.

"What was his name? Let's see. Larson. Christopher Larson."

&&&

ERIK HAD ARRANGED TO MEET THE ATTORNEY at a quiet outdoor café and was glad to see him still there waiting for their appointment. He drove up and found a parking spot by the sidewalk, close to the man with whom he came to meet. He used to be self-conscious about driving an old Volkswagen camper, but he was beyond that now. It had proven very useful in the past week, and he expected it to help him out one more time.

He realized the attorney had gained some weight since the last time he had seen him, and he noticed that the man was now balding on top with a lot more white hair than brown on the sides of his head. Time seemed to change everything. The added weight may prove to be a challenge that he didn't plan for, but Erik would make it all work out.

Erik stepped out of the van and walked up to the table, offering his hand to his old acquaintance.

"I'm so sorry for keeping you waiting. I appreciate you staying a few minutes longer."

"No problem. It's such a gorgeous day today, and this is much better than sitting in an office. What can I do for you, Mr. Johnson?"

"Please call me Erik. I see you've already ordered a drink and almost finished it off. What did you get?"

"Oh, I just got a whiskey and coke. Actually, this is my second, but who's counting?"

The attorney laughed and Erik smiled, nodding his head

confidently.

"Perfect. Hey, have you been keeping up with the Cubs this season?"

"Of course. I've got tickets for their game this week-end against the Cardinals. How did you know I liked the Cubs?"

"Everybody around here supports the Cubs, don't they? I used to go to Wrigley Field quite a bit, although I haven't been to any games this season."

"Well, they've got a good team this year, but they end up losing anyway. I can't understand it. It's not like the days when they had Grace, Sandberg, Dunston, Dawson, Sutcliffe, and Maddux, but this year's team is still worth watching."

"Yeah, I remember that team. They were a great combination. I can't believe they traded Maddux to the Braves."

"Oh, I know. Then of course the Braves went to the playoffs every year after that."

Erik laughed and stared right through the man's soul, digging deep to see what was really going on in this guy's mind. Everything seemed to get quiet for a moment as Erik remembered the pain this man allowed him to go through when his former lawyer was bribed by the gas company. The attorney lifted his glass to finish off his drink, while Erik never took his eyes off of him.

"Listen Erik, I need to use the restroom. If the waiter comes by, would you ask him to bring me another? I'll be right back and then we can get down to business."

"No problem. I'll wait here enjoying the breeze."

&&&

TAMI PICKED UP HER PHONE AGAIN AND dialed a number.

"Hi this is Officer Tami Anderson. I have reason to believe that an attorney named Christopher Larson is in danger and needs to be put under police protection immediately.

Yes, he was involved in a case several years ago, with a judge, a politician, and a company executive. I'm investigating a new case where they're all being targeted by the man who lost that old case. I believe Larson will be the next victim unless we act now to prevent it. Of course. What's the address? OK, I'll meet you there as soon as I pick him up. Thanks for your help."

She couldn't wait for John now and wondered if she should give him any of this new information anyway. It was bad news if she couldn't even trust her own partner. Tami stood up and left the station as quickly as she had come in. She needed to get to Erik Johnson's residence before Officer Hultgren, but she had to protect the attorney first.

She checked the address on her way out to her car and got on her way with determination to make it in time. However, she wasn't so sure she could beat Erik to the next target. He seemed to have all of the cards and was at least a few steps ahead of them, actually stringing them along with clues and bits of information that the police wouldn't even have without help from the suspect. As luck would have it, the traffic lights worked against her. No surprise there. All she could do was hope that she found the attorney in time to save him from a fate worse than death.

&&&

ERIK GLANCED ACROSS THE ROAD AT THE fine row of maple trees along the sidewalk and appreciated the autumn-colored red and orange leaves that had still not fallen to the ground. He hadn't been to this part of town in years, but it looked like it was still a nice area. The waiter soon brought Erik an iced tea and his friend a third whiskey and coke, while Erik used stealth to add a little something special to the other man's drink. He stirred it briskly, figuring the strong alcoholic content would help to cover up any bitter taste, but knowing that since the man had already drank two, he may not notice anyway. Erik preferred adding this concoction to spicy food, but he didn't have that luxury this time so a stiff drink would have to do. Besides, he estimated this mixture would work almost right away, whereas he had planned the others to take a couple of hours before affecting his old acquaintances.

Erik stared down the street for a few minutes while he waited, and the attorney soon sat down with a big smile and picked up his drink.

"Now that I've made some room, let me fill 'er up again," and he gulped over half of it down right away.

While he was still drinking, Erik asked, "How did you get here today? Did you walk from the office?"

"No, I drove my black BMW convertible over there," pointing just a few cars down.

"I figured it was such a nice day that you might have strolled around the corner on foot."

"Well Erik, tell me what's going on and let me know what I can do for you."

"Yes, I've wanted to talk to you for a long time. You probably don't remember me, but you and I worked together many years ago."

"No kidding? You don't look familiar. When was this?" Erik watched as his old friend blinked repeatedly and tried to make sense of his surroundings, knowing that he was starting to feel the effects of the additive.

"Oh, it was about fifteen years ago. I didn't have a beard then, and I went by my first name, Victor. You don't look so well. Here, I'll take you over to my car. Maybe you shouldn't be driving."

Erik stared deep into his eyes, assuming that his vision was blurring and he hoped the man would recognize him before he lost consciousness. The attorney appeared to be in a daze, but froze and gave Erik a look of horror.

"You're Victor Johnson? Oh no!" slurred the attorney, but Erik already stood beside him, helping him to his old Volkswagen camper as the man passed out in his arms.

Chapter Twenty-Five

WHILE SHE DROVE INTO THE nicer part of town, Tami had too much time to think at each of the traffic lights she visited. Someday, she needed to look into the timers on these things and do something to get them all synchronized or whatever needed to be done. There were a few more turns to make before she would be there at the attorney's office and she impatiently tapped her fingers on the steering wheel. She watched a mother and daughter strolling on the shaded sidewalk and it took her back in time when her mother took her hand-in-hand in this same area. This truly was a great place to raise a family.

Checking the light again, Tami lurched forward once it turned green and she sped away. She considered turning on her siren so she could race through the red lights, but for some reason she didn't use it. Maybe she needed this time to think about what was about to happen and what her reactions should be. Things moved very hurriedly now and she needed to be able to maintain a level head to keep up. She was on her own with this now.

It occurred to her that even if she was too late to save the attorney from being taken by Johnson, she could at least show up during the man's funeral and possibly find him alive. That would be an interesting scenario to witness, and it brought out a rare laugh as she pictured herself waking up the lawyer at his funeral. She wished she had the results from the toxicology report on Judge Lewis, and hoped that the chemical mixture used on these men was something that eventually wore off, where the victim would be able to fully recover after a specified amount of time. However, it was possible that the chemical was a poison and eventually led to the victim's actual death anyway. If she could just figure out the chemical, could she get an antidote soon enough? She needed to know what chemical he used on these men but she was losing her patience and running out of time.

Pulling into the parking lot near the law firm, she looked up at the names on the front of the building. She hoped Christopher Larson was still in the building, even though she didn't have much respect for the man if he was involved with payoffs and influencing the judicial process. She would still protect this potential criminal from the vigilante justice of Erik Johnson, only to work her best to really bring the man to justice legally through the court system based on what she's learned about these men. That may prove to be a challenge if these people were able to pull strings and manipulate the court system as well as they appear to have done over the past decade or two. It didn't matter. She had a responsibility to see that the laws were upheld and charges brought against those involved. It occurred to her that these people were powerful enough to ruin her career if she got too close.

She rushed inside and confronted the receptionist.

"Hi I'm Officer Tami Anderson, and I have reason to believe Christopher Larson is in terrible danger. Is he in?"

The receptionist stammered and was at a loss for words, but she picked up the phone. Obviously nervous, she probably hoped to get her boss out there as soon as possible. Tami wondered if she made it here in time.

"Hi, Mr. Larson. A police officer is here in the lobby and says she urgently needs to speak with you. She says you're in some kind of trouble. OK, thanks."

Turning back to Tami, the receptionist said, "He'll be right out. You can sit over there if you would like."

"Thanks. I'll just stand here if you don't mind."

Tami was relieved that Larson was in the office, which meant he was still alive. Her first goal of getting here in time was successful. Had she actually beat Erik Johnson to the next step? She considered how she would present this situation to the lawyer, whom she suspected of being an arrogant criminal, but she tried to give him the benefit of the doubt. She chided herself for being prejudiced against the lawyer and stereotyping him before even meeting him. She glanced around the lobby, admiring the professional décor and refined selection of furniture and paintings. This guy certainly had good taste, so she gave him credit for that. She then wondered if he paid for it with bribe money.

A very well-dressed man soon came through the door and she thought he looked very distinguished, with a full head of grey hair and handsome smile. He walked toward her with his hand outstretched, and Tami thought of it as a peace offering.

"Hi, I'm Christopher Larson. To what do I owe the honor of this visit from one of Stockton's finest?"

"I'm Officer Tami Anderson. Can we go back to your office to discuss it?"

He gave the receptionist a glance and a smile and motioned toward the door with his outstretched arm.

"Sure. Please follow me."

Once behind the closed door, Tami got straight to the point.

"I'm sure you've had so many cases over the years that you can't remember them all, but I need you to think back around fifteen years ago to a gas explosion on Eighth Street, involving Senator Jerry Grant and the gas company CEO, Ed Stewart. Does that ring a bell?"

She noticed a surprised look on his face and he nodded. She thought everything came out rushed, so she took a breath and forced herself to slow down while she waited for his response.

"Yes, I do remember the explosion. How could anyone forget it?"

"Do you remember the details of the case and the owner of that building, the person who lost the case against the gas company?"

"I believe that person was held responsible for negligence with the gas leak. What's all this about and why would you come to me?"

"We believe the owner of that building may have gone after the key people in that case, with the suspicions that they were involved with a payoff and manipulation of justice."

"What? That's absurd. From what I remember, the evidence presented was overwhelming against that guy. Besides, I heard that Senator Grant passed away recently of a heart attack."

"Yes, as did Judge Frank Lewis and Ed Stewart from the gas company. All supposedly from natural causes, but there's evidence suggesting that these men had been tortured before actually being killed. We believe two were cremated alive and one was buried alive. "

Larson's mouth dropped open, and he sat down while all the color left his face.

"You're the last person I've found still alive who was linked to the case, and I think this man may be coming for you next. I raced here to get to you before this man did, so time is of the essence. Now that you know a little more about what we're up against, I absolutely need your cooperation."

Larson began to say something, but just stuttered a few syllables of nothing, shaking his head.

"Mr. Larson, do you remember this man at all?"

He looked up at Tami, who still stood beside his desk, and replied, "No, I hardly remember the man and can't even picture his face. It just seemed like an open and shut case. So what do we do from here?"

"I would like for you to come to the station with me and we'll keep you safe from this man for a few days while we try to track him down."

"I'll need to make some arrangements. Can you give me a few minutes?"

"Of course."

Larson went out into the lobby, almost expressionless, and discussed the plans with his secretary. Tami watched him, wondering about his involvement in that case, and she finally exhaled her relief that this man was indeed still alive and could be protected. He didn't seem like a criminal so far and his actions appear to be those of an honest person. Even so, maybe Erik Johnson still thought he was involved in the payoff.

Larson stepped back into his office and stood in front of Tami, looking into her eyes.

"Officer, I appreciate you following up with this case and getting here before your suspect did. I'm ready to go, but I hope you can enlighten me about what happens next on the way to the station."

"I will, but first you need to be aware that someone may be trying to kidnap you at this very moment. We have to be careful and alert on the way to my car. Stay right with me and walk quickly."

He gave her a nervous look while Tami smiled at him, and they walked out the front door to her car. She immediately took back all of the rude thoughts she had about this man before she met him and actually saw him as the nice guy he appeared to be. Glancing around as they walked through the parking lot, she tried to spot anyone who might have been staking out the office and waiting for a time to surprise Larson. She looked into a few faces walking on the sidewalk and standing beside some cars, but none of them stood out as a potential threat.

Her heart pounded because she had a feeling Erik might be around, waiting for the chance to snatch Larson from her, so she hurried him along toward her car. The tension was high, and she could tell the attorney felt anxious during their rushed, silent walk. Once he was inside the car, Tami ran to the driver's side, still keeping a watchful eye on her surroundings, and she got in and hastily started the car.

"This is spooking me out. What's going on here?"

"We suspect that the judge, the senator, and the CEO of the gas company were involved with payoffs in order to manipulate court cases certain ways, and they were all targets of that one victim I mentioned to you."

"But I've never been involved with such bribery. Why would I be targeted?"

"The fact that you were the prosecuting attorney for that case puts you in a bad position, whether you were paid off or not. You're the one who helped make sure the man didn't get compensation for his building, so in his eyes, I believe you're still in danger."

"I just want to make sure everyone knows that I was never involved in any illegal activities. Something like this could ruin my career."

"You should be more concerned with surviving the next few days rather than worrying about your career."

Silence.

She thought about the man's reaction when she mentioned the payoff's and was surprised at his insistence that he wasn't involved. Tami was often a good judge of character and he honestly appeared to be insulted that he had been lumped in with three potential crooks. Even if he wasn't involved in the gas company cover-up, he was probably still the most logical next victim, wasn't he? She didn't want to think about what would happen if she was now protecting the wrong man.

Chapter Twenty-Six

ERIK STRUGGLED TO PUT THE ATtorney into his own VW camper, then went back to explain to the waiter, who stood by a table with a red umbrella on the sidewalk.

"I'm sorry, but my friend's not feeling too well. We won't be able to order lunch today after all."

"Probably three whiskeys didn't help."

"I agree. Would this cover the bill?" and he handed the waiter two twenties that he had pulled from the attorney's wallet.

"Of course. I hope he's feeling better. Have a great afternoon, sir."

He went back to his car, figuring that he could return with the attorney's keys before the dinner rush and drive the BMW back to the office. So far, everything was working perfectly.

&&&

WITH THE PROSECUTING ATTORNEY SAFEly protected by the Stockton Police Department, Tami felt relieved and was now on her way to the address of Erik Johnson. It was the same one given to her by both Bella's Ristorante and the Stockton Funeral Home, and it matched the address given to her by another officer who had looked up Erik Johnson in the city directories. All points led to this one spot. If this was indeed the home of the person responsible for faking the deaths of three prominent citizens and torturing them before they died, then she was potentially walking into the spider's web. Unfortunately, she didn't feel as though she could trust the help of her partner with this task and kept it to herself.

However, she feared that Officer Hultgren might have already visited this address and carried out some kind of vigilante ritual himself on this guy. That would explain why she was able to get to the attorney before her suspect did, but she wanted to think she might have actually beat the man to his next target in this game of chess. Was she really that smart or was she just fooling herself? This guy always seemed to have the upper hand against everyone, and that's what made it seem like something was wrong now.

What if her partner beat her to Erik Johnson's house and was still there? She didn't know which would be better – walking in on Erik Johnson alone or walking in on her partner at Erik's apartment. Tami calmed her nerves as she approached the neighborhood by taking special notice of the old, two-story houses that lined the streets. These houses were here when the Swedes immigrated to the United States over a hundred years ago, and many of these immigrants lived in this neighborhood for decades. Some of these houses may still be in the same family that originally purchased them.

The towering oak trees by the sidewalks were probably only saplings back then, so they were very much a part of these people's lives as they drove by them on their way to work every day or on their way home from work. They probably played with their kids and grandkids out in these yards. The limbs touched as they reached across the road, providing a canopy covering which shaded the street almost any time of day.

Tami thought back to her own visits to her grandparents'

house in one of these neighborhoods, and remembered their voices and accents. It brought out a smile as she pictured their faces and relived the feelings she experienced as she came into their house. She especially enjoyed her grandpa's flower garden out back and was always impressed by his skills in growing the most colorful flowers. Climbing the trees in the front yard was another activity that surfaced in her vast bank of memories and she instantly missed her grandparents.

She stared out her car window at one of the houses and was reminded what her grandparents' house looked like, since they all looked so similar. She couldn't remember any arguments between her grandparents and her siblings, and always looked forward to spending the day visiting them. This was almost like going back in time being here now, because her grandparents had been in the large cemetery up the road for the past ten years or so. She enjoyed these memories and decided she would make a point of visiting their actual house in the next week to see if the current owners would let her walk around inside.

As she came to the end of the street, she saw that the address for Erik's house was the last structure on the left and her smile left her at once. She had to bury her memories for the moment and deal with the business now at hand. Parking in the street a few houses away, Tami turned off the car, going over the address again to be certain. Most of the houses were wooden two-story homes, but this one was a two-story brick home. It almost didn't fit in with the other ones and she wondered if the original home might have burned down decades ago. This building may have been built on that spot back in the 1930's or so. While confirming the address, she noticed that Erik had the second floor of the house and understood that someone else probably rented the first floor. That was common here with the economy being what it was. Most families here couldn't afford the price of a home, but they could rent out part of one.

Carefully checking the area for anything out of the ordinary, she got out of the car and walked across the street, heading toward Erik's house with caution. With each step, she became more and more apprehensive but was determined to confront this man if she had the opportunity. Relieved to find that her partner's car was nowhere to be seen, Tami was still concerned that he may have already been here to 'visit' Mr. Johnson. What would she find inside?

Tami knocked on the door and was greeted by a young lady, who showed obvious surprise to see a police officer at her front doorstep.

"Um, hi. Is something wrong officer?"

"Good afternoon. I'm Officer Tami Anderson. I'm looking for Erik Johnson, whom I believe lives on the second floor. Do you know if he's home now?"

The young lady glanced over Tami's shoulder, which startled her and caused her to look behind her.

"I'm sorry. I was just looking to see if his white VW van was parked outside. It looks like he's not back yet. He works two jobs, like a lot of us around here, so he's gone most of the time. He rents the place from me. Did he do something wrong?"

"It's possible, so I have a search warrant to look around. Do you have a key to his apartment?"

The woman showed uneasiness and nodded, stepping away from her door to get the key. When she returned, she opened the door for Tami and led her up the stairs. The place appeared to be in good shape, not run-down like some of the old houses in the neighborhood, and she noticed the quality of Erik's front door. She was glad she had the key and didn't need to try and kick this one down. Once at the top of the stairs, she stepped up to the door in front of the lady.

"Let me knock first, just to be certain," and Tami rapped

her knuckles on the door to listen for a response. There was none, so she nodded to the young woman. "Just unlock it and don't open it. Step away immediately and I'll open it then, OK?"

Tami saw how nervous the woman appeared and while the woman had her back to Tami, she pulled out her handgun quietly so as not to alarm her more. The woman stepped back away from the door to let Tami come forward.

"Thank you, ma'am. Please go back to your apartment and I'll look around for a few minutes. I'll stop by the first floor when I'm finished."

The young landlord obeyed without a word, while Tami took a deep breath, tightening her grip on the gun and turning off the safety. In one swift movement, she opened the door and glanced around the room before stepping inside. Simple décor. Not much furniture. It was obvious that a guy lived here because it didn't seem to have the touch of a woman's tastes. Why did she seem to notice things like that? She thought it was funny that she could always tell the difference.

"I'm a police officer. If there's anyone in this apartment, please show yourself now. I'm armed, so don't do anything foolish."

She paused momentarily, then pointed her gun inside and passed through the doorframe, taking in the location of the window and two doors on opposite walls. It was now or never and she moved with a purpose, without hesitation. She progressed quickly across the room and peeked into the first doorway, noticing the place was tidy but empty. Bed made, no sign of clothes out of place. At least this man wasn't a slob. Moving along to the kitchen area, she could tell it was empty as well. Dishes washed, nothing piled up. There was one door remaining, so she kept up her pace and came up beside it. This door was closed, so her lips tightened while she reached her left hand to turn the knob. This would be where a cornered animal jumped out and made one last desperate attempt to escape. A couple of deep breaths here first.

She flung the door open with her gun aimed straight ahead and paused as she absorbed the contents of the room. If a gunman had been inside, he would have had an easy kill with Tami staring around the room, mouth open, not paying attention to the corners or blindsides. Instead, she was met with a wallpaper of newspaper clippings, photos, and assorted articles. She held on to her gun and tried to grasp what faced her, knowing for certain she now stood in the lair of the man who had taken revenge on three of the people who had wronged him. His story was fleshed out here on the wall, with details of each of his victims from before and after the case involving the explosion on Eighth Street.

Tami clicked on the light switch so she could read the text of the newspapers and made her way into the room. Some of these articles looked familiar, since she had seen many of them in the packets she received from Erik. She was now fully convinced this was indeed the man who sent them to her. There was a strange fascination as she realized that Erik had tracked the careers of each of these men, apparently stalking them for more than a dozen years.

Interestingly enough, these were not the original, yellowed newspapers, but copies made from what looked like printouts from a computer. Perhaps he had only researched all of this in the past month or so, discovering the truth for the first time, and put his plans into motion since then. It seemed he gloated over and saved stories that came up in the news about any of these men, and accusations came up against them several times over the years. This blatant disregard for the law also increased her anger over what these men did to Erik, and the fact they got away with it for so long.

The suspect could be back any minute, which increased

her anxiety a bit, but she was drawn to the details that were highlighted and circled. Apparently, her partner had not beaten her to this apartment, since he would have probably destroyed this evidence before she arrived. She needed to get a team here right away to make sure this was all preserved, since it would prove to be very useful in court once they caught Erik Johnson. Although, this would incriminate the three victims as part of a conspiracy and they were now dead. Maybe that's all Erik wanted done at this point, since he had already taken care of the final judgment for each of these men.

Tami attempted to take it all in, but there was so much to read. A pattern came out as she realized there were four separate parts to the story. One section was dedicated to Judge Lewis, another section dedicated to Senator Grant, and there was a photograph of Ed Stewart from the gas company, surrounded by many newspaper articles. She took a step closer to the wall so she could see the details about the fourth person when the apartment phone rang and startled her.

Instinctively, she stepped back and followed the ringing, zooming in on a spot by the couch in the other room. She went to it, but glanced back at the articles on the wall. She wondered if she should pick it up or let it keep ringing, assuming an answering machine would interrupt soon. It rang again. Tami hesitated for a moment, but then answered it.

"Hello?"

Silence.

"Hello?" Tami repeated.

"What are you doing in my apartment?"

Chapter Twenty-Seven

TAMI'S HEART ALMOST BURST from her chest as she looked out the window to see if someone was out there watching her.

"Hi Erik. This is Officer Tami Anderson from the Stockton Police Department. I'd like to ask you a few questions if you could come on up to your apartment."

"Why are you in my apartment?"

She stretched the phone cord as far as she could, but still didn't see anyone with a phone on the sidewalk or in the street nearby. She was hesitant to stand where she would be visible to a gunman from outside, so she was cautious as she surveyed the area from the window.

"Some very disturbing things have happened recently, and I urgently need to talk to you. I tried the funeral home but you weren't there, so I stopped by Bella's. They said you had called in sick. It's so important that I got a search warrant. Can we meet somewhere?"

Silence.

"Erik, we need to go over the details of the case with you and confirm everything you've presented to me about Judge Lewis, Senator Grant, and Ed Stewart. I believe they were involved in a cover up in order to keep the gas company from being responsible for the explosion of your building. Can you help me with the details?"

"I sent you everything you need to know. Do you believe me?"

Finally he admitted something. He was definitely the one who sent those envelopes to her.

"Yes, and that opened my eyes to what really happened. Thank you for sending them. Listen, I really need to know if you deliberately drugged these men to fake their deaths."

"Everything I've collected in the past few months is on the wall in the small, closed room of my apartment. I'm sure you've seen it already."

"Yes, and it will help with the case."

"No, didn't you notice that people have been bringing this information to the newspaper and even to the police for years, and it always gets brushed aside. The only way to get justice in this city was for me to take care of it myself. I think there is corruption in every level of our local government and even in the Stockton Police Department."

Tami thought about her partner and was now sure that he was also involved in payoffs and cover-ups.

"Erik, I'm not like that. You've shown me the truth and I'm going to make sure something gets done about it. Can you confirm anyone else who was involved?"

"Well you know some of the people who were on the gas company payroll, like Lewis and Grant. You may not realize it, but your partner frequently met with Ed Stewart and other powerful people who sought police help to quiet things over."

"I appreciate that information. Do you have any proof that can be used in a court of law?"

"I've already told you that we can't get justice from the courts or the lawyers in Stockton. I even paid a visit to my old lawyer on the case about my photography studio, and I believe he's still just as crooked as ever."

"Wait a minute. What lawyer? Christopher Larson?"

"No, my so-called friend and defense attorney, Danny Clark."

Tami closed her eyes and hit the wall. The room spun out of control as her mind raced through these new details. He wasn't after the prosecuting attorney after all. He wanted his defense attorney. Now she understood the conspiracy. His own attorney took a bribe to make sure Erik lost the case. She had protected the wrong man.

"Oh, Danny Clark. I thought you might have been interested in the prosecuting attorney."

She immediately took the phone as far as she could into the room with the newspaper clipping wallpaper, and read the name Danny Clark several times in various articles. She had blown it and now another person was probably going to die a horrible death.

"No, my lawyer is the one I need to talk to. We'll discuss old times and come to an understanding. Actually, I have an envelope ready to go out to you on the desk in the kitchen. You might as well pick it up while you're there and save me some postage."

"OK thanks Erik. I appreciate it. Is there any way I can talk to Danny Clark right now?"

"No, he's really not up to it now. Do you want me to give him a message? He may not say much, but he'll be all ears."

"Erik, I just want you to meet with me and talk about this rather than hurting Mr. Clark. It's wrong to take justice into your own hands, and I promise I'll do everything I can to make sure he gets what he deserves."

"Oh, I won't need your help with that. I'll make sure he gets what he deserves. Thanks for your concern, but this is something I must do on my own. While you're there, would you vacuum the carpet? I haven't gotten around to it this week. Listen, I've got to go now. Don't forget your envelope of clues."

"Wait, we need to talk about Danny Clark. Don't hurt the man, please. We can work together to make sure he has all of the charges brought against him, and justice will be done. Erik. Erik. Don't hang up."

Too late. He was gone. Tami slammed the phone down and ran to the front door, down the steps to the front porch, scanning the street for any movement, but saw none. He must be close by, but she couldn't tell where he was. She went back into the room with the articles on the wall, and called someone on her cell phone.

"Hey James. This is Tami Anderson. Please send someone over to 2012 Seventh Street, Apartment B right away to gather evidence. Yes, thanks. You won't believe what's on the walls of one of the rooms in here. This is the apartment of Erik Johnson, who has just kidnapped Attorney Danny Clark, and was probably involved in the murder of three other men. OK, I appreciate it."

She took one last pass through each room for anything that stood out, and snapped a few pictures of key newspapers with her cell phone. Moving past the bedroom, something caught her attention and she couldn't help but stop and stare at it. On the wall, there was a beautiful family portrait of Erik, back when he went by Victor, with his wife and daughter. She recognized him clearly now and realized that his wife truly was as striking as Tami had remembered. When Tami was not even ten years old, she thought that Erik's wife was the most beautiful woman she had ever seen. Their daughter was so cute and so much fun to play with at the studio when Tami was there for Christmas photos with her own family.

Mesmerized by the photograph, she didn't realize that tears streaked down her face until she snapped out of her trance. She couldn't picture Erik with a beard, which is the way his co-worker described him, since she remembered him clean-shaven, just like in this portrait. So much had changed since this picture had been taken. Mr. Johnson didn't deserve the treatment he received by the court system. It just wasn't fair that he went through what he did.

Wiping her eyes and then walking into the kitchen, she found the envelope Erik mentioned, and took that with her out the door. Tami stopped by Apartment A downstairs, knocked on the door, and waited for the owner to answer it.

"I want to thank you for your help with the apartment upstairs. Another crew from the police department will be here soon to do more investigating, so please help them in any way you can."

The young woman nodded somberly, but didn't have anything else to say as Tami handed her a business card.

"If Erik comes back here, would you please call me at this number right away? I really need to talk with him."

She nodded once more, and Tami walked back out toward the tree-lined street. As she made it to her car, she kept her eyes moving in order to spot any sign of Erik in the neighborhood. She drove down the street slowly in an effort to see anyone who could fit the description she received from his co-worker at the funeral home of a tall, bearded, white male with medium length brown hair. To her disappointment, there was nobody walking around, and she couldn't find anyone in the parked cars either. He must have arrived at home, saw a police car near his apartment, and called his own phone from a safe distance, yet he was nowhere to be found. He had eluded her, but she still felt he was somewhere nearby, still watching her as she drove out of his neighborhood.

Tami proceeded with caution, but had little hope of finding her suspect at this point in time. Banging her hand on the steering wheel, she pulled over to the curb and put the car into park while she opened the package she took from Erik's apartment. Seeing the attorney's name, she felt terrible that the department had protected the wrong man upon her recommendation, and knew that it would be her fault if Danny Clark became the next murder victim. As she skimmed through the articles, it filled in some of the unknown aspects of this case, confirming that Clark was also an unethical lawyer who accepted bribes. He fit right into the group of men who had already died horrible deaths as a result of their involvement in the case with Erik Johnson.

It was remarkable that Erik made sure he left his name out of the articles that he provided to her, but still had plenty of material over the years to paint quite a picture of these characters. He must have really had a tremendous amount of bitterness to take out such a vengeance on these men so many years later. She couldn't blame him though, since it looked like they all made a mess out of Erik's life after the explosion. She wondered if that was truly the case, or if Erik had somehow manipulated the facts to make it seem like he was the fall guy. Carefully sliding the newspaper copies back into the envelope, she figured it would be better to review this data some other time. Right now, she couldn't stop kicking herself over making the call to protect the wrong attorney.

Moving back into drive, Tami continued up the street to the intersection and noticed the large church taking up the entire block. It was interesting that Erik lived so close to St. Mark's. After a moment of hesitation, she decided to stop in to pay Father Bill a visit. She didn't think he would have anything new for her, but she could at least share some of the new information she had learned. That might spark some clues from the priest.

Parking at the curb beside the church, she got out of her car and walked up the path from the sidewalk, enjoying the colorful leaves that had fallen around the ancient trees lining the yard in front of the church building. She thought back when she met Bill Ljunglof, and how she never expected him to go into the priesthood when they were in school together years ago. She figured he would have ended up as a business man, since he used to talk about becoming a millionaire someday. Probably the only millionaires she knew of in town were Ed Stewart and Jerry Grant. Not good company to keep.

Stepping out of the sunshine and birdsongs into the silent and austere building was quite a contrast, and she made a face when the door thumped closed behind her, fearing that she might have disturbed someone's meditation. Looking around sheepishly, she quickly walked toward the office where Father Bill would most likely be if he was here. He was easy to find the last time she stopped by.

"Tami."

That got her attention, and she spun around to her right, spying the very priest she came to talk with.

"Hey Father Bill. I was just looking for you. Do you have a few minutes to talk?"

"Yes, I do. Let's go to my office."

She followed her priest-friend, and for some reason felt odd in her uniform inside the church. Glancing around, she hoped people didn't think she was interrogating Father Bill for anything he might have done wrong. She hated giving people the wrong impression, and wished she could announce to the curious people scattered around the church that she just came to talk with an old friend.

"I assume you haven't heard from your mysterious confessor lately."

"No, I don't think I will either, based on the way he left in such a rush the last time he came in, plus the last time I talked with him wasn't even in person. He called my office phone and hung up on me."

"I found out who he is, and why he has such a grudge against some people."

Father Bill stopped and turned to look at her.

"Really? I'd sure like to know what happened to this guy to make him so angry."

Continuing through the church and then stepping into his office, he offered Tami a seat while he stood in front of his bookcase.

"Do you remember the explosion on Eighth Street years ago?"

"Sure. Who could forget that?"

She laughed. "Everyone says that. Anyway, the owner of that building tried to get the Stockton Gas Company to pay the costs of rebuilding his business, reimburse the people who rented office space from the building that was no longer there, and basically get them to accept responsibility for the losses incurred from the gas leak that led to the explosion."

"OK, so what happened to the owner?"

"He lost everything. He was sued by the renters because he couldn't fulfill the rental contracts, and had no insurance to pay for the lost equipment and property. However, based on information he sent me recently, I believe he was setup to take the fall. The gas company paid off his judge and his defense attorney, and a politician got involved to make a phony investigation that cleared the gas company of any fault."

Tami saw the wheels spinning in Father Bill's mind as he moved to his chair and sat down while processing these facts.

"I get it now. I can see how that could lead to the ideas for revenge. I wonder why it took so many years for him to want to get even."

"Good question. Anyway, three of the men involved with the cover up have already died, which he confessed to you about already, but it looks like he just took the fourth man as a prisoner yesterday or today. I'm concerned he'll torture this man as well."

"Torture? Are you serious?"

"I can't reveal details, but it looks like he buried one alive and cremated the others alive."

"Oh dear God. This is unbelievable. And I talked to this guy. I thought he was feeling bad about his vengeful thoughts and was close to turning his life around."

"I talked to him just a few minutes ago on the phone when I was searching his apartment, and I believe it'll take a miracle to turn this one around. You'd better pray hard. I found where he worked and where he lived, but I suspect he won't be coming back to any of those places again."

Tami got up from the chair and stood in the doorway to face the priest.

"I've kept your name out of the police reports, so right now you're an anonymous tip. I'm hesitant to give too much information to my partner, Officer John Hultgren, since it seems as though he would actually go after our suspect with vengeance on his mind. I believe he'll shoot first and ask questions later. Be careful what you say if he finds out who you are and pays you a visit, OK?"

The priest had a stern look on his face, but responded, "Thanks for not using my name. And thanks for the warning."

"As always, please let me know if your confessor contacts you again. I don't think we even have two days to save this latest victim."

"Of course. I appreciate the information, although it wasn't what I'd wanted to hear. I'll be praying for the man and his captive. Can you tell me the name of the person who came to confession?"

"Yes, he's Erik Johnson. He used to go by Victor Johnson."

"What? I remember him. He's the photographer at the old studio. I didn't realize that he owned the building too. He and his wife were good friends of my parents."

Chapter Twenty-Eight

ALREADY KNOWING IT WAS TRUE, she was glad to hear it come from Father Bill too, but she had to make sure. She asked, "So you're certain the photographer was Erik, I mean Victor Johnson?"

"Yes, I'm sure of it. He had a beautiful wife and a little girl who was a bit younger than us. I remember listening to him and his wife talk Swedish to each other sometimes, and he called his daughter 'his little Svenska Flicka,' whatever that meant. It struck me how his eyes lit up whenever his daughter came up to him, and I was just a little kid back then."

"I suspected as much but you've confirmed it. Thanks for the additional information. I remember going to that studio with my parents, but I didn't realize our confessor was actually this same man. So the building owner was actually the photographer too. He always made me laugh when he took my pictures, and I liked him a lot."

He watched as she stepped toward his office door, still thinking about the photographer, and added, "Bye Tami. Remember to use caution, even though I don't think he would harm you."

Tami gave him a nervous smile as she left his office and disappeared into the church sanctuary. Father Bill still sat at his desk, when there was a knock on his open door, not more than a minute after Officer Tami Anderson exited through that same door. Father Bill looked up, assuming Tami had forgotten something, and then froze when he realized that it wasn't her.

"Hi Father Bill. We need to talk."

The last person he expected to see in his office was Erik Johnson, especially so soon after Tami had left and he didn't know what to say as Erik quietly shut and locked his door.

"I had a feeling you'd be talking to the police, and it looks as though Officer Anderson has worked hard at gathering the facts."

Father Bill stared at Erik's face, trying to see the man he once knew and was impressed with how different he looked from the man he remembered so many years ago at the photography studio. Unfortunately, the beard and the lines around his eyes did a good job of hiding that person.

"Mr. Johnson, do you speak Swedish?"

Erik looked up at him, apparently surprised by this question, and laughed out loud. Wait. The priest finally caught a glimpse of the photographer from his memories when he showed a twinkle in his blue eyes. Father Bill was now almost certain this was the same person he once knew. Erik immediately recited something that sounded like nonsense with a lot of 'when' 'what' 'where' 'why' sounds.

"Sju sjösjuka sjömän sköttes av sjuttisju sköna sjuksköterskor på det sjunkande skeppet."

Father Bill smiled back. This had to be the photographer. But what could have made this kind man turn into a murderer?

"What was that?"

"It's an old Swedish tongue twister about seven sea-sick sailors on a sinking ship that my grandfather taught me when I was little. I'd forgotten all about it until you just brought it out."

"I remember you at the studio. You knew my parents."

Erik paused and looked at him, nodding his head.

"Yes, I remember you as a boy, and was a little disappointed when you started going astray. I was so glad that you finally got your life together and went into the priesthood."

Father Bill was silent and wondered how Erik would have known about that. Again, his past came back to haunt him, and he wondered why this man would bring it up. It was in the past and he had already been forgiven of his actions. This was too painful to endure. Bill's eyes welled up and he believed he might actually start crying, so he rubbed them and turned his head.

"Is it true that you've killed three men?"

"Straight to the point. You should read the papers, Bill. These men died of natural causes."

"You told me you took revenge on three men. If they died of natural causes, then what kind of revenge could you have had?"

Father Bill kept his eyes on Erik as his visitor moved toward the bookcase, appearing to be interested in some of the books on a shelf that was eye-level, and the priest wondered if he should stand. He wished Tami would come back in now, and shot a quick glance out his window to see if he could spot her walking to her car. No sign of her. She must already have gone.

"You know, I really enjoyed your parents' friendship. They were two of the few friends I still had after the explosion when I lost everything. I felt like Jesus in the Garden of Gethsemane, deserted by all who knew me. But those friends didn't really know me, because I would never have falsified anything like they said I did. They said I knew about the gas leak for days and deliberately covered it up. I was an innocent victim of the gas company's negligence, and Ed Stewart used his money to pay off key people in the case to make me out to be the bad guy. I couldn't believe it. I didn't know what to do. I had no money, no business, no studio, no equipment, and my reputation was down the toilet."

Erik continued walking slowly beside the bookcase toward the window, appearing to admire the priest's collection of books, never looking at Father Bill.

"I remember hearing that you moved away to get a new start. Why come back with a vengeance all these years later?"

"Those men were all so smug about burying me and ruining me. I just wanted to see them get caught in their web of lies and get what they deserved. I've looked up the old Stockton Newspapers, poring over details about each one, hoping to see these men get caught. Every time someone tried to pin something on them, they slipped out of it. Every time!"

Now Erik stood by the window, next to Father Bill, but his eyes were far off, somewhere down the street, somewhere in the past. He gently touched the window sill and Bill thought about finger prints. Was that really important at this point? He knew exactly who this man was now and there was no doubt. Father Bill experienced a new courage and was instantly given something to say.

"Sometimes bad things happen to good people, and we can't understand why the bad guys get away with things that they shouldn't. God is still the one who will judge these people, as well as the rest of us, so we all need to do the right things, even when it seems as though justice is not being provided. Some people make mistakes and can be forgiven if they're truly sorry for what they've done. Others, like the men who hurt you, are just plain bad news and will do bad things. They will see justice at the end of their lives. We just have to deal with them when they affect us, but keep doing the right thing no matter what."

"Deal with them. Interesting choice of words. I used to

be a good person, Bill. I used to go to church regularly with Kiersten and Brita. I knew God but He abandoned me along with everyone else. He left me when I needed Him most."

Father Bill stood up cautiously next to Erik and tried to look eye-to-eye, but Erik kept gazing into the window, almost as though he looked into another world. He never turned to face Bill even after the priest stood up.

"No, He was there with you every step of the way but you refused to acknowledge Him. You took things into your own hands and deserted Him. I believe He's still waiting for you to turn away from these evil thoughts and actions you've been involved with, and will welcome you back. No questions asked."

Erik now looked directly into the priest's eyes and fear covered Bill for some reason. He prayed for courage and wisdom.

"Bill, you don't know the depth of my thoughts and my actions. I'm beyond help and any kind of reconciliation."

"No, I disagree. No matter what you've done, if you turn away now, it can all be erased. You'll still have to accept responsibility for your actions and go to court for any laws you may have broken, but your conscience can be clean. If you really mean it, God knows your heart and you can still go to Heaven someday."

Erik casually stepped across the room and opened the door which he had locked behind him earlier.

"If only it was that easy."

"It is. I know it for a fact. I did some things I wish I could change, and I've knelt before God asking Him to forgive me. And you know what? He did. I'm a new person, and even though Satan keeps reminding me of the way I used to be, I know deep in my heart I'm forgiven."

"You're a good man, and I know your parents would be proud of you."

Erik stepped through the door again and Father Bill stared at the spot where he was just a couple of seconds earlier. It felt good to hear those words and he knew they were true. It also occurred to him that the kind man he remembered was still inside this Erik. He had hope that Erik would still change for the better. He couldn't give up on him now and raced out the door after him, only to find an empty sanctuary again.

Chapter Twenty-Nine

FATHER BILL COULDN'T BELIEVE his eyes when he realized that this man had disappeared in the church a third time. How could it be possible? This man was flesh and blood, not a ghost or an evil spirit. He was only inches away from him a moment ago. Bill stood there facing the back of the church scanning the large open room, only to observe a quiet yet very vacant sanctuary. Not even one person walked down the aisle or sat in reverence. He sat down on the first row, still looking toward the church's main doors with his elbow resting on the back of the bench. He tried to figure out how this person who had come to him several times could simply vanish. It occurred to him that something unusual could be going on, like a visit from an angel or even a demon, but he looked deeper. Could Erik have only been a figment of his imagination, and all of these visits were in his own head? He went over it all once again, focusing on the words that he believed were spoken by Erik in his last few conversations, and tried to figure out what was going on.

He needed to call Tami and let her know that Erik was just there, so he went back into his office and dialed her number.

"Officer Anderson."

"Tami, this is Father Bill. Where are you? Right after

you left my office, Erik Johnson came in and locked the door. He must have been watching us, waiting for you to leave."

"Incredible. What did he want? I assume he's gone already?"

"Yeah, he just left. I asked him some questions, some of which he didn't answer, but it sure seemed like the old Victor Johnson is still there. I think I can reach him and convince him to turn himself in to you."

"That would be awesome. Did he say anything about the attorney that he took?"

"No. Sorry about that. He talked about the people who he felt had left him when his building blew up, and I could see how much that hurt him."

"OK, please let me know if anything else comes up. I'm at the defense attorney's office now to find out what the receptionist knows about his disappearance, but we don't have much time. Any clues would be much appreciated."

"I understand. I wish I knew how to get in touch with him, but he didn't leave me with any contact information. I didn't expect it, but it would sure be good to talk with him more. Wait a minute. I saw him touch the window sill in my office, so you should be able to get a print from it."

"Thanks Bill. I'll send someone over now to get that and will call you later."

Father Bill tried to convince himself that he had indeed seen and met with Erik Johnson, despite what his mind told him, and a new wave of sadness came over him when he was reminded about what his visitor had said about his parents.

Erik probably knew Father Bill's parents better than anyone, and when Bill was a young teen-ager, trouble seemed to come easy for him. He had put his parents through a tremendous amount of grief back then, but what hurt the most was that they both were killed in a car accident before Bill turned his life around. He knew they confided in Mr. Johnson since they were such good friends, and realized that he could learn some important things about his own parents from Erik. If only he could talk with him more now. He hoped he would be able to catch a glimpse into their lives at this key point in time, and get to know them a little better. He had to find this bridge to his own past, if he truly existed.

&&&

ERIK WALKED AROUND THE OLD STRUCture as if he understood everything about the layout; where the hidden rooms were, which doors had been sealed shut, where there were dark areas that couldn't be reached by the light. It was an old basement with no windows and no visible doors, but he was aware of a way in and a way out. He would have to make use of this place for a while, since the police knew about his apartment as well as both places of employment, so he couldn't go back to any of them. It was a shame, since he had made friends at each place, but he recognized that he was only there for one reason, and that was revenge. His mission almost complete, he only had a few loose ends to tie up, with his former defense attorney as the final piece to his puzzle.

He walked around the brick pillars that ran from floor to ceiling, shining a flashlight to lead his steps. There was a hidden room that he had already picked out in this secret basement, and he planned to use some of the loose bricks to conceal it even more. This place would work fine, and nobody would even suspect him of being here. This evening, under a cloudy and moonless sky, he would bring his guest to the new location to discuss old times with his former defense lawyer. He spent a few minutes making the final arrangements for his so-called good friend.

&&&

TAMI QUESTIONED THE RECEPTIONIST AT the defense attorney's law firm, only to discover that he went to one of the outdoor café's around the corner to meet a client for lunch. His car wasn't in the law firm's parking lot, but the receptionist was certain he had driven it to the café.

"He always likes to show off his fancy sports car, even if it was just a short walk to the café."

"I appreciate your help. If you hear from Mr. Clark, please contact me immediately," and Tami handed the receptionist her business card. On her way out, she glanced around at the gaudy paintings and ungodly color combinations in this law office, and thought it explained a lot about what this attorney was like. She already didn't like him without meeting the man, but knew that wasn't being fair. She hoped there would be a chance for him to prove her wrong.

As Tami walked outside, she looked toward the street where the outdoor café was and decided to walk to it. The sun was out, the breeze comfortable, and she needed the walk to sort out events in her head. She now understood that the wrong man was put into protective custody, and as a result, Defense Attorney Danny Clark had been kidnapped by her suspect. She had blown it, and now this man's life was in grave danger.

At the corner, she looked both directions and crossed the road without thinking about traffic. She noticed the café as she looked up, and saw that it was only a few shops down the road. Certainly an easy walk from the office, but if he was the type of person who wanted to show off, she could picture the lawyer driving here, parking at the curb in front of everyone, and getting out so they could all see who he was. For a moment, she believed he deserved what he was getting, but she quickly backed that thought out of her head. She had to get to him in time, whether she liked the guy or not, and was uncomfortable thinking about what would happen to him if she didn't.

At the café, a pretty waitress came up to her and asked, "Just one for dinner?"

Tami smiled and responded, "No, I need to talk to someone about a customer who was here for lunch today. Is your manager here?"

The waitress looked inside, and pointed to a young woman near the back.

"That's who you want. Her name's Beverly."

"Great. Thanks."

Tami noticed a dark colored BMW convertible parked at the curb, and figured it probably belonged to Danny Clark. It occurred to her that she could have it dusted for fingerprints, but realized they probably wouldn't find anything. She headed toward the inside part of the café, and walked up to the manager.

"Good afternoon. I'm Officer Tami Anderson, and I need to find out about a customer who ate here for lunch today."

Beverly reached out her hand and met Tami's.

"I'm Beverly Meeks. I'm not sure I can help, but I'll try. We had dozens of customers today. Is there anything descriptive you can give me about him or her?"

"I've been told he has a brown beard, medium length brown hair, maybe mid-forties or fifty. He met with an attorney, who was in a dark suit, probably drove here in his BMW and parked out front for all to see."

"Doesn't ring a bell."

Just then, a waiter walked by from the kitchen on his way to the sidewalk and she looked over at him.

"Hey, Don. You were here for lunch, weren't you?"

He stopped in mid-stride and came over to the booth.

"Yes, I was. What's up?"

Tami took over and repeated her description of the two men to Don.

He laughed, and looked back and forth between Tami and Beverly.

"I think I know who you're talking about. I had a sloshed guy in a suit that ended up getting sick and not buying anything to eat. Just had a few drinks."

Tami's eyes narrowed, and she asked, "Was he alone? How did he leave?"

"There was a man with a beard with him, who paid for the drinks and put him into a white VW van. That's all I saw. He gave me a nice tip, by the way. Oh, I've noticed there's been a BMW parked out front all afternoon, so maybe that's his."

"A white VW van. OK, thanks Don. You've been a big help."

Don continued his quest toward the front, while Tami smiled at the manager.

"Well, you asked the right person. Thanks for bringing him into the conversation."

Beverly shook Tami's hand again and replied, "Anytime officer. Would you like to stay and have dinner on me?"

Tami looked around the room at the wonderful décor of the café, clearly done with a woman's touch, but frowned. "Very tempting, but not today. I need to find this man as soon as possible, so I'd prefer to take a rain-check."

"It's a deal. I'll look for you in the next week or two."

Tami hoped it wasn't too late for Clark.

Chapter Thirty

LOOKING OUT ACROSS THE CHURCH graveyard at night, Erik noticed there weren't many people about, so he was confident he could do what needed to be done without getting noticed. He'd been concerned about the loud engine of his VW camper, but it didn't seem to draw attention when he parked it at the curb. He gazed out over the rows of graves on the hill from the road to the church, but couldn't see much in the dark under overcast skies.

It was a bit eerie sitting here in the cemetery in the blackness, never knowing who or what could come creeping up to him when he least expected it. Glancing in the back of his van, it occurred to Erik that this situation was even more unusual with a man lying in the back seat who had the appearance of being dead. He obviously didn't want a police officer to stop him under suspicion of grave robbery or murder when this guy was actually still alive, so he proceeded as planned.

Getting out of the car, he headed straight through the graveyard toward a specific tomb that was above the ground and stood in front of it momentarily, using a small flashlight to read the names 'Mr. and Mrs. P. A. Olson.' Since it was taller than the others, this grave was easy to find even under a starless night. This was the original cemetery for the church, but once the dead population of the congregation reached a certain point, the church elders bought property down the road a ways for a larger cemetery. They evidently needed it, since that cemetery was also filled up now. Erik was glad this was a small cemetery, since it didn't take long to locate what he was looking for. Moving a stone, the front of the tomb opened and he briefly searched for any witnesses before passing through a full-sized doorway. This was an ideal night for clandestine activities, since it was very dark with no moonlight, and there weren't many streetlights nearby that lit up the graveyard.

Erik thought it was odd to have a walk-in crypt here in Stockton, but he was thankful to Mr. P.A. Olson for having this one built over a hundred years ago. Almost as though it was made specifically for him to use, he took full advantage of it now. He had learned about it when he photographed the church and one of the elders told him about the secret basement when they had a few minutes to chat. Apparently, that elder went to his grave without telling anyone else. Erik found that the basement and the secret door into the church hadn't been used probably since that same elder showed him the hidden entrance from the graveyard almost twenty years ago. He wondered why that memory came back to him, but he didn't complain. Of course, not many people had tried to open Mr. Olson's grave since it was sealed after he passed away.

Olson was one of the elders of the church and designed his tomb to have a passageway into the church. Only he and one other elder knew about this passageway and that elder was one of the builders of the church. The man who told Erik about it years ago, that elder's son, wasn't sure why, but he suspected the man secretly visited his wife this way after she died. The story he heard was that the man was heartbroken and didn't accept her death very well. He was also told that Mr. Olson had a fear of being buried alive and wanted to make sure he had a safe way out if that ever happened to him. Either way, it gave Erik the entrance he needed this evening, so he didn't care what the man's reasons were.

The wealthy man's grave was about ten foot by ten foot, with a fancy stone burial chamber on each side of the room. Mr. Olson was in one, and Mrs. Olson was in the other, with room to walk in between and behind each chamber. The smell was musty, and there were quite a few spider webs draping from the seven foot ceiling as though they were decorations for the small room. He didn't want to look too close for fear that he might actually see some of the spiders crawling around. He never cared much for spiders. The tomb looked larger from the outside than it did while standing in it, and Erik was one of the few people who knew why that was.

He ambled to the back of the above-ground grave and with significant effort, pushed another stone, revealing a second concealed entrance there as well. The tomb was well designed, with strategic lines in the interior décor that brilliantly disguised where the doorway existed. When the door was closed, nobody could ever guess there was a hidden opening and most people wouldn't notice that the inside of the tomb was several feet smaller than what it appeared to be from the outside. He cautiously stepped down a staircase into the darkness of the newly revealed room and lit a couple of torches cleverly placed along the walls. Once he was satisfied there was enough light, he came back up to the grave, exited into the dark cemetery and continued to the curb where he had parked. He figured his guest hadn't deserted him.

Opening his van, he lifted out the captive attorney who looked like he should be a member of this exclusive country club known as the cemetery. He strenuously carried the dead weight that was Danny Clark, dragging the man's expensive shoes up the hill through the grassy graveyard.

"We can thank Mr. P.A. Olson for this nice entrance to your final resting place, Danny."

He took Clark into the grave, and carefully maneuvered him down the stairs with the assistance of the dim firelight. The stairs proved to be quite a challenge, but he made it to the bottom without dropping his quiet friend. The light flickered as he dragged the attorney's shoes through the dirt floor of the basement and it gave the peculiar appearance of a ghostly audience. Working silently while the fire danced, he found the room he had prepared and laid the man down on a concrete slab, taking time then to finally catch his breath.

"Danny, I appreciate you coming to visit me. Let me go and park my van and I'll be back to talk more with you tonight. Don't go anywhere, OK?"

Erik laughed while he walked through the basement toward the hidden stairs and he rapidly ascended them, moving out into the open air within seconds. He started up the van and drove it to a nearby neighborhood, hiding it in the back where it wouldn't be easily seen. Then walking briskly in the chilled autumn air, he arrived back at the church and disappeared into the open grave once more. This time, however, he closed the front of the tomb and it went back to looking like an undisturbed grave, as it had been for many years.

Erik put out the torches hanging on the walls, using his flashlight to guide him back to the hidden room. As he came around the corner, he saw Danny Clark lying on the slab, looking like he was ready for his own funeral. Erik walked across the room to a collection of water bottles, snacks, and camping supplies, picking out a drink and relieving the bottle of its precious contents. He set up a camping lantern and extinguished the torch in the room, making the lantern the only source of light in the basement. He then sat next to the attorney and stared at his ashen face.

"Danny, I was so surprised when I found out that you

had betrayed me. I could understand those rats accepting payoffs, but not you. I trusted you to get me through that mess so I could start rebuilding my life again. How much did he pay you? You were Judas to me and I was so happy when I found that you had been accused of something unethical several times over the years. I couldn't believe you were able to get out of them all and still keep a clean reputation, but I shouldn't have been surprised. The other guys always seemed to slip out of sticky situations as well. You sure had a system in place, didn't you? It was like you were protected by the Mafia. You probably were."

Erik looked around the room at the shadows on the wall and was reminded of being in a cave. He considered what he should do with Danny, since he couldn't take a chance going to the crematorium. The police were probably watching for him to return there, just like they were doing at his apartment. He figured Bella's Ristorante was off limits now as well. Things had indeed changed, but he expected this would happen at some point in time.

"I guess when three prominent citizens pass away within a couple of weeks, it's only a matter of time before someone connects the dots and realizes that they all had their last meal at the same place."

He realized that the police officer he had contacted was very astute and did an excellent job of taking his hints on each of these citizens. She now knew who he was and would most likely provide the investigation that never happened. She seemed to have taken the details he sent to her and ran with them, following the leads and building a case. He knew she was after him, but hoped she would also investigate his motive and expose the criminal involvement these men had in this town for decades. It was too late for him, and nothing she could do would ever change what happened to him in the past, but if justice was finally served after all these years, then at least something good would come out of all this.

Focusing back on his visitor, Erik moved a little closer to make sure Clark could hear him clearly.

"Your buddies and I all had some nice talks about old times before they died, although they couldn't respond. Much like you, they were paralyzed by this concoction I was given by a friend of mine in Upper Michigan a while back. Remember how we used to talk about going fishing up there for long week-ends? I had forgotten about that until just now. It seems as though I remember a little more about my past every day. Anyway, the idea of faking someone's death worked for Juliet in Shakespeare's famous tragedy and it has certainly worked on you guys."

He pondered for a moment about how badly that strategy turned out for Romeo and Juliet in the famous story, and immediately changed his train of thought to get back to his former friend.

"I put Jerry Grant and Ed Stewart through the crematorium while they were still alive and I buried Frank Lewis alive. It was a very satisfying revenge and I had something similar planned for you. Although, plans have changed, so I'll have to come up with something different now. Not to worry. I'm a creative guy and I'll think of something."

He patted Clark on the chest and stood up.

"I'd like for you to reflect on what you did to me and how that must have made me feel. You know it helped to ruin my life and as a result, there was no way for me to rebuild. You knew my wife, my daughter. You pretended that you enjoyed our company. You knew what this did to my family. I'm going to make you pay for what you did and it won't be a pleasant death for you, my old friend. Just be aware that you'll spend time with those men in Hell very soon and there's nothing you can do about it. You're at my mercy now and I don't seem to be very merciful anymore. Have a pleasant night's sleep, buddy. It will be your last."

Erik walked over to a place he had cleared for himself to sleep, and laid out several blankets. It would be cold down here, especially this time of year, so he came prepared. He thought about what he had already done to the other three men and wondered why he didn't feel good about it all. He tried to convince himself that revenge was the best solution, and with Danny Clark's demise close at hand, his payback would be complete. He would be entirely justified. However, it just didn't feel as he had expected and it bothered him. It must have been what Father Bill told him, about letting go of the vengeance, and those words from the priest angered him now.

Taking the lives of those evil men was a service to society, yet it was wrong of him to do it. In the law's eyes, he had committed murder and would need to be punished. He would have to pay for his crimes and would burn in Hell just like the men he helped along to get there, and he knew that he was no better than they were. Erik had done just as much evil as they had, and he would soon join them there, separated from God and from his family. He wept bitterly at the irony of his situation and fell asleep, terrified that there was no way for him to escape his punishment.

Chapter Thirty-One

OFFICER JOHN HULTGREN WAS frustrated when he found that Tami had already been to the suspect's house without informing him and knew that she was suspicious of him now. He walked by the officer at the door and his eyes interrogated every aspect of each room, searching for a clue that his partner might have missed. They darted here and there, hoping to capture something that would give him an opportunity to reach the suspect before Tami but knew that she was very good at what she did. Despite his best efforts, she always stayed a step ahead of him in this case. He thought he had a break when the funeral home worker revealed the name of his co-worker, and Tami confirmed the man's name at Bella's. Yet, Tami still got here ahead of him.

He stopped and stared as he walked up to the doorway of Erik's extra room. He saw photographs of various people who were involved in the cover-ups, most of whom John knew well and had since passed away. As he read the newspaper clippings on Erik's wall, he fumed because he knew he couldn't cover up this evidence and he wished he could have gotten here first. The investigation team had already been to Erik's apartment, photographing everything they could find, especially the newspaper articles on the wall, and the cover up was about to come out to the public.

Hultgren thought he could prevent it all from seeing the light of day by taking the copies Tami had stashed in her desk drawer, but now those packages she received in the mail didn't matter anymore. All of it had been seen and documented when the team came and searched the apartment for evidence, and as he glared at the news clippings, Hultgren now saw the writing on the wall in more ways than one. Everyone who was involved in payoffs, the cover-up that included a judge and a senator, as well as the CEO of the gas company, even information about himself being bribed to allow certain things to go undisclosed was about to be front page news. How did Johnson get all of this information? Standing alone in the apartment, he stared at the newspapers without really reading anything as his mind raced through several scenarios.

This was all Erik Johnson's fault and he hated the man for exposing a very successful and profitable enterprise for so many people. Hultgren was obsessed with retaliation because he realized it wouldn't be long before the police made the connections to him and the game would be over. He needed to work fast and find the mysterious informant before Tami did, but it was obvious to him that she had been working without keeping her own partner in the loop. She linked the attorney to the cover up, although he found it humorous that she initially protected the wrong one. He read about the defense attorney in the articles on the wall and found out at the office that while Tami was out saving the prosecuting attorney, the killer snared Danny Clark to be his next prey.

Hultgren didn't care one bit about the life of the defense attorney and wasn't concerned that this man would be dead soon, the victim of a horrific torture. Three others that were part of the cover up had already faced a similar fate, and he knew that he could be next on the list if he didn't strike first. All he wanted to do now was get to Johnson and make him pay for exposing the whole business. Hultgren's career was over and prison was a certainty in his future if he didn't get out of town soon. Yet he had to get to Erik Johnson first. A game plan developed in his mind as he processed the whole scene in front of him, and he was satisfied these were the next steps needed to bring it all to closure.

Storming out of the apartment, Officer Hultgren drove to Bella's to see if Erik had returned or contacted the manager, but there had been no calls or visits from the ex-waiter. No surprise there. Johnson must know that they were on to him and may have even skipped town already. He probably came back to his apartment, saw police swarming the area, and may have been warned by the restaurant owner that the police were looking for him.

Next, John drove over to the funeral home and considered taking in the employee that he had already visited once. There was enough suspicion to detain him for at least a few hours, but Hultgren thought about taking him somewhere private and roughing him up to make the man talk. He had to know more, since this guy had worked with Johnson for several months. He stood out in the parking lot for a moment as he finalized his game plan in the event that Keith Ellis was there. The clouds moved swiftly across the overcast sky with a chilling wind, which didn't help to get Officer Hultgren in a better mood. The weather seemed to affect everyone's attitude these days.

The big policeman was furious to find that Keith had the day off and the funeral home had not heard from Erik Johnson for a couple of days. He should have expected this but it ticked him off even more. Johnson definitely knew they were after him. He politely thanked the receptionist and walked out to his car, hitting the roof with his fist before getting in and slamming the door. He started the car and sat there to catch his breath. He could tell that his frustration shocked the receptionist but there was nothing he could do about it. This was not turning out as he expected. In the past, the group of men who worked the system so well for years were somehow able to weasel out of tough situations every time they came up, but it sure looked like Erik Johnson would have the last laugh this time. Not if he could help it.

Hultgren wasn't sure where his partner was, since she hadn't answered his calls, and that ignited his temper even more. He tried again to reach her but it went straight to voicemail. He threw the phone down to the floor of the passenger side and left the parking lot with a fury that revealed his true self. Glancing up in his rearview mirror, he noticed the wrath in his eyes and he chose not to hide it like he usually did. He didn't care anymore and just wanted to finish off this serial killer that he had never even seen.

The strange thing was that the public wasn't aware that a serial killer had been working in the area, since the deaths were all supposedly from 'natural causes,' and details from the one that was exhumed had been kept quiet to all but a few people. Maybe he needed to let some key people at the newspaper know about Erik Johnson's evil activities so he could be exposed as the real criminal. Then if he could get to Johnson first and put an end to this guy's spree, maybe the city would look at Officer Hultgren as the hero who stopped a terrible serial killer. Not much of a chance for that if his partner exposes the whole network of payoffs first.

He wished he knew who Tami had been talking with about this case, but she hadn't revealed her sources to him. Maybe she had suspected him all along of being part of this. It didn't matter anymore. He'd make sure she wasn't able to tell anyone as soon as he found her. She was nobody. Just like Johnson and they'd both be gone once and for all as soon as he found them. He wouldn't be the only one going down and was determined to take a few of his enemies with him if it ever came to that.

It then occurred to him that the prosecuting attorney might know more than he initially led on, so he decided to pay him a visit and have one last round of questions. The prosecuting attorney was being released from protective custody this afternoon, since everyone now realized the actual target was the defense attorney. He was just in time for that. Besides, he was close to the location now anyway and it would only take a few minutes. He pulled into the parking lot and found an empty spot. Running up to the door and showing his badge, he was glad that nobody stopped and questioned him. The news obviously hadn't traveled here yet or they hadn't put the pieces together enough to connect him into this giant web of cover-ups. It was only a matter of time though.

"Hi, I'm Officer John Hultgren, and I'm investigating this case involving the attorney. I need to ask him a few final questions now. It's urgent."

"Go ahead. He's in the first door on the right. He'll be leaving soon."

"OK, thanks."

Hultgren walked into the room as soon as the door was unlocked, and he stepped up to the attorney with his usual intimidating approach.

"I need to know anything you can recall about Victor Erik Johnson who owned the building on Eighth Street that exploded around 1998."

"Listen, I know all about that case and I've gone through everything I can think of. It seemed like an open and shut case, with nothing unusual."

"So nobody approached you with suspicious evidence that appeared to easily lock up the case?"

The attorney remained very professional and stared at his interrogator for a moment while he thought about that.

He then shook his head and looked away.

"A tremendous amount of evidence was presented to me and I didn't think there was anything suspicious about any of it. If there was a cover up of some kind, I wasn't aware of it then and I'm still not aware of it now. As far as I can remember, the man knew about the gas leak, falsified records regarding inspections, and was negligent in getting the right people involved in time to resolve it. Probably tried to collect an insurance settlement."

Hultgren bored into the man's eyes and was satisfied with the answers, although they didn't do anything but confirm that this attorney really wasn't involved. Interestingly enough, the man was unaware that Johnson had no insurance on the building and would not have collected any insurance settlement.

"I appreciate your time."

Hultgren quickly left the room without giving the attorney time to respond and he nodded to the guards at the door. He was getting nowhere and time ticked away. He called one of his friends at the police station.

"Officer Hoffman. This is John Hultgren. Have you seen Tami today?"

"Hey John. No, I haven't. She's probably with her new boyfriend, that priest."

"What priest? "

"You know, a couple of days ago, I told you she had a visit from a priest, all dressed up with his white collar and dark robe, and she took him into one of the offices."

"Oh yeah. I remember you mentioned that. Do you know what he wanted?"

"Maybe she was questioning him or he had some information on a case she was working on. I don't know. I think he was probably an old friend from the way they talked and smiled at each other. We thought it looked kind of funny at the time, especially the way she led him into the back room and closed the door."

"OK, thanks man. See ya."

Staring aimlessly out over the roof of his car into traffic, John realized that he had overlooked this contact his partner had made recently. He had to find out who this priest was and how this man was involved.

Chapter Thirty-Two

OFFICER HULTGREN HAD HIS LAP-top, and started researching his partner's personal background. He found out where she went to school, who her friends were back then, which of those friends she kept in touch with now, and where she went to church. Strange. She went to a Baptist Church, but the man she met was most likely a Catholic priest. Maybe the priest outfit was a disguise. He should have checked out this priest when Officer Hoffman first mentioned him.

So out of this list of names, how many could have gone into the priesthood? After searching several, he only found one that became a priest. That person was Bill Ljunglof, who currently worked at St. Mark's Cathedral in the downtown area. Bingo! Wait a minute. That name sounded familiar for some reason, but he couldn't put his finger on it. How would he be familiar with a priest? He did some more searching on this priest and after several minutes, he smiled at what he found.

&&&

FATHER BILL KNELT AT THE ALTAR AND asked for guidance and help with Victor Erik Johnson. He sought wisdom for himself, protection for the attorney, and asked for a miracle in the life of Mr. Johnson. While he was at it, he asked for forgiveness once again for the many bad choices he made before he became a priest. Surprisingly, he experienced a warm assurance, like a gentle hand on his shoulder. It was so real, that he opened his eyes and glanced up to see if someone had entered the room. Nobody was there, so he smiled and ended his prayer.

As he walked back to his office, he recalled how Mr. Johnson had disappeared three times after visiting him here at the church, and he knew it couldn't have been his imagination. There must be something outside of the confessional that allowed Erik to hide or maybe even an unknown door that's been out of sight for years.

Bill followed the aisle in front of the confessional, and then stepped to the left into an area where candles lined a small open prayer room. There was a statue about seven feet off the ground, and a rail that prevented him from getting close to it. His eyes explored the area beyond the rail, but found nothing suspicious. Following the rail to the wall, he touched the cold stones, not really sure what he was looking for. Could there really be a mystic lever or button here that would open a hidden doorway?

The candlelight mesmerized him as he stepped softly, his hands feeling the smooth wall all the way to the rear of this small room. He had prayed in this alcove several times, but never thought there was anything secretly concealed here. At the wall, there was a tapestry that covered the stones from floor to ceiling, and he absent-mindedly rubbed his hand along the cloth as he walked toward the center of the alcove. Halfway to the aisle, it came to him that he had never looked behind the tapestry, so he took a few steps back and carefully lifted it to gaze at the wall behind it for the first time.

There was nothing unusual, as far as he could tell, but as he blindly touched the dark wall, his fingers went into an opening that he wasn't expecting. Stepping fully behind the tapestry, he continued following this hole with his hand. When his arm reached all the way inside and he felt up and down the opening, he realized it was a small doorway. Bill had been at the church for several years, and nobody had ever mentioned this before. There was no button or lever, but a secret entrance was indeed hidden behind this large cloth.

Father Bill stepped out from behind the tapestry, hoping nobody had seen him fumbling around with it in the dark, and was determined to find a flashlight to see if his new discovery led anywhere. Perhaps Mr. Johnson knew about it, and used it to hide in until a more convenient time when nobody was around, then slipped out of the church unnoticed.

He rushed back to his office, and went straight to the bottom file cabinet drawer to pull out a flashlight. Clicking it on and off, he was ready to see what was in the opening behind the tapestry. Remembering that Tami asked to be kept in the loop if anything new came up, he decided to call her from his desk to let her know about the secret opening and how Erik might have used it to escape. The phone went straight to voicemail, so he left her a message.

"Hi Tami. This is Father Bill Ljunglof. I just found a hidden opening in the wall around the corner from the confessional at St Mark's, behind a tapestry. I'm going to investigate now, but I wanted to let you know about it in case it means something to you. I think Erik knows about it and has used it to slip away from me after his confessions without being seen. It could be nothing, but it could lead somewhere. I'm going in now."

With the excitement of a schoolboy on an adventure, he made his way back to the alcove and glanced around to see if anyone was watching him. His hands were slippery with sweat, and suspected that his forehead was probably moist as well. Satisfied his secret plan was safe, he slipped completely behind the cloth again, and shined the light into the opening. His eyes grew large when he considered that this wasn't just a small hiding place but was actually a doorway that led down below the church.

&&&

Officer Hultgren had come in the front door of the church just in time to see Father Bill rush to his office, then come out looking like he was up to something. He immediately sat in one of the back row seats, keeping his eye on the priest, and hoping this was the one who was Tami's friend. The priest stood with his back to Hultgren in a small room to the policeman's right, just barely within his line of sight. He appeared to be studying a large tapestry hanging on a wall. Hultgren watched him for a moment, and then noticed the priest stepped out of sight, so he leaned to the left to get a better view. The tapestry moved slightly as if someone brushed against it, but the man was gone. He waited to see if he came back into view as the large cloth became still again, but the priest didn't reappear.

Hultgren promptly stood up and walked to the small room, not understanding what had just happened. As he stood in the entryway, his eyes explored every inch of the alcove, but there was nobody else there. The priest had walked in this room, looked at the tapestry, and vanished. Impossible. He walked to the back of the room, looking up at the statue across from the tapestry, noticing no real places to hide. Touching the cold stone wall, he kept his eyes on the statue, and then turned to look back at the decorative piece that hung on the back wall.

He didn't care how ornate the cloth was or how old it might be. He just wanted to find the priest and question him. He had to know something, and the fact that this man seemed to act suspicious before disappearing convinced the determined police officer that this was the man he was looking for. He touched the cloth, glancing out into the sanctuary to see if anyone was watching him. Not that he cared, but just from habit. He didn't like people to spy on him.

Pulling the cloth away from the wall about waist high, he looked behind it and saw nothing but black. It didn't look like the man was behind the cloth, but he wasn't anywhere to be found in the alcove either. There had to be a doorway. He reached farther, sliding his hand along the unseen wall until he sensed an opening. His eyes widened as he comprehended the fact that the priest must have a hiding place and secretly slipped away using this concealed entrance. This guy really was up to something.

Officer Hultgren moved completely behind the tapestry and felt his way through the open door while getting his flashlight out. Once he could see the small doorway with a little bit of light and started following the steps down into the basement, he also unholstered his pistol and pointed it in front of him so he'd be prepared for any surprises.

Chapter Thirty-Three

ERIK THOUGHT ABOUT MEETING HIS wife and daughter and wondered if they would like to go shopping in some of the old stores in the downtown area. After that, they could also have lunch at one of the places they used to enjoy years ago. He wasn't sure which restaurants were still open and paged through his mind seeing all the places that had closed since those days. Ancient memories came back to him for the first time in years as he saw him and his wife at various restaurants in the area. These were pleasant reminders of how good his life used to be and he savored each one.

As he visualized the neighborhood and each shop on every street, he ended up back on Eighth Street and the little restaurant that was no longer there. What a shame it had closed down. That was probably their favorite. He saw the front of the restaurant next to his studio and another old home movie started playing from his memories. He needed to meet his wife again today but he couldn't resist another brief trip through the past.

He watched himself hurriedly walking on the sidewalk, going straight into his studio's front door. The memory followed him closely and zoomed in as he stepped through the lobby, picked up a present from the desk drawer of his office, and moved on through the front doors to walk around to the back of the building. Silently he continued in the rear entrance door, making it to the top of the stairs of the basement, and then he maneuvered down the steps. There was the man from the gas company and Erik could tell something was wrong. The man seemed to yell, although no sound came from his lips, and he now moved in slow motion, pointing to the stairs with his eyes wide open. How could he ever forget the fear in the man's face?

Erik watched himself from behind as he slowly ran up the stairs two at a time, then was propelled through the glass of the back door and over the white concrete wall by the alley behind his building. He landed hard on the ground amidst the chaos of fire, smoke, and debris and then everything went black.

Suddenly, he was being carried on a stretcher toward an ambulance and the noise was now deafening. He was back on Eighth Street in front of his old building, with ambulances, police cars, and fire trucks, sirens blaring. Dead people were being brought out of the rubble under blood stained sheets. Several women stood nearby, crying as the flames appeared to reach out to the smoke above the former building. Erik noticed that he didn't look fully conscious as he tried to comprehend the scene, and people ran in different directions around his stretcher. Confused, he realized that he could smell the burning chemicals, probably from his photography studio. It seemed odd to be able to relive these smells through a memory.

His studio was now a pile of bricks and rubble seen only through a veil of smoke, and he began to comprehend that his magnificent three story building was now in ruins, collapsed into a giant hole that had been opened up from the gas explosion. Covered in blood and broken glass, he noticed that his shirt had been burned off his back, only hanging in blood-red strips on his arms and chest. He could tell his leg was broken and it occurred to him that he probably had a lot of other broken bones, since he was in pain all over.

Every part of his body, especially his head, felt as though he had been hit by a truck and he couldn't get the burning smell out of his mind. He detected pieces of glass and gravel embedded in his hands and arms and he knew that he was about to pass out.

A paramedic ran up to him from the ambulance and said, "Wow, someone must have been watching over you today. You're the only one we've found who's still alive."

Erik tried to understand what this meant and couldn't respond as the ambulance worker continued talking. What about the man from the gas company? He was just right behind him on the steps. What about the people at the restaurant on the first floor of the building? His wife and daughter were in there.

"The whole place was demolished. Some kind of gas explosion. Everyone from the restaurant and the other building are gone, but you're going to make it. You were lucky to have been thrown clear from the building. Don't worry. We'll take good care of you."

Suddenly the home movie was over and Erik sat up terrified, his eyes opened wide in horror. He was back in the dimly lit, cool basement but he his shirt was soaked with sweat. He realized what his memories had just shown him were real, and he had difficulty catching his breath. The silence of this cave was overwhelming to him, as all he could hear was his own heart beating wildly and his rapid breathing. At that moment, he finally recognized that he was alone. All alone. Tears came out. The truth swept over him like an unstoppable avalanche.

&&&

Father Bill was fascinated with the hidden tunnels under his church and wished he had been told about them years ago so he could have explored them at a slower pace. Now he needed to hurry to see if there was something here, maybe some kind of clues that could lead to Erik Johnson and the kidnapped attorney. According to Tami, there wasn't much time. Could the photographer really torture that lawyer? Was Erik so far gone that he could attack a priest?

Fear swept over him as he imagined haunted nightmares coming to life in this dark, lonely place. What kind of horrors could come out at him from one of these openings and what would they do to him for invading their territory? It occurred to him that he should have never come down here without Tami and her gun.

His thoughts ran rampant and he forced himself to overcome each one of them with reason. There's something incredibly frightening about the unknown, especially in the darkness, and based on what little information Tami had revealed to him about this case, his fears were indeed justified. He prayed for protection and guidance but felt neither right away.

The smell of burnt wood seemed very fresh and he suspected that Erik had been down here in the past day or two. How would Erik know about these passageways while people who were members of the church weren't even aware of them? Someone else had to know about the opening behind the tapestry, since the giant cloth had to be cleaned once in a while, right? It was dusty, so maybe it hadn't been touched in years, maybe decades. He would talk with some of the elders later and see what they knew about it. From the way things looked down here, he had good reason to believe nobody else in the church knew these passageways even existed.

He touched the cold stones along the stairs but they weren't as smooth as the stones inside the church. Down here, they were coarse, since much of this place appeared to have been left unfinished. As he reached the basement floor, he stopped to shine the flashlight and see what was around him. Just a narrow hallway with stone walls and dirt covering the floors. He wondered if there were graves down here for some of the early leaders of the church, but didn't see any sign of them at this point. There may have been several burials down here a hundred years ago, but he had never heard of even one. Yet that was a common practice in many churches over the centuries, and it was especially honorable to be buried under the altar. His fear got the best of him again and he wondered if he was going to die here, only to be buried under the altar; his final resting place unknown to the world.

His shoes crunched on the dirt floor with each step he took, and he strained his eyes in the faint light to notice that footprints led the way in front of him. Someone else certainly knew about this room and had been here. His light revealed that the basement was not one big open room but appeared to have a corridor that led through the middle of the large room where he now walked. Several additional hallways meandered off into the blackness from the main corridor, but he couldn't see anything of interest when he shined the light into each one. He did smell smoke from something burning and speculated that a person might have lit a torch.

What was that? He heard a noise behind him, so he stopped to listen. It was quiet and he wondered if noises from the great church above would echo down here. Possible. He kept moving down the long corridor, occasionally admiring the stone supports that appeared every few yards from the floor to the ceiling. Not as impressive as the beautifully decorated columns up in the church, but still there was a masterful pattern to the stone pillars. Those builders knew what they were doing back then.

He jumped as something touched his face but he knew right away it was just an old spider web. Hoping the occupant of the web was long gone, he laughed to himself for a moment before sobering up again. It looked like this might turn out to be a wild goose chase down here, with nothing but a big, empty, hidden basement. However, he still figured that Erik had been down here at some point in the past few days. Disappointed there wasn't any great archaeological discovery to be made, or a hideout where Erik had been holding his hostage, he was almost ready to turn around and go back to one of the other dark hallways. This one seemed to be a dead end.

Before he changed direction, however, he was convinced he heard voices and immediately turned off his flashlight. Standing still with his back against the cold corridor wall, he listened again to see if his mind played tricks on him. He thought it might be possible in the basement to hear people talking in the church above, and he tried not to jump to conclusions.

Silence again.

He reached his finger to turn the flashlight back on, but before he could press the button, he distinctly heard a voice coming from the end of the corridor where he now stood. Someone else was definitely down here with him in the dark.

Chapter Thirty-Four

FATHER BILL CREPT SLOWLY AND silently toward the end of the corridor, realizing there must be a doorway down there that had been blocked, perhaps by Erik to hide his new home. The blackness touched every part of him as he searched for some kind of sign down here below the hallowed grounds. He didn't like being in the dark, where he was afraid of being visited by demons from his past, but he resisted the urge to turn on his light. He didn't notice it when he had the flash-light on but was confident there must still be another room left unexplored ahead of him. He touched the walls in the dark for a while before he noticed a faint light that appeared to come from an opening at the very end of the tunnel. He was certain now that someone was speaking from just around that corner, so he strained to make out what was being said. It sounded like Erik, but he still wasn't positive. If he could just get a little closer.

As quietly as he could, Bill stepped up to a stack of bricks that he could now tell blocked the entrance to another room and he listened. These bricks were obviously placed here to hide this doorway, and that voice had to be Erik Johnson's. It sounded like the man was crying, and not just a little bit but with great sobs. Was he too late to save the attorney?

"Danny, I'm so sorry I dragged you into this after all this

time. I should have just forgiven you and left it at that. I'm sorry."

More sobs and crying. Father Bill wondered if Danny was the attorney's name. Maybe he wasn't too late after all. Or maybe Erik was sorry that he killed the man already. To his astonishment, Bill couldn't believe how remorseful Erik sounded now and listened as he forgave the man who had hurt him years ago. This could be a turning point in Erik's life and Bill's eyes tried to focus on the bricks in the dim light ahead of him.

"I felt betrayed when I found out you were working against me. My own lawyer. I hated you for taking a bribe from the gas company to turn the case against me. I used to wonder how much they paid you but now I don't even care. I went away and forgot about everything. I began my life all over again and could have stayed there in peace if I hadn't started remembering these things that happened to me back then. Once pieces of it came back to me, all I wanted to do was get my revenge and make you pay for what you did to me. Now I wish I had never even came back to Stockton and put all of this into motion. None of it was worth what I'm going through inside now. It's tearing me apart, what I've allowed myself to do to those men. And to you."

Bill figured the lawyer must be in the same room, but he didn't hear another person's voice. That man was either gagged or drugged or worse. He didn't want to think about the third option and stayed optimistic. He waited out of sight, just listening and trying to determine what he should do at this point. He could come in and surprise Erik and since the tone of his voice didn't sound angry, it could turn out to be a positive meeting. However, if Erik had already killed the attorney, he could turn out to be on the defensive and become a very dangerous threat.

"Danny, I know you've been listening to me for the past

day or so and I know I told you how much I wanted you to suffer. Well, now I've changed my mind and I take all of that back. I want you to live and I want you to know that I've forgiven you. I've done some terrible things to several other people who were involved with my case, but I'm finished. I'll accept my punishment for those actions and I apologize for putting you and your family through this. My family's gone and it's not your fault. Nothing you or I can do will bring them back but I know I can change so that I can see them again someday in Heaven. That's the most important thing in the world for me now so you're free to go as soon as you wake up. I'm so sorry for doing this to you."

Father Bill heard this and couldn't stop his own tears. Erik had asked for forgiveness and was letting the attorney go free. That victim was still alive and Erik was going to turn himself in to the police. Father Bill fell to his knees and prayed a prayer of thanksgiving for this miracle and for the change in Erik's life. Bill knew that even the worst criminal could be forgiven if he truly was sorry and was willing to turn his life around, but he had never seen it firsthand like he was witnessing now, especially to this extent. Erik was a murderer who may have tortured several people and was now asking for forgiveness. This was probably the happiest day in his entire life and what made it even more special is that it was a reminder that he himself had been forgiven for his own past behaviors as well.

Just then, a noise from the beginning of the hallway caught Father Bill's attention and he turned around to see a light pointing at him. He stood up and walked toward the light, wondering who else knew about this secret basement of the church. The light provided an interesting view of the circular ceiling, showing the brick pattern that someone had once put a lot of effort into many years ago. For a moment, he was glad to see something more than the darkness and some dimly lit piles for bricks.

"Hey priest. Surprised to see me down here?"

Father Bill couldn't see who this person shining the light in his face was, but didn't like the tone of voice that was threatening this situation. He instantly feared for Erik's safety and tried to lead the man away from the room at the dead end of the corridor. His moment of relief had left him and he prayed for guidance and protection for himself and Erik.

"I can't see who you are. Do I know you?"

"Let's just say we haven't seen each other for a while but I remember you back before you went to hide behind a priest's collar."

Father Bill still didn't recognize the man's voice but he kept walking toward the light in hopes of seeing the man's face and getting him farther away from Erik. He remembered Tami said she feared that her partner would take his own revenge on their suspect and figured this could be him. Another police officer, but one with his own agenda. He wondered how this man would have known him before he became a priest.

"I didn't hide behind the priesthood. I'm a changed person and ..."

"Yeah, yeah. A changed person. I don't think you can do some of the things you did and suddenly somehow get it all wiped clean. You're just as guilty as this guy who's been killing these city officials and you know it."

"What kind of things do you think I did?"

The policeman's voice now turned into evil laughter as he slowly shined the light on his own face.

"William Ljunglof. Take a look at my face and let me see your reaction."

Father Bill knew in an instant who this man was and his heart pounded a rhythm that he figured the policeman must be able to hear. The eerie light illuminated a familiar demon from his own past and he didn't want to face this man now. He knew he should run and just forget about it all, even though he realized he had been forgiven for the things he had done when he was younger. He wondered briefly about Erik and what this man might do to him, but what was more important?

"I thought that might bring back some memories. Remember some of the things you did as a teen-ager? I could have busted you for selling drugs but I protected you so you could do bigger and better things in this town. Didn't we pay you well enough back then?"

"What I did was wrong and I recognized it. I knew I needed to get my life back on the right path, so I changed. You should have done the same."

Fear covered him at first like a mist and then more like a blanket of perspiration as he seriously considered running toward the man to escape past him. Something about the light in front of him comforted Bill and he stood his ground.

"Well, listen to the little priest lecturing me. I think you'd better think twice before telling me what to do with my life."

Father Bill heard the click of a gun and saw a pistol pointing at him. Suddenly he was filled with courage and he didn't care about the gun. He didn't care about the past and he knew this man had no power over Bill's soul. His heart still beat like a fast drum but the fear had left him. He was right with God, just as Erik Johnson, who was guilty of multiple crimes, was now forgiven, and this man in front of him was not.

"I don't know your name, but I know that you're a bad cop who's always been a bad cop. I've asked God to forgive me for my actions and I know in my heart that I'm forgiven. I pray that you'll recognize your own crimes and turn from the evil that leads you to do those things."

The policeman gave another laugh that started almost like a low growl and became louder until the corridor echoed with an explosion. Father Bill's body was blasted back against the wall as he watched smoke from the powerful handgun dance gracefully in the light held by Officer Hultgren. Grimacing, his head hurt from hitting the wall with such force and there was a tremendous pain in his heart as he crumpled to the ground, unable to breathe, and then closed his eyes. For a brief second, he wondered if this was what it felt like to die but he was no longer afraid.

Chapter Thirty-Five

As Tami walked near the confessional inside St. Mark's Cathedral, she heard a gunshot below the church and knew she had to act fast. Where was this hidden doorway Father Bill told her about in the voicemail he left her? Why wasn't he answering her calls? Her eyes raced around the room, desperately trying to locate any clues. She saw the tapestry he mentioned and briefly admired the design sewn by its' creator. It was impressive, but she would have to look at it more closely some other time. Right now, she had to find the opening so she frantically touched the cloth and pushed it occasionally, feeling the resistance of the wall behind it. She didn't notice anything unusual, so she carelessly lifted the side near the corner of the small alcove and looked behind it, not really caring if she pulled the huge, dark fabric down by accident. Taking out her flashlight, she shone it in front of her as she stepped completely behind the tapestry and walked toward the center. The flashlight suddenly went out and for a moment, she became claustrophobic as the cloth enveloped her in the darkness. Banging the flashlight, she was rescued by the return of the light and quickened her steps toward the middle of the tapestry.

She didn't believe her eyes when she actually came to a small opening and her jaw dropped in astonishment. This was just like in the movies but there were real people's lives at stake here. Someone nearby had fired a gun, so time was of the essence. She needed to hurry and find out what Father Bill had discovered down there before it was too late. Her eyes took in every part of the scene and she leaned over with her flashlight to peer inside the opening. It didn't seem to go back very far but she noticed that the floor disappeared momentarily, until steps descending into the darkness, came into view when she pointed the light downward. She immediately took out her phone and punched some numbers by the light of her flashlight. Not an easy task with her hands trembling the way there were.

"This is Officer Tami Anderson of the Stockton Police Department. I need backup right now. I'm at St. Mark's Cathedral on Springwood, near Tenth Street, and I've just heard a gunshot coming from the basement. I believe there's a murder suspect down there now and one of the priests had already gone down to investigate before I arrived. The entry to the basement is hidden, so go to the confessional, and then step around the corner to the small prayer room. There's a large tapestry on the wall and the opening is behind the tapestry. Bring flashlights and an ambulance. I don't know if someone's been shot already but let's be prepared just in case."

Contemplating the gunshot from a couple of minutes ago, she wondered if Father Bill had accidently surprised Erik, and ... She didn't want to think about that. Besides, Erik wouldn't shoot a priest, would he? Although she had to admit that he did put several people through a crematorium fire alive and buried another man prematurely, so the capability for murder did exist. She didn't know what to expect and swiftly moved down the stairs, not wanting to consider what she was about to walk into.

&&&

OFFICER HULTGREN KICKED THE FALLEN priest, looking for any sign of life, but there was none. He noticed blood on the ground and smiled, while smoke from his gun surrounded his face and glistening teeth in the softly lit room.

"I guess you'll meet your Heavenly Father sooner than you thought. Let's see if he really has forgiven you for your past."

Hultgren chuckled as he looked down the hallway where he had seen the priest on his knees a few minutes ago. He quickly lit one of the torches he found hanging on the wall and then took a few steps in the direction from where the priest had come. He strained his eyes to grasp what was down there since it seemed like there was some kind of light coming from the end of the hall, although it was very faint. He hurried down the corridor, knowing that if the suspect was down there, he must have heard the gunshot and was already warned that someone was coming. The last thing he wanted to do was scare off this guy and let him get away. The policeman hoped the suspect was cornered now and had no way of escape, especially with his own six foot-five frame blocking the corridor and a smoking gun barrel welcoming the former funeral home employee to try it.

He was taken by surprise as his ears picked up a shout, almost like a groan, and he tightened his grip on the weapon. He slowed down and stepped carefully, keeping the gun aimed straight at the light up ahead. He wouldn't give anyone an opportunity to come rushing out at him and get away alive. There would be no prisoners today.

&&&

TAMI FOUND THE BOTTOM OF THE STAIRS and followed the corridor as fast as she could without hitting her head on any low ceilings or tripping on bricks that were hard to see in the indistinct light. It looked like Father Bill may have helped her find her way, since she saw a light, and she hastily quickened her pace. Sure enough, there was a lit torch hanging on the wall up ahead, so she sped past the two dark rooms that reached off of the main corridor, only giving them a brief glance. Since they were still dark, she assumed Father Bill had wanted her to keep going down the main hallway. She hated to think that as she passed the rooms, her back would be to each of them and someone could potentially come out of one and surprise her. She was reminded about her nightmare of being captured and tortured and her adrenaline increased at an overwhelming rate. She needed to control her senses and be aware of her surroundings, but it was no easy task with everything going through her mind.

Passing the torch, she could tell there was another light flickering in front of her, so she kept her current speed toward the light, which appeared to be beyond the next corner. Slowing down to carefully peek around the bend, she made sure her pistol was ready and she backed up against the wall. Listening for voices or anything that might indicate there was someone close to her, she waited impatiently, hearing nothing. Taking several deep breaths, she popped her head out past the corner and promptly pulled it back, her expression registering the surprise of what she had just seen. Someone was lying on the floor, dressed in black. It looked like a priest and it appeared as though he was lying in blood.

&&&

Officer Hultgren heard another groan and stepped up to the pile of bricks that were blocking the doorway. Studying the neatly stacked bricks, it was obvious that someone had used this pile in an attempt to block most of the light in this room from being seen down the hall. Eyeing the crude structure, he walked gently around it, keeping his ears open for any sudden movement toward him. He cautiously peered in and saw light painting the walls and ceiling. This room had the appearance of a cave but the light didn't move like a campfire. This was a solid, steady light. At first, he couldn't see anyone, but a yell through clenched teeth surprised him and drew his attention further into the room. His fingers tightened on the gun as he fully expected to fire it at any moment. He finally saw someone on his knees, head wrapped by his arms and he wondered what was going on. Was this the next victim Tami had mentioned, going through some kind of torture? Could this be the attorney? He had to find the suspect before rushing in; otherwise he could be stepping into a trap. That's the last thing he wanted and the thought of Erik Johnson winning now, getting the chance to torture a bad cop, was enough to bring a hint of fear into the big man's corrupt heart.

He continued looking around the room from his vantage point but was resigned to the fact that he would have to go inside to see the rest of it. It was dangerous but he was certainly no coward. A liar, a cheat, and a thief, but no coward. His eyes made one last survey throughout the room but all he saw was the man in pain, sitting on the floor with his back to the door. Where was the suspect? He carefully moved his head past the hidden doorway and thought he noticed someone. Pulling back, the adrenaline rushed throughout his body. He was ready for this. He burst in, gun pointing in front of the kneeling man, surprised when neither of the two men even acknowledged his presence.

"This is Officer John Hultgren of the Stockton Police Department. Put your hands where I can see them. Now!"

One man just continued to lie on a make-shift bed made out of bricks and the other kept his head cradled in his arms while kneeling on the floor. What was going on here?

"I said get your hands up and I mean it."

Again nobody moved, so Hultgren stepped up behind the kneeling man and kicked him to the ground, keeping his gun aimed at the man's head as he sprawled onto the ground and rolled over with another yell.

"Who are you and what happened to the man that's lying down? Is he dead?"

Hultgren glanced over to the wall but the horizontal man had still not moved. He definitely looked dead and appeared to be lying on some kind of makeshift altar. Could it be a human sacrifice? Maybe this was the attorney and the killer was the guy on the ground. The officer's nerves were on edge now, since he couldn't make sense of the situation.

"The man over there isn't dead. He's been drugged but will be waking up in a few hours."

The sudden outburst startled Hultgren, but he checked the aim of his gun and made sure he could see both hands of the man on the ground.

"OK, who are you?"

"My name's Erik Johnson," was all he could respond.

After all of the searching for this man, Hultgren finally had him, but for some reason he was apprehensive, even though he had his gun pointed at the man's head. Something didn't seem right here. Had he stumbled into the murder of the attorney, just in time to save him? Why was Johnson screaming like he was in pain if he was indeed the killer? Maybe he was crazy as a loon and needed to be locked away in a padded cell with a nice wraparound white jacket.

"Erik Johnson. Did you kill Senator Grant, Judge Lewis, and Ed Stewart?"

He kept his eyes closed, causing Hultgren to not trust his next move, and Erik finally nodded.

"Yes, I killed them. I wanted revenge so badly at the time but now I realize it wasn't worth it. I almost killed Mr. Clark here but Father Bill helped me to see that I can be forgiven, even though I've done some terrible things. I'm a changed person now. I've committed some crimes and need to be punished, but I also know that I'm a new man and that's all that matters to me now."

"Enough of all this forgiveness garbage. Yeah, you're gonna pay alright, you psycho. You don't even deserve prison for what you've done. Get up. On your feet now. You're not leaving this room alive."

Chapter Thirty-Six

TAMI HEARD VOICES AT THE OTHER end of the hallway but wasn't sure whose they were. Suspecting the body on the floor was Father Bill's, her anger reached the same level as her fear. This was truly a good man, and there was no reason Erik Johnson should have shot him. As much compassion as she felt for Erik after all that he had been put through, she would be forced to shoot him if confronted. None of that justified shooting an innocent man, especially a priest. But could she do it after all she had learned about him and what he'd been through at the hands of those unethical men?

She peeked out into the dark hallway again, trying not to look at the body in black, but her eyes were drawn to it. Closing them and focusing her attention on the situation again, she cleared her mind of emotion, getting herself ready for a confrontation. She leveled her gun at shoulder height and rushed into the fire lit corridor to check for a pulse, never taking her eyes from the light at the end of the hall. She watched the reflections from the fire create images on the ancient brick walls on both sides of the corridor and imagined she could see faces mocking her, daring her to go further.

Knowing this could be a trap, using the priest as bait to lure her out in the open, she had difficulty trying to stop her hands from shaking. Keeping her back to the wall, she squatted down to touch the man's carotid artery. Glancing momentarily at the unmoving face of the man on the ground, she saw that it was definitely Father Bill and noticed the back of his head was covered with blood. It didn't appear to be a gunshot wound, especially an exit wound, although she surely heard a gun go off a few minutes ago.

Wait. There was a pulse and it seemed strong. He was still alive. Tami was engulfed with relief but knew he still needed medical attention. Where was her backup that she called for a few minutes ago? This man needed a paramedic right away. Holding her phone in one hand while her other held the pistol, she made a call, trying hard to keep her voice from shouting. Even little more than a whisper echoed down here and she figured someone else in the hallway could easily hear every word she was saying.

"Yes, this is Officer Tami Anderson from the Stockton Police Department. I have an emergency in the basement of St. Mark's Cathedral. A man's been shot and is down, but he's still alive. I've called for backup and an ambulance but it hasn't arrived. There's a hidden entrance to the basement, around the corner from the confessional and behind the large tapestry. Please hurry. The man's bleeding, and..."

The sound of a gun reverberated throughout the corridor and Tami jumped to her feet, on full alert again. Her first thought was that Erik Johnson must have shot the attorney, since he couldn't safely get back to the funeral home. She saw nobody in the hallway and gave Father Bill another look of concern. She didn't want to leave him alone but knew that she needed to see what was happening where that gun went off. With some hesitation, she ran toward the pale light, hearing an angry man's voice talking through the echo of the shot. It sounded like her partner's voice, which threw a wrench into the situation. How did he get here and who was with him? Did he know that Father Bill was out here?

She would find out in a matter of seconds as she came upon the stack of bricks covering the small opening at the end of the hall.

Why were these bricks placed here? Maybe to hide this room. What would Hultgren do when he saw her come through the doorway? She was initially concerned about surprising Erik in the middle of something but walking in on her partner was a whole new ballgame. If there was anything left of the kind photographer she once remembered, he wouldn't hurt her. On the other hand, she didn't know if her partner would really shoot her, but she didn't want to take any chances. She hoped he wouldn't go that far but if he was wrapped up in the bribery and felt threatened that Tami might expose it all, anything could happen.

The rush of adrenaline was overpowering now as she stopped and hurriedly glanced into the room from behind the wall. Erik Johnson stood with his left arm sleeve soaked in blood, his hair a mess with sand sticking all over his wet face, but she didn't see anyone else. This man didn't have a beard like Father Bill had told her but she figured he must have shaved it off so he wouldn't be recognized easily. It amazed her at how similar he looked to the man she remembered from over a decade ago. He had not aged much after all this time and she experienced compassion right away. Someone must have shot him in the arm but he looked defenseless. She popped her head out a little farther this time, noticing a police officer pointing a gun at Erik. It looked like Hultgren and she knew this was not going to end well. He must be torturing Erik before killing him. She planned her next move and was about to step through the doorway, when Hultgren's voice boomed from the small, cavernous room.

"So Erik Johnson, how does it feel to be on the receiving end of a slow and painful death? Didn't think you would get caught after all that you did?"

"Listen, I'm ready to turn myself in. I'm not resisting arrest at all and I don't have any weapons. I'll confess to what I did and why I did it."

"It's too late for that, my friend. You know a little too much about how things are done in Stockton, and I can't let you leave quite yet. You've messed up a good thing that we had going here and I'm not too thrilled that you're trying to accuse some of my friends of bribery and fixing the court system. I'd like to know what you used to fake their deaths so convincingly. You must have given it to them at the restaurant, right?"

Erik was quiet, and Tami knew she needed to rush in to stop her partner, despite the danger he presented to both Erik and her. She swiftly stepped through the door and saw the surprise in Hultgren's face, watching his gun shift from Erik to her and then back to Erik.

"Well, well, well. This is a new development. Tami, I'd like you to meet Erik Johnson, the murderer and torturer we've been tracking. He has his next victim over there behind me, but I'm not sure if he's still alive."

"He's alive, Tami. I only drugged him and even though I was planning to kill him, I've changed my mind. Father Bill helped me to realize that I can still turn my life around from the revenge I've been seeking, even after the terrible things I've done. I'm ready to do that now."

"Yeah, well I think it's a little too late for that, and I think the only reason you haven't killed this man is because I interrupted you. Don't try to weasel out of it with a pitiful 'I've changed my ways and I'm going straight now' story. I don't buy it."

"It doesn't matter if you buy it, Officer Hultgren. This is between me and God, and I know I've been forgiven. You can ask Father Bill. He'll explain it to you."

Tami pointed her gun to the ground, since it seemed like

the situation had become diffused and said, "Father Bill is laying out in the hall bleeding. I don't know if he'll survive."

Erik glared at him and said, "I thought I heard a gunshot a few minutes ago. You shot Father Bill? You shot an innocent priest and you're lecturing me on right and wrong?"

"Listen here. You're the one on trial now, and I'll ask the questions. And your priest friend is not as innocent as you think." Looking over at Tami, her partner added, "Tami, you really don't need to be here. Why don't you go and see what you can do for the priest. I'll stay here with the suspect."

Erik continued talking and Tami was surprised at his boldness toward a big man pointing a gun at his chest.

"Officer Hultgren, I think you realized that Bill knew all about your involvement in bribery, police brutality, and you figured you had to silence him. Isn't that right?"

"You can think what you want but it's you that's going to fry now."

"No, just wait until Tami sees the information I saved for her on your interactions with Ed Stewart from the gas company and the bribes he gave to you to cover up things, to make certain situations go away. I've put together a nice package showing how you've encouraged criminals that have money to slip some of it to you in exchange for you letting them off the hook. You'd be surprised at how many enemies you've made over the years."

Tami couldn't help but smile at the look Hultgren gave Erik but she was now concerned that his anger had reached its limits. Suddenly, four shots rang out in rapid fire before Tami could do anything and Erik was shoved backward against the wall by an unseen force.

Chapter Thirty-Seven

AS THE ECHOES STILL RANG IN her ears, Tami instinctively raised her gun as she watched Hultgren turn to point his gun at her, and she instinctively fired twice. They both seemed to move in slow motion and she saw the fury in her partner's eyes, glaring at her. Bracing herself, she expected to get hit by a bullet from her partner since he was moving so fast and had the advantage of surprise. However, he collapsed on the floor without firing a shot and she rushed over to kick his gun away. Tami cuffed his hands behind his back, staring at the blood covering Erik's chest from multiple entry wounds.

She looked at Hultgren's wounds, one in his right upper arm and the other under his right collar bone, but neither looked life threatening. Good. She wanted to see him charged for crimes and face the punishment he deserved, so she would do everything she could to make sure he lived to see that happen. She couldn't wait to see what Erik had sent to her on this bad cop.

With her partner secure, although alert and fuming over the change of events, Tami got up and ran over to Erik. He was still conscious but his breathing was labored. He probably had damage to at least one of his lungs and other internal organs. Not good. How would the EMTs get down here in time to save him?

"I'm glad to see you smile, Mr. Johnson. We have an ambulance on its way right now, so the EMTs will be here any minute. Just hold on."

Erik tried to speak but she could tell it was difficult for him at first. She guessed that he also had the wind knocked out of him but that was the least of his concerns. She didn't know what he said but found that she couldn't speak herself, as tears welled up in her eyes. She cleared her throat, thinking about all of the bad things that had happened to him years ago. She shouldn't be vengeful, but in her heart she was glad that the men who caused Erik so much pain and suffering had died terrible deaths. They all deserved it.

Blood came out of his mouth so she held his head up gently in an effort to make it easier for him to breathe.

"Tami, I'm glad you're here with me now. I'm so sorry for doing those horrible things to those men and causing so much agony."

This stunned Tami, since deep down it was her impression that the murders were justified. She smiled back at him as she supported his head with one hand and unsuccessfully tried to stop the bleeding in each of the wounds with her other hand. Her shirt darkened with his blood but she didn't care as she helplessly watched this man's life ebb away with every heartbeat. It was as though Erik's life was flowing out of his body and into hers, but she pushed that thought out of her mind.

"I wish I could have thanked Bill Ljunglof in person. He's the one that showed me how wrong it was for me to carry out those actions; and I owe him so much for turning me around."

He had a difficult time completing that sentence and tried to catch his breath.

"Don't try to talk right now. Let the EMTs get here and start patching you up."

Erik blinked his eyes and looked around the room as though he couldn't tell where he was. The dim light gave an eerie glare off of the stone walls. His eyes met with Tami's and he smiled.

"You're a good cop and a good person. I wish I'd never hurt those men but it's too late for that. I'm sorry, but there's nothing I can do to change things." He gave a chuckle and added, "I thought I'd end up going to prison for the rest of my life and I was OK with that. I deserved as much or worse. This way is better."

Tami couldn't say anything in return and tears covered her face. She made an unconscious attempt to wipe them with her hand, adding Erik's blood to her watery cheeks. He gasped again, trying to catch his breath.

"I was in so much pain every day I almost couldn't take it. Thanks to Bill, I know I'll be with my wife and daughter again soon and that fills me with so much joy you can't imagine. I'll be eternally thankful for that gift."

He clenched his eyes in pain, coughing up blood, as Tami used her fingers to apply pressure onto the bullet holes. It just kept seeping from all four wounds and she knew there was nothing she could do for him.

"Mr. Johnson, I've been meaning to tell you that I remember you from the photography studio and I know how much you loved your family. I saw it in your eyes when my parents brought me there for our Christmas portraits every year." She stopped and laughed, and then continued, "I had the biggest crush on you when I was a young girl. I didn't realize it was you who we were searching for until just recently. I wasn't aware you also owned the building that blew up, so I didn't expect the building owner and the photographer to be the same person."

He smiled and responded, "I liked your parents so much. They were good friends to me, just like Bill's parents. That's one of the main reasons I picked you and Bill to get hints from me."

He stopped suddenly and coughed more, and Tami's sobs became more noticeable.

"Tami, please tell Bill that his parents knew he would get past that phase he went through when he was making bad choices and they loved him very much. Bill never got to tell them how sorry he was and how thankful he was for their love and dedication to him, even when he was at his worst, but they knew. They both somehow realized that he would get his life back on track. They just didn't get to see it. He needs to hear that."

She nodded. Tami didn't want to think about Father Bill lying out in the corridor but she suspected he could already be dead by now. It angered her that Officer Hultgren actually shot Bill but she had to hide her feelings from Erik right now. This was too much for her to handle. Where were the paramedics? Bill couldn't die now. Neither could Mr. Johnson, not after the tremendous change he'd gone through today.

When Erik turned his head away from her and a big smile lit up his eyes, Tami wondered what was happening. She looked where he was looking but didn't see anything but the wall.

"Are you OK?"

"I'm better than OK. My wife and daughter are standing right over there and I know it's not just a memory or a vision. This is the real thing."

Tami stared in the same direction but saw nothing. She wiped the blood from his face, watching tears of joy flood everywhere she smeared. What was going on here? Could he really see something or was this just an end of life hallucination? She had read about those things with some dying patients. She believed in life after death and had seen several people actually die in front of her. Yet this was the most amazing thing she had ever experienced. She wished Father Bill was here now. Tami knew in her heart that Erik truly did see his family and was convinced that she was in the middle of something special.

"Kiersten said that she remembers you when you were little, especially when you brought in that little white bunny with the rattle in his belly and wanted it to be in your family picture."

At first, Tami thought Erik was getting delirious and wasn't sure what to make of this comment, but the memory came to her as though it occurred yesterday. He still looked toward the wall and Tami noticed he still had a smile as he continued.

"Brita said she loved your bunny so much that he's the reason she asked for one the next Christmas. I don't remember your bunny but I know we did get Brita one for Christmas. After all these years, I never knew it was your bunny that gave her the idea."

Tami gasped and stopped breathing for a couple of seconds as she let that sink in. She looked at the wall again and knew that his family must be there to escort Erik to Heaven. She could picture them standing there, exactly as they looked when she came to the studio for portraits, and she remembered her little stuffed rabbit. She had forgotten all about that. Tears kept pouring out as she caught her breath and a peace came over her as she looked back down at Erik's face.

"Tami, thanks so much for being here with me now. You've brought back some wonderful memories just by sitting here with me and I'm filled with a happiness I haven't known in fifteen years. It's funny. Brita would actually be close to your age now, but I kept seeing her from exactly as she was back then before the explosion. I should have known they had to be memories and couldn't have been real."

He coughed again and she felt so good that nothing

could have wiped away her smile. This troubled man was finally at peace. He turned his head to look into her eyes again and she wondered what he would think about her own tears.

"I have to go now but I have a feeling I'll see you again someday. Tell Bill I'll see him again and that's a fact."

Tami nodded and noticed his head quickly moved back toward the wall. His eyes followed something up a little higher and then closed, leaving a hint of a smile on his wet and blood smeared face. He was gone but she knew exactly where he was now.

Chapter Thirty-Eight

AT THAT MOMENT, SEVERAL PO-lice officers rushed into the room, each with a gun focused on a different part of the bricked basement. Tami observed the leader assessing the situation as he motioned to allow the medical team to enter. Everything seemed quiet to her while she looked around as though she was watching a play. One team went to Officer Hultgren, who was semi-conscious and handcuffed, while another rushed to assess Danny Clark. Two men knelt down to check on Erik and she didn't understand what they said. Looking into one's eyes, she struggled to focus. She felt more like a spectator in this situation and found it difficult to bring herself back into the reality around her.

"Officer, are you OK?"

Tami stared at him but noticed that one of the EMTs shot the other a quick look. He shook his head while testing Erik for a pulse. Tami already knew that Erik was dead and she was numb just sitting there beside him. Glancing down at his face, she tried again to wipe some of the blood and sand from his chin but only succeeded in smearing it more. Her hand was already covered in his blood and the lead police officer gave her a cloth to clean up.

"Tami, you have some on your face and I assume it's the victim's blood. Use this to wipe it off. Do you need any medical attention?"

She looked up at the policeman with a blank expression, recognizing him as Officer James Harrison, then saw him kneel and move the white towel closer toward her. Shaking her head, she took the towel from him with no verbal response, immediately turning it red, and then rubbed it gently against her own cheeks. She used it to clean off Erik's face and only then did she finish wiping her hands. She absentmindedly touched the red cloth on Erik's chest, not realizing what she was doing. So much blood on his chest, the ground surrounding his body, and soaked into the dark sand. It looked like someone dumped a bucket of red paint on his chest and it spilled everywhere, coating the ground, staining his clothes as well as her own clothes. There were only a few places that revealed his dark, wet shirt was actually white a few minutes ago.

"We need to take him to the ambulance now. Are you going to be OK?"

She slowly stood up with Officer Harrison's help and watched as two paramedics carefully lifted Erik to a stretcher.

Another officer came up to them and said, "The man lying on the stack of bricks is dead but not from a gunshot wound. The EMTs can't tell what killed him yet."

Tami looked up at the man, torn between watching Erik being carried out of the room and providing a response, but finally said, "No, he's actually still alive but he's been drugged with some kind of substance that makes him appear to be dead. I don't know exactly what it is since I'm still waiting on the toxicology report from one of the other victims."

"Ma'am, we've checked him thoroughly. There's no pulse and the man's not breathing. I think we could tell if he was still alive."

Tami could have easily snapped back at this man. However, she just calmly replied, "Please get him to the hospital. If you've seen what I've seen this past week, you'd understand."

There was doubt in the EMTs eyes as the officer looked back at him, and she added, "Believe me. The chemical or herbal mixture is so good that it's caused three other people to be declared dead even though they were all still alive."

Officer Harrison commented, "Do what she says. She's been closely involved with this case and knows more about it than any of us," and they nodded as they returned to the attorney's apparently lifeless body.

She smiled at Officer Harrison and noticed that he looked at her with concern.

"I'm alright James. I'm not bleeding anywhere. It's Erik Johnson's blood all over me. This just isn't how I expected it all to end."

She glanced to her right as Officer John Hultgren was carried by two EMTs on another stretcher, but he didn't appear to be conscious. Hatred welled up from within her but she didn't say a word as he disappeared through the doorway to the dimly lit hallway.

"I never really trusted Hultgren but I didn't think he was capable of doing all that he's done. Wait until you see what Erik Johnson, the victim who was shot to death, gave me on him. Hultgren tried to shoot me right after he killed Erik but somehow I hit him first. I don't know how. When he turned his gun on me, I waited to feel a bullet hit me." She paused for a moment, and then added, "I think he'll be put away for a long time."

"Yeah, the priest in the hall warned us that your partner was determined to kill that guy, which he did, and wouldn't hesitate to shoot you too."

"Wait, is he OK? The priest?"

"Yeah, you won't believe what happened with him."

Tami then stepped out into the corridor, leaving Officer

Harrison to finish up in the hidden room, and ran down the hall to where Father Bill was being lifted up on a stretcher. He gave her a weak smile, bringing a smile to her face when she saw his eyes open and a white bandage wrapped around his head.

"So, Mr. Johnson's dead now. I just saw them carry his body down the hall."

Tami knelt down to take hold of his outstretched hand but didn't stop smiling.

"Bill, his wife and daughter were in that room with us and he went with them to Heaven. I know it."

"What? Did you see them?"

"No, but he did, and it was real. They were there with us and Erik was so happy. He asked me to thank you for helping him to forgive those men who caused him so many problems. He made the decision not to kill that defense attorney and I believe he was truly sorry for all that he had done wrong. I honestly think he's in Heaven with his family now. It was an awesome experience."

Father Bill stared at her as new tears of happiness rolled down her cheeks and she noticed the paramedics were watching her as well.

"Unbelievable," Bill finally said as he shook his head.

Tami heard voices behind her and turned to see the attorney being carried out on a stretcher. She moved up against the wall so they could get by. Officer Harrison and another officer came up behind them and Harrison stopped beside her. "Tami, I'll be right outside when you finish up here. Could you stop by and fill me in on the details before you leave?"

"Of course. I'll be there in a few minutes."

He smiled and continued on behind the other men, disappearing around the corner and leaving the hallway echoing with the sound of their voices until it was quiet again. She turned back to look at Father Bill and thought about what she had seen when she first came around that corner. It was a priest lying motionless on the ground.

"Bill, what happened to you? I saw you on the floor and thought Officer Hultgren had killed you."

"Well, I want you to look at this Bible."

"Why?"

Bill picked a Bible up from the stretcher and handed it to her. The first thing she noticed was a large hole in the front cover and she looked up into his eyes again.

"I don't get it. What's this?"

"Tami, that cop shot me in the heart and left me for dead. I had this Bible tucked in my inside pocket, right here over my heart, and it saved my life."

He placed the book over the left side of his chest with the hole facing her and she knew instantly what had happened.

"So when the bullet hit me, or actually when it hit the Bible, I fell back and smacked my head on those bricks," he said while pointing up at a couple of bricks that stuck out from the wall, "and it knocked me unconscious. Your partner must have left me for dead."

"When I saw the blood on your head, I first thought he had shot you, since I heard a gunshot, or maybe hit you over the head with something. When I checked your pulse, I didn't think you would be alive much longer."

"Tami, open the Bible to the page where the bullet stopped."

Bill held out the book and Tami took it, not knowing what she was looking for, and she found the first page that had not been punctured by the bullet.

"Read the verse right where the bullet was pointing." Tami stared at the page but Bill chided her, "No, read it out loud."

"Isaiah 43:25. I am the one who wipes out your offenses for my own sake and I will not remember your wrong-doings."

"I've been struggling with wondering if I could truly be forgiven for the things I did when I was younger, and for the past few weeks a voice kept telling me that I would never fully be forgiven, even though I've asked for forgiveness and felt that He had. I believe this is a reminder for me to never doubt my forgiveness. I also believe this is what Erik needed to hear, but from the sound of it, I think he finally realized it for himself."

"Well, he said it was all because of whatever you told him. He's with his family now and at peace finally all because of you."

Tami saw that Father Bill couldn't hold back his own tears as he stared into her eyes, so she gave him back the assaulted Bible and held his hand again.

"Excuse me, officer. We need to get him to the hospital, since he may have a concussion and internal bleeding."

Tami stood up and nodded, while the two men picked up the stretcher with Father Bill on it and walked with him down the corridor.

Before they made the first turn, she called after them, "How are you going to get him up the stairs?"

"We'll just drag him up by his ankles, ma'am."

The thought made her laugh, since it reminded her that some EMTs have a good sense of humor, and she figured they must have something at the top of the stairs to help them get the men back to the church sanctuary. Within a few seconds, it occurred to her that she was alone in the corridor, as everyone except a couple of the police officers had gone upstairs. She heard their voices faintly as they documented the crime scene and she tried to grasp what she had been through in the past hour.

Chapter Thirty-Nine

TAMI AND FATHER BILL FACED THE cool autumn breeze as they stood in the freshly mowed grass at the cemetery where Judge Lewis had been buried recently. However, this was a much nicer location than the Judge's gravesite. Bill had finished his eulogy and the few people who had remembered Victor Erik Johnson as the good man he truly was were already gone. They stared at the gravestone which was now complete with the names and dates for a husband, wife, and four-year old daughter, listening to the beautiful sounds of the birds in the nearby trees.

"I believe Erik would have enjoyed seeing the sunshine above us now. He preferred the sunny days to the overcast ones and this was a perfect day for his funeral."

Tami looked at the priest and smiled as she took in the scene. White billowing clouds moved swiftly across a blue sky, with a view of the park and a lake across the green grass of the cemetery. Large hardwood trees, probably elms, oaks, and maples, lined the path with decorative colored leaves waiting to fall to the earth in their annual ritual, and she watched a young family holding hands with their little girl off in the distance. That could be Erik with his wife and daughter, finally at peace and together for all eternity.

"Father Bill, you did a great job with the eulogy. It's a touchy situation to say such positive things about a man who killed three people, but you told it like it really was. He was a wonderful man who made some terrible choices and deserved to be executed or die in prison. Yet he finally turned his life around before it was too late. It was very moving."

"What I said was so personal that most of it applied to me. It came naturally and I knew I could have never come up with those words myself. They were for Erik but were also for me as well."

Tami remembered some of Bill's past and had an idea about what he was referring to, but didn't want to ask anything further. This wasn't the time to bring it up.

"The warmth of the sun does feel good against the cool breeze, doesn't it?"

Father Bill looked at her and nodded. He seemed to be off in another world.

"Tami, what'll happen to John Hultgren?"

"Well, there's so much evidence against him in the package I received in the mail from Erik the day before yesterday, I think he's going to be behind bars for many years to come. He also shot and killed an unarmed man when the situation was under control, so I'll testify against him. Your testimony against him will help as well, both from when he tried to kill you under the church and when you were a teenager dealing with him."

"Good. That man was bad news. I can't believe you actually had to work with him."

Tami laughed and continued, "Oh, and you know that defense attorney, the one who Erik dragged down into the basement? The effects of the drug wore off and he came out of his death-like trance crying tears of joy that Erik had changed plans. Confessed everything he had ever done, including the payoff during Erik's case fifteen years ago.

Apparently, Erik's one-on-one talks with him under the church made a lasting impression and he's a changed man. You may want to visit him and fill him in on what you and Erik went through. Even though the attorney will be going to jail, you'll probably have a new member for your church, although he won't go near the basement ever again. The attorney was there and alert in the basement when Hultgren came in and shot Erik, so he heard everything. The state actually wants to use him as a witness to what happened, even though he didn't see it. He heard it all. Isn't that awesome?"

"I'm learning to expect miracles nowadays and not be surprised by them anymore. I've experienced some and they are truly amazing."

The sun's rays came out from behind a cloud, causing them both to squint as they continued talking. Tami closed her eyes and faced the sun directly, enjoying the moment.

"Bill, the attorney told me something odd about when Erik took him into the basement. I had figured he must have gone through the same entrance we went down, the one behind the tapestry from inside the church. It would be difficult to carry someone down there, but it's feasible."

He looked at her with his hand blocking the sun, trying to understand where she was going with this.

"Yeah?"

"He insists that Erik parked his van somewhere and dragged him uphill through grass, pointing out that he now has grass stains on his shoes, with pieces of grass still stuck in the end of both."

"OK, so what are you saying?"

"He insists that they never went inside the church, but came to the basement from some other entrance outside the church. He could be so traumatized that he's getting things mixed up, but he thought they went into a secret, musty smelling room that led into the basement. Is that possible?"

"Anything's possible, but I don't know what other room he could be talking about."

"Does the name 'P.A. Olson' mean anything to you?"

"Olson? He was one of the founders of St. Mark's Cathedral. Why do you ask?"

"The lawyer mentioned that Erik thanked P.A. Olson for providing Clark's final resting place. What do you think that means?"

The priest thought for a few seconds and looked into Tami's eyes.

"P.A. Olson has the only above ground crypt in the old church cemetery, the small one behind St. Mark's. You don't think that crypt has a hidden passageway under the church, do you? How would he have opened the tomb?"

"I don't know, but I plan to check it out. Are you interested?"

"You bet. I never knew the church had a hidden basement, and if there's an entrance from Olson's grave, that's even more fascinating."

"Let's set up a time to meet at St. Mark's and find out more of the secrets of the old church. I've got to get back to the station now, so I'll talk to you later."

"Bye Tami. I'm going to stay here a little while longer if you don't mind."

"I understand."

Tami walked away from the gravesite on her way to the car and she looked out over the rows of headstones. Following the cemetery across to the park, she noticed the young family again near one of the large elm trees. The school-aged kids must have been in class now, so there weren't a lot of people roaming the park at this time of day. She watched the little girl roll down the hill to the delight of her parents sitting at the top, and smiled at memories of herself doing that same thing when she was little.

She stopped walking and just stared at the family as the little girl ran back up to give her mother and father kisses. It surprised her when they all looked over toward the cemetery and waved at her and she wondered how they noticed her watching them. Hesitantly, she looked around but saw nobody else nearby except Father Bill, who was kneeling and not watching the park. Tami waved back at the family and they continued playing on the hill. She smiled and walked over to her car, amazed at the resemblance they had to Erik's family from so many years ago. It occurred to her she may have just had a glimpse into Heaven.

Rick Gangraw lives with his wife and children on the East coast of Florida, and wishes he could spend more time at his family's cabin on a lake in the Upper Peninsula of Michigan. He has traveled to over twenty-six different countries and has visited almost all fifty states in the US. When he's not dabbling in fiction, he enjoys sports, hiking, kayaking, camping, and researching family history.

Rick is the award winning author of *Secrets in the Ice* and you can find out more about him at www.RickGangraw.com.

www.ingramcontent.com/pod-product-compliance
Lightning Source LLC
La Vergne TN
LVHW091038080826
845145LV00002B/537

* 9 7 8 1 6 1 8 0 8 0 8 5 1 *